Homer's
ODC

Michael Yates

Nettle Books

Dedicated to my wonderful family: Pam, Dan, Matt
and Tracey

Published 2015 by Nettle Books, Yorkshire
nettlebooks@hotmail.com

©2015 Michael Yates
ISBN: 978-0-9561513-7-7
Classification: Fiction

Contents

Homer's ODC

Homer

Greek *Homeros* (c 8th century BC) The Greek poet to whom are attributed the great epics, *The Iliad*… and *The Odyssey*…

…The Penguin Concise Encyclopedia

ODC

(meaning Ordinary Decent Criminal). The acronym given by the Royal Ulster Constabulary to any professional criminal who was not actually a terrorist.

Prologue: Charlie Pickett

IT'S LIKE A FILM to Charlie. A film he's seen lots of times.

The grey walls, the windows with those funny screens to keep out the sunshine, the folding metal tables, the files, the folders, the computers, the desk lamps with their spidery arms. And here he is sitting on one of those metal chairs with the canvas seats like they have in hospitals. The only difference today is the Christmas decorations – a couple of red and gold streamers and four blue and green paper bells that open up like concertinas stuck in the corners of the ceiling.

And he thinks: It won't be much of a Christmas. But at least it'll be better than last. Fuck Millennium. Fuck fireworks all the fuckin time. At least it'll be back to normal this year. Goodbye 2000, start of the fuckin new century. Hello 2001, it's got to be better. Hasn't it?

That Millennium rubbish was the wrong year anyway. If you count it up right, 2000 isn't the start of the new century at all. It's the end of the old one. You've got to see that. It's *this* year that'll be the real new start.

He's been in places like this lots of times. Times immemorial, as his Mum used to say. She always wanted him to work in an office, and times like these are the closest he's come. He reaches for his cigarettes in the torn side pocket of his jacket, then stops himself, rubs a hand on the shiny knee of his trousers instead. Better not. He could use a piss as well but decides against asking. And his arse aches. These canvas chairs don't give you no support. He knows he's in trouble. And when you're in trouble, better keep mum, as him Mum used to say. He sighs, pats down a loose strand of his wispy grey hair and rubs a sudden itch on his bristly chin.

The other two are both standing, looking at him. Now the older one, the one with the red face and the beer belly, has started talking again. "Look, Charlie, we know it's not your caper. It's not your style. I mean, what are you, Charlie? Apart

5

from shitting yourself? You're a petty thief, a small-time con merchant. Get your way into some old biddie's sheltered bungalow pretending to be the gas man and make off with her life savings that she keeps in an Asda bag. And even then it's only thirty quid. No, this isn't you. I know that, Charlie. It's a top batsman, a real Geoffrey Boycott, that's what we're looking for."

Charlie grins. The older one, that Mr Dexter, Bradley Dexter, he's the one that matters. If he says it's OK, you walk out of here with a clean sheet. Look at him. Big man, lots of muscle, even if it is all running to gut now. Dark blue suit, light blue shirt that's come undone, showing his belly button. Charlie knows he's got to say something. "Then why'd you bring me in, Mr Dexter? Why'd you make me come here?"

Mr Dexter sucks in his breath. His face gets redder. Charlie looks down at his shoes again, the faded brown suede of his Hush Puppies.

Mr Dexter says: "Because I want to appeal to your better nature, Charlie. Because I know, deep down, that you want to help me find the bastards who did this."

Charlie looks up again. "I don't know nothing, Mr Dexter. I wasn't there."

Mr Dexter steps closer to Charlie, leans over him. "No, you *weren't* there. We know that. We know where you were because we've seen the arrest report."

Mr Dexter picks up a folder from the desk, glances at it, hits Charlie – *smack*! – over the head with it before putting it down again. "Oh, you want to stay away from ten-year-old girls, Charlie, you want to stay away from school playgrounds. Still, it gives you an alibi. No, you weren't there, Charlie. Not on the day. But you know somebody who was."

Mr Dexter turns to the young one, the quiet one. "Play it again." The young one wears a tatty pullover and Michael Caine specs. He goes over to the video player, presses the button and the screen comes alive. All gorgeous Technicolor now.

The man on the video, thin body and long, wavy black hair, is running, wearing a tracksuit, carrying a Nike sports bag in one hand and a gun in the other.

Mr Dexter says: "Look at him, Charlie, take a good look. What do you think?"

"I don't know, Mr Dexter.".

Mr Dexter does more leaning over. "Good investment, them security cameras. This one's outside the bank. Above the billboard for Janet Reger. You'd be surprised how many men can't help having a look at Janet Reger. OK, give us the slo-mo."

The young one fiddles with the video. He has short brown hair, gelled like they wear it these days so you can see bits of his scalp shining through. He's wearing brown cords and a blue polo shirt and that pullover. Not smart like Mr Dexter. Meanwhile, on the video, the man with the sports bag slows down, his running gets slower and his facial expressions exaggerated.

Mr Dexter sits on the table next to Charlie. "See it better now, Charlie? Recognise him?"

"I don't know. I can't be sure."

"Freeze it."

The young one hits the button. The man with the bag is frozen on the spot, his face a bit fuzzy.

"Got him now, Charlie? We know that face, don't we?"

Charlie says: "It *is* a bit fuzzy." Then he hears another sharp intake from Mr Dexter. Charlie says: "It looks like... it could be..."

Mr Dexter shouts so loud that Charlie puts his hands over his ears. "*It looks like! It could be!* It *is*, Charlie! It's your mate Dave Castle."

"He's not my mate."

Mr Dexter smiles a satisfied smile. "Then you won't mind shopping him. You won't feel bothered about telling us where we can find him."

"I'm not a grass, Mr Dexter."

"Yes, you are, Charlie. You *are* a grass. And a pervert. And a junkie. And a bucket of dogshit. Now I want to know where Dave Castle is, Charlie. I want to know what he's done with two million quid that him and his mates nicked from the local branch the Royal Bank of Cumbria. *My* local branch, as it happens. I've got my mortgage with them. So I've a personal interest. As well as a professional one."

"Please, Mr Dexter..."

"*Two million pounds!* On *my* patch. And guns! Shooters! Waving 'em about in public, frightening the shoppers, laughing at me, Charlie! I can't have that, can I?"

"No, Mr Dexter!"

"*No, Mr Dexter!* So where is he? And who else was there?"

"I don't know! Honest! I've not seen Dave for... years."

"Years, Charlie?"

Charlie takes a deep breath. He tries to think what his Mum would say. *Honesty's the best policy.* Alright then... "OK, it's been months! Well, a year. Exactly a year. Last Christmas. We had a drink last Christmas."

Mr Dexter's smile turns into a laugh. "*God rest ye merry gentlemen!* OK, turn the bloody thing off. So... who are his mates these days? Who's his woman if he's got one? Where does he get his stuff? Because he's still on the needle, isn't he? He'll be looking for a good score. With two million quid, he will!"

"Mates? I don't know..." Suddenly something in Charlie gives way. "A Geordie called Teague. Used to go to school with him."

"Old boys' reunion then."

"And a black bloke. He palled up with this black bloke in the nick last time. Dockie. That's what they called him. Used to work on the docks, you see. Then he went into the fight game. Didn't do no good. Dockie Williams."

"A real boys' reunion. Keep thinking, Charlie. There'll be a woman."

"No, no, Dave don't like women."

"There'll be a mother. Or a sister."

The word *sister* presses the button. "I can't remember. Lauren. Laura. Lorraine. Yeah, Lorraine."

"What's her married name?"

"She's divorced, that's what Dave said. I don't know her married name. I can't remember."

"Do better."

"She's registered. She's an addict. She's got a file."

"There's lots of files."

Charlie slumps in his chair. "I don't know. Honest. It's the best I can do."

Mr Dexter stands up again. "A Geordie called Teague. A blackie called Dockie Williams. An addict called Lorraine. And that's all, Charlie? You don't know where they might be staying over?"

"Honest, Mr Dexter."

"And you've told Mr Dexter the truth? You've not misled poor Mr Dexter by giving him silly names? The cast of Coronation Street? The Albanian national football team?"

"Yes, Mr Dexter. I mean *no*."

Mr Dexter sits on the table again. "Charlie, I believe you. I believe you don't know where they are because nobody would trust a dung beetle like you with information like that. And I believe you've told me the truth because I know you're too afraid of me to do otherwise."

"Yes, Mr Dexter. Can I go now?"

"The only thing that bothers me is that Dave Castle is down at your level. *He's* a bag of bollocks as well. So who

9

got him involved in a job like this? And why him? I don't suppose you'd know that, would you?"

"No, Mr Dexter. Can I go now?" He wants Mr Dexter to nod, to agree with him, to let him go. He wants that more than anything.

Mr Dexter stands up again. "Well, Charlie, I've got no further use for you."

Charlie smiles. He's OK. He can go to some pub and get that piss now. He starts to get up. He looks across at the young one. But the young one won't meet his gaze. Charlie is enjoying the thought of taking that piss when he notices a movement out of the corner of his eye and tries to turn. He doesn't see Mr Dexter, only Mr Dexter's hands and the bit of wire, very fast, very fleeting as his Mum would say, feels it bite into his throat and he grabs at his throat, grabs at the wire, tries to scream, feels the pain, the terror, the pounding, only a moment or two, but stretched out, like the slo-mo on the video, stretched out like a film, only one he's never seen before, only dreamed about, but knows the ending to, the red spot, the blackness, the absolute nothing.

And he pisses.

Part One: Christmas Eve

"The very first thing a team captain has to be is decisive. He must be prepared for every eventuality within a game, and be undismayed when, as chance would have it, an evil fortune mars his innings or an unforeseen happening strikes his stumps."

— **Arthur Tetley, My Bat and Me, Pheasant Press, 1976**

1 Raymond Dexter

RAYMOND FELT SCARED. Sick scared.

He watched his Dad as his Dad strangled Charlie Pickett. Raymond wiped his forehead with the back of his hand and adjusted his Michael Caine glasses and coughed.

Maybe *strangled* wasn't the word. Didn't *strangled* mean you had to do it with your hands? But it wasn't *strangled* when you did it with a little piece of piano wire that Raymond's Dad always carried round with him.

He'd have to look it up in Chambers or the Oxford one-volume. Ah! *Garrotted*. That was the word. That's what his Dad had done. He had *garrotted* Charlie Pickett with the piece of wire weighted at both ends with two old fashioned pennies that had holes drilled through them.

Once the coppers had nabbed Raymond's Dad for something, something minor, something not worth shouting about. And they'd gone through his pockets and they'd found the bit of wire. And they'd said: "What's this?"

And Raymond's Dad had said to the stupid coppers: "I use it to mend me bike."

Oh, how Raymond's Dad laughed when he told that story! Oh, how Raymond laughed when he heard it! And Harry Fountain. And Shoulders Greenberg, the enforcer who often came round on a Sunday to play cards with Raymond's Dad. And Joey "The Mouse" Michaels, who was his Dad's main collector and often stayed after business meetings for a salmon sandwich and a glass of Bell's. How they all laughed!

But it wasn't really a joke to Raymond. It was terrifying. His Dad's sudden movement, the bit of wire in his big ham fist. Charlie's look of surprise, the way he half got to his feet, stumbled, raised his unavailing hands to his throat, staggered slightly, gasped and turned purple, slumped and hung and fell and lay still. How many minutes? Less than two.

What was it scared Raymond? Not the enormity of killing someone. No. He'd seen plenty of people die on TV. *The Bill* and *NYPD Blue*. OK, they were actors. It wasn't real. But the idea was real. It didn't bother him.

Nor the fear of discovery, the knock on the door and the boys in blue, the days in the dock watching old men in wigs and the 12 years banged up in a cell with – as his Dad always joked – all mod cons.

No. What scared Raymond was the beauty of his Dad, the beauty of a man in control. What scared him was the speed, the grace, the surprise. Raymond knew his Dad had put on a lot of weight in the past five years, had got himself a regular belly. He knew his Dad needed reading glasses by the way he held his *Daily Telegraph* at arm's length. But there were times when his Dad was still his old Dad – that is to say, his young Dad – fearsome and filled with power. And his Dad was most like his old Dad when he dealt with his enemies, when he took them to task for whatever he thought they had done, and he destroyed them. In a moment. In no more than two minutes.

Raymond had heard about it enough times, from Shoulders and Joey The Mouse, and three or four other hangers-on, about the way they'd all started out, first small-time, then up-the-ladder, then top-of-the-heap, with his Dad leading them, protecting them. They went on about it for two reasons. First, to impress Raymond with how close they were to his Dad, how they could be trusted, how they would one day be as close and useful to Raymond as they had been to his Dad. Second, to size Raymond up, to see how he responded, to see how much like his Dad he was.

Oh, the tales they could tell!

How his Dad had ambushed the Bentley Brothers in their own scrapyard and tied them up in their own motor and set fire to them with their own petrol from their own cans!

13

How his Dad had taken Mo Ridley to one side one summer night at Kinsley greyhound track and slit his throat with a cut-throat razor (*what other kind would you use?* they laughed) and shielded himself from the sudden rush of blood with Mo's red PVC umbrella. *Good job about the colour*, they agreed.

And the things Raymond had seen for himself.

When Moss Trent, the used car dealer from Headingley with a sideline in drugs, had cheated Raymond's Dad out of his cut from a heroin deal. "I want you to watch this," Raymond's Dad said to Raymond as they waited outside a working men's club in Chapeltown along with Harry Fountain and two other hard men whose names Raymond couldn't remember, "because it's what I do for a living. It's not that I got anything personal against old Moss. He's a nice bloke to have to a party. Good at the old karaoke. Sings *Old Man River* like he was a coon himself. And it's not that I wouldn't do what he's doing if the shoe was on the other foot. But you see, son... if he gets away with it, then everybody will do me down. You understand?"

This time it was a gun, a Browning 9mm, fixed with a silencer. And as soon as Moss Trent went down and the ones whose names Raymond couldn't remember picked him up by the arms and dragged him through the puddles to the waiting Range Rover, Raymond's Dad had handed the gun to Harry Fountain who walked briskly away.

It was Raymond's 16th birthday when his Dad properly showed him – and Moss Trent – what business was all about. Afterwards Raymond and his Dad went for a curry followed by a drink at the Albert in Rotherham Street. Raymond was sick when they got home. "Don't blame the drink," Raymond's Dad told Raymond's Mum, "It was something in the curry. I felt pretty bad myself."

Now the bit of wire round Charlie Pickett's throat. And it's nobody's birthday, thought Raymond, so there's no rites of passage stuff. Raymond had studied the modern novel at school as well as Milton and Wordsworth. So he knew about such things from reading DH Lawrence and Nick Hornby.

What also scared Raymond was: he knew he could never be like his Dad, his beautiful Dad. He could never put a wire round a man's neck with such speed and certainty, never shoot a nice man who sang *Old Man River* behind a boozer in the rain.

And he knew that the others knew it. The ones who joked about red umbrellas and scrapyard fires.

"I'll give Harry a ring and we'll get rid of this heap of shit," said Raymond's Dad, kicking the body of Charlie Pickett as if to make sure he was dead, and Raymond nodded. "You get us a drink, son, OK? A Bell's with soda would be nice. That would set me up proper."

Raymond nodded, pushed a tinsel streamer to one side, walked out of the room, down the tiled steps and into the basement office his Dad used as a private sanctum. It was crammed with gadgets and furniture: a portable TV, two portable CD players, a VHS recorder, and a DVD player, all lying on a heavy pine desk with three large drawers either side. There was a high-backed executive chair and two small office chairs on castors, a glass-topped coffee table, a wooden cupboard with a padlock and a green four-drawer filing cabinet. Raymond went over to the filing cabinet, pulled out the top drawer. There was a copy of *Wisden*, Dickie Bird's *White Cap and Bails*, *Boycott on Cricket*, Alan Hill's *Hedley Verity* and *My Bat and Me* by Arthur Tetley. There were also four videos, three of them about the Yorkshire cricket team, the fourth on the history of the Ashes. Raymond found the bottle of Bell's, a bottle of soda, the metal tray and the glasses. He knew two of the drawers were empty. The last and lowest contained the Browning 9mm and ten rounds of ammunition in a Huntley & Palmer's biscuit tin.

15

Raymond put two of the glasses on the coffee table, poured out two whiskies, added the soda – a drop or two for his Dad, a fair amount for himself – and carried them through to the small kitchen next door where he added ice cubes from the freezer drawer.

Suddenly he felt his breakfast rise in his throat. He leaned over the sink and vomited, briefly and sourly. All that fry-up. He wished he'd gone for the muesli now. He turned on the taps, washed it down, rubbed his lips with his wet hands.

You can't blame the curry this time. He picked up the whiskies and walked up the steps.

2 Barry Oldham

BARRY OLDHAM WAS in trouble. Joe Clark was mad at him. Joe stood in front of him now, filling the ginnel next to the fire station, not letting him pass. Joe's thin drawn face, spotty skin, short, greasy hair and scrawny arms made him look more sad than angry. *Vulnerable* was the word Barry called to mind, a word Dr Hardy used a lot. But Joe Clark must be angry with Barry because he was calling Barry names like "shithead" and "fuckbrains" and looking round at his mates to see they were approving. Barry thought hard about what he could have done to make Joe Clark angry, but then he hardly knew the lad. Occasionally he would see Joe and his mates wandering round the town centre like *he* did. Sometimes he'd say hello, sometimes not. He sighed.

Barry Oldham used to be a big lad, the biggest of his Dad's three sons. He used to be proud of being big, much taller than Andy and Richard, his brothers. Then they grew up, and it all levelled out. Well, Barry and Richard levelled out at just under six feet. But Andy got taller than both of them. So Andy was the big boy now. Whenever Barry thought about it, it puzzled him. How could he be the big boy one day and not so big the next, even though he was bigger than what he used to be?

And he was still a handsome lad in his twenties. Wasn't he? His hair was thick and wavy and blond, the only blond in the family. "Milkman's son," his Dad used to say. But his Mum, embarrassed, had replied: "Don't go making jokes. Our Barry'll take it serious." Because he *did* take things serious.

In one respect, of course, Barry was still the biggest. But nobody at home talked about that. He'd put on a lot of weight when he left school. "Puppy fat" his Mum had called it, though his Dad said: "He's getting a bit too old for a puppy." Almost overnight, his waistline had ballooned, his hands grown pudgy, his face broad and fleshy. It seemed he had become someone else, unrelated to the schoolboy who had once won Flaxton School's English prize.

That was a thing about growing up, about leaving school. You couldn't be sure of anything any more. There was nobody to tell you things. No teachers. His Mum and Dad tried. But you couldn't expect them to be any good at it. They weren't professionals, they weren't trained.

No, it was better with the professionals. He felt more secure when he was with Dr Hardy or Mrs Gulliver. Dr Hardy would always make him comfortable, letting him sit in the white leather chair.

He wished he was with Dr Hardy now in the white leather chair. Not with Joe Clark in the ginnel by the fire station. Not trying to figure out what it was he'd done that made Joe mad at him.

"You know what?" said Joe, "You're an ugly fat bastard. Isn't that right?" He shoved Barry in the chest with the flat of his hand.

"Yes," said Barry. No point disagreeing. And it was true. At least the *ugly fat* bit. The *bastard* wasn't worth

17

worrying over. Barry had read somewhere that it was a term of affection in Australia.

When Barry said "yes", Joe Clark laughed. And his two oppos, Ernie and Jason, laughed too. Joe leaned over and brushed his hand across Barry's upper lip. Barry started back.

"What the fuck is that?" said Joe.

Barry wondered whether he should answer at all. If he did, he couldn't just say "yes" again. He would have to give a proper answer, and then Joe would make another nasty comment and ask another question and then... the conversation would just get away from Barry, go on and on and on. Barry said: "It's a moustache."

This time Joe and Ernie and Jason went ballistic hysterical. "Call that a fuckin moustache?" screamed Joe, "Anybody got a magnifying glass?"

Barry saw his chance. A small chance but worth taking. "Actually, they sell them at WH Smith." He pointed across to the bus station and the Father Christmas under the shop sign.

Joe and Ernie and Jason suddenly stopped being hysterical. Joe said: "You being funny, fat boy?" and made his right hand into a fist. Barry thought about it. Was he being funny? And should he say he was being funny even if he wasn't? Which was more likely to get him a fist in the face? It was a tough one.

Then a voice interrupted. A voice with a German accent. The voice of Erwin Rommel, second world war Field Marshal defeated at Alamein by Britain's Field Marshal Bernard Montgomery, or Monty for short. Barry had first come across Rommel in a school history book. Rommel had been brilliant and chivalrous, respected by the British as much as by his own people, but he had killed himself after joining a failed plot to kill Hitler. Just like Barry, he'd started out so well and then...

"Vot is dis dot dey do to you, Barry?" Rommel asked. He was blond like Barry, though a lot slimmer in his grey *Vermacht* uniform. Barry said nothing. Rommel went on: "I vud not stond for dis, Barry. Dey are only boys, only 14 or 15 years. You are a man, are you not? Vy don't you smack dem in der face? It is only tree against von, and I have myself succeeded against much greater odds. You know dis is true because you haf read it in your schoolbook."

And then another voice chimed in, a voice which still retained a Liverpool nasal twang. "Take it easy, Barry. You know what Jesus would have done? He'd've turned the other cheek. And Martin Luther King? He'd've sat down in the street and refused to be moved. And Gandhi would've done the same. Don't listen to those mothers, Barry. Give peace a chance."

Barry thought: *that John Lennon talks a lot of sense.* But he knew Rommel wouldn't agree with it. "Vot is dis nonsense, dis pacifist garbage? *Gott in Himmel!*" The German war hero had gone red in the face. He slapped his black leather gloves against his thigh. John meanwhile raised his fist in the solidarity sign. And stroked his Zapata moustache. Barry was pleased that John had grown a moustache too.

Joe Clark said: "Cat got your tongue, fatboy?"

Rommel said: "Gif him a smeck, Barry. It's vot ve gif der desert rats in my day."

John said: "Don't listen to the bloodhungry warmonger, Barry."

Ernie said: "Kick him in the balls, Joe."

Jason said: "If you can find 'em!"

At this last remark, Jason, Ernie and Joe laughed fit to bust. Barry laughed too. The others stopped.

"What you laughing at, fatboy?" asked Joe, "You laughing at me then?" He shoved Barry in the chest again.

Barry struggled to find an acceptable answer. Finally he remembered something he'd read: "Laughter is infectious," he said. "Like the flu," he added.

There was a silence. Joe and Ernie and Jason looked at Barry. They looked at each other. Rommel and John stayed quiet. The phrase "pregnant silence" came into Barry's mind.

Then another voice interrupted. It was a man's voice, an angry voice. "What you lot doing?" They all looked up at the window in the fire station wall. It was open now – and a large, crew-cutted fireman was looking out.

"Clear off, the lot of you!" shouted the fireman, "Or I'll be down."

"Fuckin cunt!" shouted Joe.

"Right," said the fireman, *here I bloody come!*" And he closed the window.

Joe and Jason and Ernie looked at each other.

"He's not coming down," said Joe, "He's just making a fuckin noise. He wouldn't dare come down against the four of us." After a pause he added: "We're only just standin here. What's wrong with standin? He can't do fuck all about people standin."

The four of us. It was not lost on Barry that be had suddenly become part of the gang.

"Fuckin hell! Is that the time?" said Jason, "I've got a bus to catch."

Ernie said: "My Mum's gone to Morrison's. I've got to go and help her with the shopping."

"He's not coming down," said Joe, "he's not got the guts. So I'm not gonna wait around for the turd, that'd be stupid." He and the others had now started moving away in the direction of the supermarket and the bus station. *Sidling* was the word that sprang into Barry's mind. He himself started walking briskly in the opposite direction towards the bingo hall, past the life-size plastic Santa which would call out Merry Christmas if you put a 10p coin in it.

He felt light-headed. "I think that fireman *is* coming down," he said to Rommel and John. They nodded. It was something all three could agree on.

3 Bradley Dexter

BRADLEY DEXTER SIGHED. Dexy loved his son. He thought the world of Ray. One day, he told himself, Ray would take his place. Ray with his two A-levels. But that was the trouble. Ray was clever, but he was clever in a wait-and-see sort of way. He couldn't just get on with it. This was the bit about Ray that Dexy didn't like. The standing-around-waiting-to-be-told-what-to-do that was not the mark of the leader, of the Captain.

Dexy looked down at the crumpled figure of Charlie Pickett, the piss seeping out of his trousers along with the blood from his neck and mouth. That carpet. Bloody big cleaning bill for that one. They should've thought about him pissing. He'd probably shit himself too. They should've made him use the bog first.

Dexy said: "Drop him out in the street. Might as well."

Ray grimaced. "Strikes me that's a bit dangerous, Dad. There's people round here know me." For a moment, a hint of attitude. Then his schoolboy face snapped back into its normal vacant expression as he realised he'd said the wrong thing.

"I'm joking, son." Dexy thought about it. It was his own fault. He'd said a stupid thing to his son. That was another thing about Ray. He took everything literally. If you told him something, he would do it. Down to the letter. It was as though he couldn't think for himself. "Not this street, Raymond. Look, son, find some other bloody street. Take him to Barnsley bus station. They'll not notice him for the next three days if he ends up there."

Ray laughed.

Dexy realised Ray wasn't taken in this time. He wasn't actually going to dump Charlie Pickett in a bus station. He could at least figure that one out. Where the hell would they leave the little toe-rag? There was a bit of woodland just outside Flaxton. Dexy and Simone had been lots of times, usually on a Sunday. It was real nice there, with a bird sanctuary and fishing, though all they did was walk round the lake and have a cup of tea and a scone at the cafeteria. Dexy liked going there but he'd been horrified at some of the stuff people dumped in those woodlands. Mattresses. Chairs. Scrap iron. Every so often a rubber johnny in the water. That sort of behaviour was well out of order. But it told him the people who ran the place didn't bother. It told him you could get away with dumping stuff. And if you could get away with a mattress or a bedstead, you could get away with losing a body.

He tried to describe the place to Ray. But Ray wasn't good with directions. "OK," said Dexy, "Just bundle him up." Ray was OK with bundling. You could trust him because he'd done it before. First, he'd put on surgical gloves. Then he'd strip Charlie Pickett of his shoes, socks, trousers, underpants and jacket, examine the insoles, turn the socks inside-out, pull out all the pockets. Just to make sure there was nothing tucked away that might survive somehow and lead the law to his Dad. Then he'd get two large polythene bags out of the cupboard under the stairs and push and pull until Charlie and his worldly goods were inside a couple of them.

Ray could put on some speed when he wanted, oh yes, when he was sure about what he was doing. But even so, it wasn't like Typhoon Tyson on a fast pitch or Ray Illingworth – after whom this Ray was named – hitting boundaries in days gone by.

Sometimes, when there was a difficult parcel to dispose of, Dexy would phone the specialists and they would come down and do a proper job. Take it well away and cut off the head and hands and burn them separately. But that was on the rare occasion when the death was likely to provoke public consternation. Charlie Pickett wasn't one of those. A petty crook. A paedophile. A drugs dealer. A grass. The law wouldn't be too interested because the public wouldn't give a damn either.

That was the reason he was giving the job to Ray. Give the boy a sense of achievement, a bit of pride. Why shouldn't Ray cope with it? He'd been with Dexy twice already in similar circumstances and seen how things were done. Not that Simone, Ray's mother, would approve. But the boy had to do these things for himself, had to grow up.

Dexy picked up the phone and dialled home. Harry Fountain answered right away as he should do. "Harry," said Dexy, "come down to the office, bring a car we can afford to give away. I've got a removal job. I want you to give young Ray a hand. Yes, it bloody well *could* take all day. If I say so."

When he hung up, Dexy got round to the paper work. That would also hone Ray's skills. "Look, Ray, that nice policeman who showed us the arrest report and gave us the video. What's his name? Rankin. We'll give him a grand. I'd like you to set that up. And see if he'll give you his account number. And the sorting code. You never know. Let's put our little deal on a proper business footing. I can tell he's gonna be useful to us in the future."

Dexy helped Ray stick down the polythene bags with Sellotape. "See they get burned. See everything gets burned. You always got to worry about prints. But you know that."

Ray nodded.

"There you are," said Dexy, "all done." He said: "You want another whisky, Ray?"

"No," said Ray, "No, Dad, not if I'm driving."

"Righty-ho." Dexy went down to the basement office and poured himself another Bell's. He went into the kitchen and got some ice cubes. On the way back, he took the Boycott out of the filing cabinet.

"Harry's coming over to help. Twenty minutes to half an hour. You'll have to leave your own car here." Dexy sat in the blue executive chair behind the desk and stretched his legs.

"OK." Ray sat down on one of the canvas chairs and looked over into the middle distance.

Dexy thought: *He's a million miles away, that boy.* Dexy opened Boycott's book. He read: "Self-discipline and a strong, clear mind are vital and those qualities are more important than quantity in terms of practice. It is more productive to work very hard one day and have the next day off as a holiday than to turn up on a regular day and be casual." He thought how true that was. Relaxation could be useful. It could actually be productive if you relaxed with the right people. And that's what he intended to do over Christmas. Eddie and Gina from Newcastle were coming down to party. And to talk. Eddie ran all the major stuff in Newcastle, just as Dexy did in Leeds. *We live in an age of globalisation,* thought Dexy, *think of Europe, for a start.* The barriers were down.

He realised suddenly that he was tired. Charlie Pickett had taken a lot out of him. He put the book down. He allowed his eyes to close. Afterwards, he woke with a start and it took him a second or so to remember where he was.

Harry Fountain was taking his time.

4 Chanelle Braithwaite

CHANELLE WOKE UP with a start. The light was still on. At least they'd drawn the curtains. What time was it? She glanced at the green display of the little black plastic alarm clock on the little white chest of drawers on her side of the hotel bed. The door side. The side she always insisted on. The clock said 10.30 and there was a dot in the top left corner that indicated it was morning not night.

Morning not night. It hadn't been the light that had woken her up then, nor the little black plastic alarm clock which she always carried with her but somehow never remembered to set. It was her internal clock, the one she knew to depend on, always geared for morning, that had brought her awake. She started the routine daily check of her bodily extremities. Legs stretch, feet stretch, toes wiggle. OK. Arms stretch down to thighs, very careful not to disturb the sleeping man by her side. Wiggle fingers. OK. She knew her eyes were OK – she was looking out at the world and it looked pretty much the way she remembered. She listened for tiny sounds and could hear the alarm clock's *dick dock*. Ears OK. She felt the back of her head, then exercised her neck, then contrived to see – by turning her head right and then left – the black tresses of her hair on the pillow. She touched her breasts, right one, left one, they weren't sore. She felt between her legs – once she had found to her horror that the rubber johnnie was still inside her, abandoned by the deflated cock of whoever the man had been. But no, not this time. Had he actually used one? Yes. She remembered now.

She remembered also how he'd bitched about it, saying he didn't usually have to pay for it and his regular women didn't feel they had to play safe with him. She had asked him where his other women – the women he didn't have to pay for – were tonight? He'd got mad then, shouted, and for a moment she feared it was getting nasty. But then he'd softened up, said the reason he was paying was because he wanted something special, something the other women wouldn't do, and he wanted to use her arsehole, only he called it *anus*, and asked how much that would be. And she didn't know right away what to say because she didn't recognise the word, but when she realised what he wanted, she said "more than you've got". If he'd been nicer from the start, not argued about the rubber, she'd have said yes. But he hadn't respected her. He hadn't respected her – so she'd be buggered if she'd let herself be buggered. In the end they did it the usual way and used the rubber.

Only now, remembering the eight or nine minutes of their conjunction, did she recall what he looked like. Middle aged, middle height, middling bald, spare tyre round his middle. And a heavy sleeper, as he would be after the whisky and the pot. He was the one who wanted the whole night, the full monty, spent the money on the room, probably reckoning on getting it off all night. But she knew he'd be one that fell asleep straight away. She also knew he was going to bitch about the bill. He was the type. Best to get the money right away then, before he woke up. Though that was risky. She thought about it for all of ten seconds before she made up her mind.

She pulled back the green flowered duvet, slowly and carefully, placed an exploring foot into the worn pile of the purple carpet, edged her full weight – seven stone six – over onto that foot. His breathing was still deep and regular, with the occasional snort and swallow, just so she knew he wasn't faking it.

It was a relief to get her second foot on the floor. She wriggled her bottom to the edge of the bed before she eased it off altogether. Once she was standing, she felt more confident. But then she knew she needed a piss. She tiptoed to the bathroom, dropped toilet paper into the lavatory to deaden the sound of it, and did it standing up, her legs wide apart. She couldn't use the flush so she dropped some more toilet paper on top of what she had done. It seemed polite.

On the way out of the bathroom she caught sight of herself in the full-length mirror. OK, her hair was a mess – whose hair wouldn't be after a night with Mr Arse-hole? – and her Ms Frantic eye-liner was dirty-streaky. But she was a beautiful woman, no doubt about that. She had the olive skin and small white teeth of a Halle Berry, not quite the arse of a Jennifer Lopez, but certainly the legs of a Nicole Kidman. And the breasts were big enough. She arranged herself into one or two poses that she practised for her modelling – hands on hips with belly forward, arms over head with legs apart, right hand coyly covering her trimmed pubic hair while she pouted and sucked the index finger of her left hand. Yeh, she would have to get something done about her pubes. Shaving was all very well but it made you stubbly. What was needed was a proper Brazilian. Well, as soon as she got a bit of money... Maybe the modelling would lead to something big. She was a professional. All the photogs said that. And she was only 15, though she always told the photogs 19, even if they laughed. Where could she *not* go with a body like that?

A high-pitched snore from the bedroom brought her back to reality. Where she might go depended very much on how she did in the next few minutes. She crept back into the bedroom, picked up from the floor her knickers and bra and slipped them on. She took from one of the armchairs her M&S charcoal grey tights, her Next black pencil-line mini-skirt and her Top Shop black sweater, and pulled them on. She went back to the floor for her BHS black leather handbag with the silver buckles on the strap, her red woollen scarf from George at Asda, and her black suede court shoes with the transparent heels from Shoe City. From the top of the chest of drawers she took her alarm clock and put it in her bag.

Now the dangerous stuff.

To get at Mr Middling Arse-hole's wallet in the pocket of his jacket hanging over the second armchair, she had to go round to his side of the bed. Put it another way. The bed would be between her and the door. If he woke up and realised what was going on, he had a good chance of stopping her.

She went over to the outside door, turned the key slowly, opened it into the corridor. All was silent. Of course, room service might come by with a clanging trolley any minute, but the chance was worth taking. She placed her handbag and scarf outside the room. She went back into the room, round the end of the bed, reached the second armchair and picked up his jacket. Quickly she searched the pockets – outside breast, inside breast right, inside breast left, left side pocket, right side pocket. She found a handkerchief. She put the jacket back on the chair. She picked up his grey cotton trousers, never daring to look at the bed but listening intently for any variation in the snore-breathe-swallow she had come to expect. Left pocket, right pocket, back pocket right, back pocket left. He hadn't left any cash or cards in his jacket or trousers. Maybe he didn't trust her.

Next to his side of the bed was another chest of drawers, twin to the one on her side. She dropped his trousers back on the chair and walked towards the chest, towards the side of the bed, towards *him*. She pulled open the top drawer, very slowly, very quietly.

The drawer was halfway open when he stopped snoring.

Chanelle froze. The only thing that moved was a trickle of sweat running down her forehead. Then the snoring started up again. Snore, breathe, swallow. Fart. Maybe the sound of his fart would wake him up. She nearly laughed. Mr Middling went on snoring. Chanelle pulled the drawer all the way out, held it in her hands. Inside lay a large rectangular brown leather wallet, a smaller fold-up black plastic wallet and a book with a hard orange cover.

She began walking backwards to the foot of the bed, carrying the drawer. At the foot of the bed, she turned and walked forward again, not turning her head to right or left. The only sound she could hear above the snoring was her heartbeat. It all seemed half a world away. Which was where she wanted to be.

She reached the outside door, nudged it with her elbow so it came fully open, then stepped into the corridor. She was facing an early Picasso – she knew it was a Picasso because it said so on the frame. It was yellow, blue and green and was called *Man Before a Fireplace*. She thought: *Man after a bomb went off, more like.* She looked down at the drawer. She knelt down, placed the drawer on the carpet, took out the two wallets and stuffed them into her handbag. Then she took a good look at the book. It was a Bible. On impulse, she tried to stuff that into her bag too but it wouldn't go. She looked along the corridor. Three doors down lay a copy of *The Guardian*, neatly folded. She got up off her knees, walked across to it, picked it up, put the Bible inside it, placed it under her arm. Then she picked up her scarf and handbag and walked quickly down the corridor to the stairs.

On the ground floor, she smiled at the plump woman behind the reception desk. The woman smiled back in what Chanelle took to be a somewhat knowing way. *But not knowing enough, you fat bitch*, thought Chanelle.

She waited until she got out of the car park and across two streets before she opened her handbag. She immediately threw the card wallet into a waste bin attached to a bus stop. OK, there were things you could do with somebody else's cards, but they were complicated things and they could be traced back to her. No, it was just the cash she wanted. And she was not disappointed. Mr Middle had over £600 inside the brown leather. Must have saved up for me, she thought.

And then the bell rang, loud and shrill. Chanelle dropped her handbag before she realised what it was. Not her mobile, which she always turned off when she was out on a job. Oh no.

She had obviously remembered to set the little black alarm clock after all. Just as well it hadn't gone off twenty minutes ago. For the first time that morning, she allowed herself to laugh. "Thank you, God," she said. When she got home, she'd have a little read of her Bible.

5 Dave Castle

DAVE HAD BEEN KIPPING. Dreaming money. And remembering. Him and Vic Taylor down the Pavilion after school, the old changing rooms where they didn't have any windows so the vandals couldn't break in. Dave always had a key because he cleaned up for Mr Randall the school caretaker. And they'd get out the pills or the glue or the needles. And they'd just drift off, start touching, start loving each other. And afterwards turn on the showers, wash it all away. *He needed some love right now*. He needed... But it was morning, bright sunshine in at his window, it was get-up-and-go time. And then the voice broke in. Loud, shrill, nagging. A *woman's* voice.

"Dave! Dave! Dave!"

He opened his eyes, took a look round the room. The bed, the stove, the sink, the electric kettle, the two half-full bottles of milk on the tray on the little bedside table, the 14-inch telly.... Not much for the rent. His eyes lighted on the scales and needle he'd left on the floor.

"Dave! Dave! Dave!" Nearer now, running steps on the stairs.

It was Lorraine. He'd better hide the needle stuff. She'd only be asking him about his stash, hoping she could use it, hoping she could owe him one. He rolled off the bed, laced up the Hi-tech trainers he'd nicked last Christmas, right out of the shop, under the noses of those stupid women, those fuckin shop assistants. They knew enough not to mess with him. Nobody should mess with him. Not now.

And that made him remember the gun.

He jumped to his feet, snatched the Smith & Wesson .38 from under the pillow. No chance to hide it in his jeans. He thought: *I'll get myself an overcoat with pockets. Now I'm into money.*

Then the door was flung open and it was Lorraine. And she saw the gun and she screamed.

"Aaaggghh! Dave! Don't do it!" She ran forward, took a hop, skip and jump at him and grabbed the gun. They fell on the bed – him, her, the gun. She screamed again: "No, Dave, no, it's not worth it!" and he shoved his free hand over her mouth, anything to stop that screaming, anything to stop Mr Ironmonger the landlord coming up to see what was happening. He pushed her head down hard into the pillow and fell on top of her, the dead weight of him keeping her down. He shouted: "Lorraine, you silly cow! I'm not gonna do *anything*! Right?"

She opened her eyes. She was red in the face and breathless. But then she was always red in the face. Because she was fat and couldn't run for a bus without coming over faint. He was her brother but he couldn't deny it. He had a fat sister.

Her little eyes lit up. But even then, even when she knew she'd been wrong, that he hadn't been about to top himself, even when she realised she'd almost landed him in the shit, almost brought the neighbours in to see him with his gun, she couldn't quite let go.

"Oh Dave! Dave! Put that down! For God's sake, put it down!"

"Yeah." He put it back under the pillow.

"Dave, what you want to do that for? Oh God, what are you on?"

Dave sat up, put his feet back on the floor. "It's not loaded. Well, I *think* it's not loaded."

"You're on some stuff again, Dave. Some shit." She looked round, saw the gear on the floor. "Why do you do it? Why can't I leave you for one afternoon without you're back on some shit?"

Dave laughed. "Only a *bit* of shit. Not shit. Not really. Expensive. Good stuff. You like it too!" Then he looked at her again, at the bulging neck, the medicine-ball boobs, the button nose, the spiky lacquered hair, the blue eyelids and orange cheeks. A rush of feeling went through him like the hot water from the geyser over the sink. "Oh, Lorraine! Lorraine!" Tears sprang in his eyes and he hugged her.

She hugged him back. "Oh God! Oh! You smell! You need a bath! Oh, Dave. You can't even look after yourself, keep yourself clean."

"*You* look after me, Loz. Like Dorothy looked after the Scarecrow. You're my Dorothy, you're my Judy Garland."

"I'm your sister, Dave. I'm not your Judy and I'm not your bloody Punch neither." She shoved him. "I'll make us a cup of tea." She went over to the kettle. "Good job I brought some teabags." She sniffed at the milk bottles, wrinkled her nose. "I've got some milk too. It's powdered so it can't go off."

"I don't like powdered!"

"It won't go off! That's why I brought it. I got it from a friend of mine. He cuts it in with heroin, sixty-forty. So he's got a lot of it and he's not gonna miss the odd tin. Here, I'll fill the kettle." She picked up the milk bottles and put them on the tray. "I'll pour this stuff down the lav."

When she'd gone out the door and he heard the latch on the toilet and he knew he had maybe a minute, he got down on his hands and knees and pulled the big Nike sports bag out from under the bed. He checked the padlock on the zip and shoved it back, then took the gun from under the pillow and hid that under the bed as well. Then he ran across to the gear, shoved the needle and the scales under the bed and sat on the bed, then thought better of it, got up, walked across the room, sat on the wicker chair in the corner, the only chair he had. But then *she'd* sit on the bed. *Lorraine* would sit on the bed. Maybe it was better she sat in the chair. But if she sat in the chair, maybe she could see under the bed. He got up, walked to the bed, walked back to the chair. Then he heard her footsteps and Lorraine came back through the door with the tray and the two empty bottles and he sat down quickly on the chair.

Lorraine dropped the bottles in the rubbish bin and plugged in the kettle. "This isn't much of a place, Dave." She went and sat on the bed like he knew she would.

"It's OK."

"It's not OK. It's a shit hole. There's silverfish on the sinktop, the stair carpet's all torn up and the flush won't work in the bog. You could get food poisoning or fall down the stairs and God help you if you ever get diarrhoea. What's that bastard charging you?"

"I can afford it. He's alright, Mr Ironmonger is."

"You can afford better. Lots better. That's right, isn't it? That's what you keep telling us." She was wearing a low-cut yellow top with WOBBLE-WOBBLE written across the front. When she leaned forward he could see lots of cleavage which meant she must be wearing one of those special bras that Dockie Williams said made lemons look like grapefruit.

"You *can* afford better, can't you, Dave?"

He remembered so many other times when she'd wheedled out his secrets. About the boys in the changing rooms. About what Mr Gringold had done to him in detention. He giggled and put a finger to his lips. "Shhh. Private. Secret."

"He charges you for keeping quiet, eh? This Ironmonger. You think you can trust him? You think he won't be looking to make a bit extra, a bloke who makes you pay through the nose for silverfish on the sinktop and a flush that don't work? Oh Dave, you'd be safe with me. And I'd keep you off *that* stuff. And I'd see you had a bath and some decent food. Oh, wouldn't you like that, Dave? A flush you can always depend on?"

Dave shook his head. "Not safe. You're not safe."

"I can look after myself. What's the law gonna do if they find us? They're not gonna bust me for looking after my own brother."

"Not the law. Other people. It's people looking for me. Bounty hunters. Like *The Fall Guy* on TV. Like we used to watch when we was kids. Looking for *it*. The money." He had said too much. He thought he might stop then, but more words broke away from him. "Bigger than the lottery, Loz. Bigger than the instants, bigger than the Saturday jackpot. Bigger than Chris Tarrant."

She snorted. "So you say. That's what I've *heard* you say. How big, Dave? I mean, really. Bigger than a grand?"

"Bigger." There. He'd said it.

"Five grand? Ten grand? You get away with ten grand?" Her eyes grew wide – disbelief mixed with hope.

"Ten grand? Grander than ten grand!"

Lorraine was almost laughing again. "Twenty grand? Fifty? A hundred grand? You didn't get away with *a hundred grand*?" He could tell how excited she was, how she was close to believing him, close to realising he was a winner, her little brother was a fuckin big shot.

And now the words went climbing. "Higher, higher! Higher than Everest! Higher than clouds and stuff!" He jumped up and down in the chair and his heels tapped on the floorboards.

Lorraine snorted again. He'd lost her now. "Higher than a kite if it's anything like you, Dave. You don't mean it? Not higher than a hundred grand! What's higher than that? You don't mean a million, you can't mean a *million*?" She rolled on the bed and her breasts wobbled like the sign on the shirt said they would.

"Yeah. A million. More. Maybe."

"How'd you stash away a million then? I mean, it must be like a bloody skyscraper, that sort of money."

"No, it's not. It's quite small really. You can get it all in a..." he stopped himself. "...in a case."

"I couldn't imagine it. The others got it then? The others split it up and took their share?"

"Others? I don't know no others."

"Did it by yourself, did you, Dave? Took a million pounds out of a bank by yourself? Now listen to me, Dave Castle, there's more truth in an estate agent's advert than there is in you. There was more truth in my two husbands on a Saturday night down the *Dog and Duck* than there is in you. And they was fully paid up members of the Union of Black-Hearted Bastards, Liars and Affiliated Trades. This whole million pounds is a pack of lies. How'd a chap like you that's been neither use nor ornament all of his life get in on a job like that?"

He jumped to his feet. "I did! I did!"

She leaned forward again, her eyes haughty and mocking, but her breasts betraying her excitement, giving the lie to her big sister detachment. "Tell me then. Tell me *how*. The one thing you've got plenty of form for is possession. All you ever done outside of that was knock over an off-licence with an airgun. Oh yeah, I forgot the time you tried to use a stolen bus pass but they twigged you wasn't 65."

Dave sat down again. "*Three* off-licences. *And* a Kentucky Fried Chicken."

"So – I suppose one day you thought: *I'll do a bank and take out a million*. You kept the airgun all these years?"

"It might be two. It might be *two* million."

"Two million then. OK. You were walking past a bank one day and you thought you'd just walk in and say: *This is a stick-up – give me two million pounds.*"

"No. I got asked. Somebody set it up. They come and asked me."

"Now I see it. You were sitting in the *Crown and Anchor* with pint of Tetleys, reading the racing page in the *Financial Times* and somebody comes up and says: *Hello, Dave, we've got a little two million bank job we'd like you to do. We heard about Kentucky Fried Chicken and you're the man for us.* Who was it, Dave? Was it Al Pacino?"

"Can't say. I'm not a grass."

"And *I'm* not a grass. I'm just trying to help you. Now you say there's people after you…"

"Yeah. *Big* people."

"What about the others? Is somebody after them too?"

"Don't know."

"But you know they're after *you*. Why you? You still got it then? You've not shared it out? You still got the money?"

"I didn't say that!"

She got up off the bed, walked across to him. "You rascal! You *have* got the money, haven't you? Not that I care about the money, Dave. You can go on saying it's a million pounds if you want. I don't care if it's a hundred grand or ten grand or just a grand. It's *you* I care about!" She looked round. "Where you got it then? You couldn't very well put it in your building society. For a start, you haven't *got* a building society. You got it in a luggage locker in Leeds Station? Course, you couldn't do that nowadays 'cause of the bombs. Where you got it then? You can't have got it in here. There's no space." But there *was* a space, of course. She went across to the bed and looked underneath. "You haven't... you haven't got a million pounds *under the bed*, Dave?" When she collapsed with laughter, burying her face in her hands, he did the same. "Oh, you *haven't*, Dave! Oh, tell me you haven't!"

And then she lunged at the bed, fell down on her hands and knees, shoved an arm underneath it. When the arm came back, her hand was clutching the sports bag.

Dave also lunged at the bed. He pulled out the gun and aimed it at her head. "Don't! Leave it alone! Don't touch!"

She got to her feet, dropped the sports bag on the bed. "Don't you point that thing at me, Dave Castle! Don't you go pointing a bloody gun at your big sister!"

For a moment he thought he would shoot her. Then he remembered that the gun wasn't loaded. *Probably* wasn't loaded. He threw it down and grabbed the handles of the sports bag. "It's mine! You've no right! You always was a bully, you always stole my things, my school things, my biros and my coloured pencils. *And* my protractor!"

She kept hold of it. She pulled as hard as he did. "Fuck your biros! Fuck your protractor! Is there money in that bag, Dave?"

"It's me towel and me washbag. And some spare underpants. And me razor. And me Lynx aftershave. That's all."

She stopped pulling but still held on. "Your razor?" She allowed one hand to leave the handles and stroke his face. "You could do with a shave right now, you could. Shall I get it out?"

Dave hugged the bag. "No, no!"

Suddenly Lorraine gave it up. He was holding it now, all of it, and he didn't know what to do.

"OK, OK. Keep your bloody Lynx." She sighed. "Still, you shouldn't stay here, Dave. It's Christmas, isn't it? You should be bloody home for Christmas! It's your sister saying this. *I'm* your home, Dave. Nobody knows about me, do they? And we'll look after you, me and Joby. You know you like Joby. And I can get you a fix any time you want. And you can't trust nobody who won't even mend the bloody flush. I bet he's seen what you've got. Somebody might nick worse than your protractor. You should come back and live with Joby and me."

"No. I don't. I don't like him. You *know* I don't like Joby."

"Joby's alright. We've been together for six months now. What've you got against him?"

Dave considered. "The way he licks my face all the time and his breath stinks. And you can't take him out without him pulling on the lead."

Lorraine sighed again. "All right, then. This is where you stay." She picked up her shopping bag, went over to the door and opened it. "But you better put that shooter away. Don't want nobody seeing you with that."

Dave picked it up, shoved it in his waistband under his tee-shirt. "Aren't you stopping for that cup of tea?"

"I changed my mind. It's all them silverfish. They've made me feel sick."

"What about them teabags? Are you leaving them teabags?"

"Of course I'm leaving them teabags. You enjoy it, Dave. I know you don't like that powdered milk. *Nobody* likes that powdered milk, do they? But it won't go off. Not many things in life that won't go off. Believe me, I know."

"*You* won't go off, will you? You won't go off and leave me?"

"You still want me coming round here? Now you've got to be so rich and so high and mighty? You don't even like my Joby."

"I don't mind him. I just don't want him licking my face."

"See you later then." She went through the door and it closed after her. He heard her footsteps down the stairs. He clutched the sports bag to his chest. After a bit he called after her, but he knew she was gone. After a bit he called: "I don't really *mind* powdered milk. Not for a little while."

6 Barry Oldham

BARRY SAT IN the café at the back of the art gallery with a One-cal Diet Coke. The café was *Ali's Place* in Grosvenor Road, Flaxton, run by an Algerian with a trim black beard, and it was the only place Barry knew which sold Genuine Viennese *apfelstrudel* with sour cream, which today came with a colourful serviette wishing him a *Joyeux Noel*. Barry liked *apfelstrudel* but knew it was bad for his diet. He ate it, but chose the One-cal Coke to make up.

Anyway, the *apfelstrudel* was gone by now. "Is no goot regretting vot has gone," said Erwin, who had eaten a lot of *apfelstrudel* as a young man, and Barry nodded. He admired the old soldier's philosophical turn of mind. Erwin remained cheerful and generous towards his enemies. "Dot Montgomery vos goot soldier," he would say and nod along with Barry.

But right now Barry found Erwin's presence a trifle disquieting. *Irksome* was the word that came to mind. The German warrior had been a considerable support during the incident with Joe Clark and his gang and Barry was grateful, even though Erwin's advice had been contradicted by John. Barry liked to be even-handed with his friends and try to find virtue in their statements even when they disagreed profoundly, as Erwin and John often did.

There were times when he would much prefer to be alone. Alone in the sense of not having to share his immediate thoughts with others. He didn't mind the other customers in

Ali's Place – now reduced to a white-haired woman in a ragged coat, who smelt like rotting potatoes, and a 13-year-old girl with a barbed wire tattoo across her bare midriff – because they didn't know or care that he was there. But he wanted to be free of Erwin for a while because he had something important to do which did not involve military leaders of the Second World War. He had something to write.

Maybe Erwin got the message, maybe it was Barry's body language. Anyway, the grey-uniformed veteran suddenly rose to his feet, slapped his glove against his thigh and said: "I need some fresh air." And he stalked out. Barry took a spiral-bound reporter's notebook from the side pocket of his green anorak, a ball-point pen from his inside pocket, placed both of them on the blue Formica table top next to his empty plate. Time to begin.

It was, after all, the day of the Poets. Every Monday evening Barry would attend the scheduled meeting of The Victoria Poets at *The Victoria Hotel* in Skinner Lane. But this year, since Monday was Christmas Day, the Poets had decided to bring their gathering forward to the Sunday.

He had been going there for 18 months and Dr Hardy approved of it and expressed great pleasure in reading Barry's verse. Often the bald psychiatrist would have Barry read out his latest work, then discuss the symbolism, and try to relate it to Barry's problems. Barry enjoyed this as much as Dr Hardy obviously did. He felt it gave Dr Hardy real insights into life and he was half hoping the verses would form the subject of some future thesis, for he knew Dr Hardy to be a man with a number of published works to his credit.

The procedure among The Victoria Poets was always the same. A chairman was elected at each event, though it usually ended up being Hal Peterkin, who was some sort of lecturer at the Education Centre.

Each member brought along half a dozen copies of an original poem and each would take a turn, pass round the extra copies and read the poem aloud. The other members would then speak about the poem, praising or damning as the mood took them. When Barry had first gone along, he was nervous about opening himself up to criticism, but his confidence had built up week by week. And he seldom attracted any vitriol. Perhaps the other poets feared his stringent judgment of their own works and consequently gave him an easy ride. More likely they admired a man whose comparative youth and limited experience had proved no barrier to a profound understanding of the human condition.

The best thing about the weekly workshop meetings was: if you wanted to take along a poem every week, then you had to write one. To be sure, Barry had started out with a backlog of verse stretching back to his sixth form days, but this had run out. So he was driven to write something new. Now he considered his subject for today.

Not that there was any doubt about his inspiration. When he went to the public library in Fox Street to borrow a book or photocopy his verse, an additional pleasure these days was Alison, the library assistant, who worked on the counter between 2pm and 4, and helped him work the photocopier. He didn't know her second name because Alison was all it said on the laminated badge pinned to her breast. She was a pretty young woman of about 23 or 24, with shoulder length auburn hair, a soft, round face and a trim figure. He knew straightaway that she liked him and he always left a copy of his current poem lying around, just so she could see he was no ordinary user of the public libraries. The poems were always gone the following day so he knew she had picked them up. But he never revealed that the poems were inspired by *her*, just as he had never revealed the fact to the previous women in his life – Mrs Moran, the English teacher at his comprehensive, whom he still saw occasionally on the street; Jean, the youth adviser at the jobcentre; or Tracy, the travel agency worker who had moved into the block of flats opposite

41

his parents' house in Old Bank Street for a few months last year.

But how to start today's poem? How to express the inexpressible, acknowledge the unknowable? That was always the problem for poets – the impossibility of what they were trying to say. That was always their pain, the thing which set them apart. Dr Hardy had been especially interested in Barry's theory of the isolation of poets. Barry hoped the doctor could be trusted – that he wouldn't steal the theory and publish it under his own name.

Barry took a deep breath. He stroked his moustache thoughtfully. He began to write:

Ashen faced, I resolve to forgive you.
I resolve to let you lead your own life,
Knowing you will have to return to me,
Knowing that we will eventually share what was
nearly ours.

I am the clown at the centre of my stage and you
Are my spotlight.
You shine for me as I reflect you.

I am a clod of lowly earth
And I bear your imprint.
It hurts but shapes me.

I always thought it would be like this,
Even though I know it can change
In an instant
And you can change
Me.

I have been without you too long

And yet I know our love will not blossom
Yet.

Take your time then.

He stopped. He put down the pen. Yes. It was good. The best poems were the ones that came in a hurry, poems you didn't have to think about. He glanced at his watch. It was nearly one o'clock. He would go and get it copied. But he didn't want to rush things. He still had all afternoon to kill. He deliberately took four separate gulps to drain his Diet Coke. That *apfelstrudel* had been really good though, the highlight of his day so far. Apart from the poem.

7 Harry Fountain

HARRY FOUNTAIN WASN'T pleased. He'd been disappointed before so he was used to it. But that didn't make it better.

He wondered for the millionth time why he was working for a stupid cunt like Bradley Dexter. It wasn't the money because the money wasn't that good. And it wasn't the job satisfaction because most of the time he just hung around the house and acted like some kind of fuckin butler.

Harry wanted something better out of life. Which is why he'd trained as an accountant. But then there was that bit of trouble with a law firm's tax returns. Not to mention his personal expenses. None of it was *his* fault, but some clever cunt made out it was. So now he had to kowtow to the likes of Bradley Dexter and his moron son Ray. Little Ray of Sunshine, that's what Harry called him. Sunny for short.

At least he'd got the afternoon off from that bitch Old Dexter had married. No better than a tart, with her bleach-blonde hair, her cleavage and her short skirts, but full of herself. He could show her a thing or two if he got the chance. Make that bitch sore for a month. But Harry was too smart to let the bitch get to him. Even if he'd fancied her. Which he didn't.

In the meantime, he'd got to do this removal job Little Ray and Old Dexter had got themselves stuck with. He turned the red Astra into the paved yard behind the greystone office that said *Dexter Investments* in Gothic type across the frosted windows. When he got out, he was suddenly aware how cold it was. He did up the top button on his buff coloured raincoat and pulled the silk scarf a shade tighter. He was a tall man, early thirties, thinning close-cropped hair, slim and well muscled from his daily workouts in Old Dexter's gym, which the old man never used these days.

He locked the car, went up the stone steps, pressed the buzzer. The door opened and *Dexter Investments* swallowed him up.

Not that it was much of a place inside. Cheapo furniture. Threadbare carpets. Only four computers. If *he* was running the place... well, he'd make it a bit hi-tech, bring in more terminals, video conferencing for long-distance stuff. Best that could be said for it was: it looked good from outside, respectable for this part of Leeds. Old Dexter didn't have any style, any presence. Oh, maybe once. When flares and Jason King moustaches were all the rage. But he'd lost it now.

There was a six-foot parcel lying on the floor, done up in black bin bags and sellotape. And another smaller parcel over by the desk. Old Dexter said: "You and Ray are gonna go over to the woods and drop this lot off. There's a couple of spades in the cellar. Ray's getting them now. Good job we've got a high wall round the yard."

"So what about when we get to the other end? It's gonna cause some people to fret a bit if they see us carrying that."

"Harry, it's a cold day and it's been raining and it's gonna rain again and nobody's gonna be walking in the woods today. The two of you go up there, you dig a hole in the ground, you slip our friend into it, you pour in half a gallon of Unleaded, you throw in a match, you wait around a while, you replace the topsoil, you sling a mattress or an old sideboard on top – there's enough furniture in them woods to open a store. Nobody is gonna be around to see you. Then you drop Ray off somewhere outside Leeds where nobody will see him and he can get a bus or something. Then you take the car out to Sheffield, some bit of waste ground round the Manor, and set it well alight. You come back by train."

"Can't I take a taxi? If it's gonna rain…"

"Taxi drivers is a nosy bunch. They remember things."

Just then Ray came in with the spades. He smiled and nodded. Harry nodded back. Old Dexter took the spades off Ray and picked up the second parcel. Now Harry thought again what a *nothing* Sunny was. Not even a long drink of water. Well, Sunny wasn't going to give *him* any orders.

"You take the legs," said Ray, "I'll take the head."

"OK." Harry bent down to get a grip on the feet. When he and Ray picked the parcel off the floor, it suddenly hinged in the middle and they fell in against each other.

"Whoops," said Ray. Harry gritted his teeth. Then they found they couldn't straighten it up again. They turned this way and that, tugging at the parcel but the parcel remained U-shaped.

"Whoops," said Ray again.

Old Dexter looked at Ray and said: "I'll give you fuckin *whoops*. I can see you two need a bit of experience in handling this sort of merchandise. Well, this is your chance. At least it'll be easier to put it in the boot while it's all folded up." And he went out the main door and down the steps into the yard.

45

It was true Harry had never carried a dead body before. He'd once carried a person up a flight of stairs at his house in the Dales, when he'd *had* a house in the Dales, before his troubles. But that person had been alive and mostly willing and it had been a doddle to a strong healthy man like himself. He'd never realised how heavy they were when they died. The good thing was that Ray was panting more than he was as they staggered down the steps. In fact, Harry was hardly panting at all, now he thought about it.

When they got the parcel as far as the Astra, it started to rain again. And Sunny let the parcel slip and they dropped it. When Old Dexter opened the boot, they picked it up again and dropped it inside and both of them managed to stand up straight at last. Harry was breathing quite heavily but that was OK, that was a healthy reaction to honest exertion. But Sunny was gasping, no other word for it. Unhealthy little sod. Harry wished he'd brought his golfing cap. He didn't like rain. It made his hair look thinner than it really was.

"OK," said Old Dexter. He threw in the second smaller parcel. He said to Ray: "When it's over, give me a call on your mobile. Wait till Harry's gone and everything's seen to. And remember – it's a special day tomorrow so I want you back home for an early night. Then it's up at the crack of dawn to open your presents."

"Aww, Dad!" moaned Sunny, "I might be going out tonight. I might have a party."

"You never mentioned this. Whose party?"

"Just some friends. I said I might drop over."

"Well, see you're not late. And not drunk. You know your mother worries."

It was all Harry could do to stop from laughing out loud.

Dexter said to Harry: "You know the way." He dropped the spades on top of the parcels and closed the boot. "Well, lock it then," he said to Harry. Harry locked it and got in at the driver's side. He turned the key in the ignition and the engine came alive just as Ray slumped in beside him.

"*Bon voyage*," said Old Dexter.

Harry drove off. *Fat bastard*, he thought.

8 Barry Oldham

BARRY TOOK A bus to Flaxton Library, a sixties building, flat-roofed and airy with a large frontage of glass, much of it cracked by the activities of drunks waiting at the bus stop outside. He went in through the yellow turnstile and up to the "in" counter. Women with badges sat in front of computers. But Alison wasn't one of them.

The library was usually closed on a Sunday but Flaxton Council had decreed a special Christmas Eve session as part of a Government-funded literacy campaign called *Yule Get Reading*. Colourful posters featuring Herald Angels delivered the news of the extra opening hours.

"Can I help?" said an older woman with glasses. Because the bottom halves of her eyes were behind the lenses, they appeared magnified and out of proportion with the top halves. Barry didn't like that. He said: "Where's..." He paused. "...Alison?"

"Is it personal?" asked the woman, then: "She's off sick." The woman was, he guessed, in her late forties or early fifties, her lightly powdered skin beginning to show the sort of lines that women his Mum's age worried about.

Personal? Was it personal? "Yes," said Barry. "No," he said as an afterthought, "It's the photocopies." He waved his poem.

The woman looked him over. It was almost as if she had recognised him. Perhaps Alison had shown her some of the poems he had left behind. Perhaps, without knowing it, he had already gained something of a readership among the staff.

He leaned over the counter, just enough to read the name on her badge. He was always careful about doing this sort of thing, looking at women's breasts. But if they *would* wear their names there, they couldn't complain, could they? *Marie* said the badge.

"Oh yes," said Marie. She got to her feet. Now Barry was sure she knew who he was. She had a nice trim figure, what you could see of it underneath her cream blouse, short black jacket and matching skirt. And she didn't wear a wedding ring.

"Well," she said, "there's a coin slot on the photocopier and we normally expect customers to do their own photocopying. But..." Yes, clearly Alison *had* talked about him.

Marie lifted the bit of the counter that you had to lift to get out from behind it – Barry never knew what they called it – and stood in front of him. "I'll take you over," she said. "You do have an Activ8 card?"

"Yes." Of course he had an Activ8 card. How else could he afford to do his photocopying? He said: "I'm a user of the mental health services."

"Yes," said Marie. She turned and walked in front of him. She had a purposeful, business-like walk but it was also surprisingly sexy, the way she moved her slightly plump bottom. Barry watched her slightly plump bottom closely but nervously. He was aware that he could never claim she wore her name on her bottom.

Barry was a poet and poets could look beneath the surfaces of things, especially beneath the surfaces of women. Barry knew all about the subconscious. Freud was the person who first wrote about it but he said later: "It was the poets who discovered the subconscious. I merely named it." Or something like that. There were plenty of things lying around in the subconscious that the conscious mind simply didn't know about. It was quite possible, for instance, for a woman to be madly in love with a man subconsciously and not like him very much on a conscious level. She might even desperately desire him physically on a subconscious level but not be remotely interested in a physical relationship consciously. Barry had come across such women.

He wondered why Marie didn't wear a wedding ring. Maybe she had been widowed. Or divorced. A new thought struck him. Maybe she had children. At first, he didn't know how to react to this thought. It seemed strange. But, after a while, quite exciting. If she had children, she might have stretch marks. He wondered what stretch marks looked like.

Suddenly Marie stopped and Barry almost bumped into her. They had come to the photocopier. "Let's have your card," she said.

He searched his pockets. He put his poem and his notepad down on the photocopier. He went through his trouser pockets again but all he could find was his pen, a rubber and a packet of sugar-free chewing gum. "I know..." he said.

Marie picked up his notebook from the photocopier. His Activ8 card fell out.

"It must have got inside my notebook," said Barry.

Marie pushed the card into the slot and the machine came alive with a display of lights and whirring. "How many copies?"

It was a bright day if somewhat cold – the rain so far had been no more than showers – so there might be as many as eight people at The Victoria Poets. On the other hand, it was Christmas Eve and some of the shops were opening late and people wanted to do their last-minute shopping. It might end up with only him and Victor Heyford. He decided to take a chance. "Ten," he said. And he would leave two copies – one for Marie and one for Alison.

Marie took the sheet of paper out of his hand, placed it on the machine, pressed a blue button, then repeatedly pressed a yellow one until the display had moved from one to eight, then pressed the green button. He noticed she had small, birdlike hands, but the skin was soft, very pink. Nothing like a bird really. He didn't know why he'd thought of birds. But poetry was often like that.

"Ve better be carful, Barry. Ve don't vant to show our true feeling," said a voice from behind. Barry didn't look at the German. Instead he surreptitiously glanced downwards. Nothing was showing in his fly area, thank God.

"Thank Gott for der medication," said Erwin. Barry felt a momentary shudder of embarrassment. How did Erwin know? Had Dr Hardy told him? No, Barry was sure Dr Hardy didn't know Erwin, had probably never studied his campaigns in Egypt and the Sudan. But how... ? OK. Be rational about it. That would be Dr Hardy's advice. Maybe it wasn't such a mystery. A brilliant military commander like Erwin would know about such things. And methods of treatment had probably progressed little since the days of the Third Reich.

"Here you are," said Marie. In her right hand she was holding out the eight copies of Barry's poem with the hand-written original on top. In her left, she held his Activ8 card. He took them from her and stood there.

"Right," she said, "because you have an Activ8 card, the service is free. But, of course, you know that." She motioned for him to walk ahead of her.

Barry hesitated. He had been looking forward to watching her bottom as they walked back to the "out" counter. It seemed a letdown if he had to walk in front of her. On the other hand, he didn't want her to think...

"Ladies first," he said, suddenly inspired. And he made the same slight waving gesture in the direction of the counter she herself had made a moment ago.

Marie smiled. She seemed impressed by his good manners. For the first time he saw she had nice white teeth, if a little small and sharp-pointed. "Right," she said and walked ahead of him towards the counter.

Now he was almost sure he could see the faint outline of her knickers. Yes, he could definitely see it. He was disappointed that they looked like standard Marks & Sparks briefs, the kind his mother wore, rather than a thong or a tanga or whatever they called them. But he couldn't see the colour. Actually, there weren't many colours you could see through a black skirt.

Still, it opened a whole new train of thought. He tried to imagine what colour knickers Marie would choose, now he knew she was the sort of woman who definitely (or at least consciously) did not want people to see the colour of her knickers through her skirt. *Using your skills and knowledge,* that's what it said in the instructions with the Spot the Ball competitions in the *Evening Post.* Using what he knew about her already (she was nearly the same age as his Mum, had a kind face, had been interested in his poems enough to remember him after Alison talked to her) Barry decided she would not wear pink knickers for a start. That would too... well, undignified. She might go for white but that was unimaginative. He wondered briefly about green, but he couldn't remember ever having seen a woman wearing green knickers, either in films or on knicker posters. It was like you never saw blue food.

By now they were back at the "in"counter. Marie lifted the bit of the counter that you had to lift to get behind it and got behind it. Barry stepped across to the "out" counter. When he had got through the yellow turnstile, he turned back to look at Marie but she was involved with another customer, an old man who was protesting vehemently that he had never borrowed *Brewer's Concise Dictionary of Phrase and Fable* and had no idea why it was marked as overdue against his ticket.

When he got outside, Barry realised he had failed to leave two copies of his poem. He considered going back but that would have been too obvious. He just hoped ten people would actually turn up to the Poets' meeting.

9 Raymond Dexter

RAYMOND WASN'T SURE about Harry driving the car. It took him a while to realise this.

First of all, it was Harry's job to do... well, to do the jobs. To make himself useful. So it was right that he should drive, take on the effort, fret about the traffic, bother himself with the stiff gear lever that he remarked on with a whispered *fuck* now and again. So that was OK.

But Raymond realised that this was *not* actually OK. Driving the car put Harry in control. Raymond thought: *I should be in control.* He regretted he hadn't made a point of driving. He hadn't been fast enough, hadn't made up his mind in time, and anyway didn't really want to drive. Not in this weather, not in the pre-Christmas traffic.

One thing he knew. His Dad would always have chosen to drive. Well, there might have been some situation where he would let a close mate drive just to show favour. There were times when you had give a little away. But Raymond's Dad would have made up his mind very carefully and very quickly on such a matter. Either way it would have been a proper decision, not a thing to go by default just because somebody else sat in the driver's seat first.

Raymond admired his Dad. And Raymond was scared of him too. Not because Raymond's Dad was violent – not to Raymond, not to Raymond's Mum. But he was in control. Oh, what it must be like to make all the decisions, big and small! And have nobody question you, nobody put themselves forward or cross you!

Raymond had made a little promise to himself. It was a sort of New Year's resolution, only he did it every morning. He called it his Daily Decider. And it was always on the same theme: that he should be more decisive, make himself more like his Dad. It had started at school. If his marks fell below the standard his Mum had set for him (it was, now he came to think of it, actually his Mum who decided things about school, his Dad was just the enforcer) then his Dad would have a word. "Ray," he would say, "you're letting the team down. Don't forget who I named you after." (His Dad had never learned to use the word *whom*.)

He knew *after whom* his Dad had named him: Raymond Illingworth. Great team player. Great leader. "There are more balls on a cricket field than the ones they hit the bails with," his Dad had said once and his Mum had rebuked him for being vulgar in front of the boy. (That was another thing his Dad had never learned – not to end a sentence with a preposition.)

So. It had started with his maths results, then his English essays, then his ability at games. His Mum wasn't actually so concerned with how he did at games, that was more his Dad. And it was here the rot had begun (because Raymond was actually pretty good at most lessons when he put his mind to it and had come out of school with two A levels – one a B grade in history.)

He remembered the first time he'd played cricket, real cricket, with a hard ball. Plenty of times he'd played on the beach or in the garden with his Dad and his uncle Billy and his cousins James and Joseph, but that was always with a tennis ball. Nobody ever told him about a hard ball, how hard a real cricket ball was.

He was seven years old and the kids were playing in the school playground with the drainpipe outside the first year block acting as the wicket, though it was past four o'clock and they should have been on their way home. And Bobby Nathan bowled a fast one and Joey Hallam hit it wide and it soared over the close-in fielders, all of them leaping vainly in the air to snatch it and suddenly it was there, over Raymond's head.

Raymond stood with his hands outstretched while the kids on his side yelled out in anticipation and the opposing team groaned in the face of impending doom. In many of the books that Raymond came to read later on – particularly those about sport – it was often said that during this or that event, as the crowd waited for the outcome of a drop-kick or a serve or a penalty, time stood still. And so it was for Raymond. The ball seemed to hover like a kestrel.

And when it hit his fingers, he screamed out and pulled back and dropped it. And it hit the ground and bounced on the tarmac, mocking him.

And then the enemy team were the joyous ones and the boys on his own side were the ones who moaned and wept and shouted. And Raymond cried. And they called him sissy and crybaby and wouldn't talk to him on the long walk home.

And Raymond tried to tell them that he hadn't dropped the ball because he was scared, because he was hurt, because he was a coward. He had dropped the ball because he was surprised. Nobody had told him it wasn't soft like a tennis ball. If only someone had told him, he would have been ready. He would have done what was expected, he would have caught the ball no matter how much it hurt his fingers.

It was so unfair.

Now, as he sat in the car with Harry saying *fuck* every time he had to move the gear lever, Raymond took a decision. He leaned back in the passenger seat, half-turned towards Harry and said in the most casual voice he could muster: "I think I'll drive now, Harry."

"What?" said Harry and *fuck* again as he changed gears.

"I said *I'll* drive now." Raymond made his voice a bit louder this time but he swallowed some spit and it made him cough.

"What you wanna drive for?"

"Because..." Raymond struggled to think of a reason that wouldn't make Harry think Raymond was calling him a bad driver. Which Raymond certainly wasn't. "Because," he said, "I think you can probably do with a rest." And he added: "For a while." Because he didn't want Harry to think he was being insulted in any way, like being called the kind of man who was so old or tired that he needed to rest all the time.

Harry didn't bother looking at Raymond, Well, thought Raymond, Harry was driving and he had to keep his eyes on the road so that was good enough reason not to look round. Harry just went on driving. After a few minutes he said: "I feel fine. Don't need any fuckin rest."

"Right," said Raymond. He knew he had handled this one badly. In particular he didn't like the use of the word *fuck*. Used as an expletive when handling the gears, it was perhaps acceptable – like a cricket player who throws down his bat when he's lbw, not because he's angry with the decision, but because he's mad with himself for not getting it right. But used in response to a suggestion from Raymond, a suggestion that Harry was not inclined to fall in with, it did have some aggressive connotations. It was not the sort of language Raymond's Dad would have put up with in the circumstances. So. Harry would go on driving. Maybe at least Raymond could save face a little.

"OK, tell you what, Harry," he fidgeted a little in the passenger seat and adjusted his glasses, "You drive this leg and I'll drive all the way back."

Harry laughed. "I'm taking the fuckin car away anyway, aren't I? All your old man's bright idea. You'll have to take the bus home on your own, won't you?"

Raymond cursed himself for forgetting. And now a terrible thought came over him. Would he be able to find his way back by himself? He hadn't thought to look at any bus timetables, hadn't even thought where Harry might drop him. He adjusted his glasses again. He should have thought of things earlier. Maybe he should suggest Harry dropped him off in central Leeds, where he knew where he was, and forget about his Dad's instructions.

But no. He couldn't do that. His Dad didn't give orders without good reason. And he couldn't speak out against his Dad in front of Harry.

He decided he didn't like Harry. He had a distinct feeling Harry didn't like him. He wondered yet again how it was that his Dad didn't care whether or not people liked *him*. How great that must be. Not to care.

Raymond wiped the inside of the passenger door window with his sleeve. But he still couldn't see much of the afternoon outside, thanks to the rain and the muddy spray of the car in front. *Fuck*, he thought, *fuckin weather*. But he didn't say it out loud. He didn't want to descend to the level of Harry.

10 Barry Oldham

BARRY SPENT A COUPLE of hours in *The Turnstile*, a café bar devoted to football paraphernalia. Huge monochrome pictures of David Beckham, Pele and Kevin Keegan in his permed days adorned the walls. Barry didn't like *The Turnstile* half as much as he liked *Ali's Place* but it was the only other half-decent café in Flaxton. *Ali's Place*, being run by a foreigner, was more exotic. And there was something distinctly uncivilised about football, with its chanting masses, burly foul-mouthed players and fists in the air, something which set Barry's well-filled teeth on edge. Oh, he knew it was very working class and he certainly admired the working classes for their struggle against bourgeous gentility and various other things, but he felt this struggle had gone astray on the football terraces and had actually caused the lower orders to score an own goal, if you could put it that way.

But he didn't want to go back to *Ali's Place* for the second time in one day. It would look soft, as if he didn't have anywhere to go. Which of course he did. Most of the time. But it was Sunday, wasn't it? It seemed daft to go all the way home and have his Mum ask him if he wanted a cup of tea and have his Dad sit in the armchair by the hearth, reading yesterday's *Sun* and ignoring him. *The Sun*, not the *son*. Now that wasn't a bad line for one of his poems about family life. It almost wrote itself, that did.

And *The Turnstile* was just down the road from *The Victoria* where the Poets always used the small upstairs room. There had been a move lately to switch to another pub with a downstairs room, a ramp for wheelchair users, and easily accessible toilets capable of accommodating the disabled. Barry was all for social inclusion, being too often one of those excluded, but he was less than enthusiastic about any move. It wasn't that *The Victoria* had such great facilities – they didn't even sell One-cal Diet Coke and he had to make do with shandy. It was just that he felt settled at *The Victoria*, the *Vic* as he called it in imitation of *EastEnders*. He didn't like change. Not for the sake of it. Not for the sake of a minority of wheelchair users who probably wouldn't come to The Victoria Poets anyway (or to the Oak Tree Poets as they would have to call themselves if the move went through).

He sighed. Right now he was nursing another Diet Coke and making hastily scribbled marks on a copy of his poem. He was always like this before a meeting – phrases which had seemed to him the height of poetic perception a short time ago suddenly seemed gross or laughable when he had to contemplate reading them out to his fellow poets in the next hour or so. Why didn't he have more confidence? Like Jim Wiggins. Jim read his work with such intensity, waving his large fist with such vehemence, that there was very little opposition from the others. "Very interesting," they would say when he had finished. That was when you knew your poem was real crap. When it was so bad that nobody dared say anything in case they had a row about it. At least it was never like that with Barry's poems.

Right now Barry was agonising over the line *Knowing that we will eventually share what was nearly ours*. He was aware of the paradox. If you are eventually going to share something with someone and you know that as fact, then it would no longer be *nearly ours* but actually and completely ours, so the sentence was illogical. That's what Fred Whittington would say. Fred who wrote sonnets about the Lake District. *Tarn again Whittington* was what Jim called him, often to his face, and Barry had to admit it was a clever pun. He allowed himself a smile at Jim's pun, then returned to the task in hand. He wrote *rightfully* instead of *nearly*.

Then there was the problem of the word *reflect* in the lines *you/ Are my spotlight/ You shine for me as I reflect you*. Somehow *reflect* was wrong. It made the clown seem merely a mirror image of the spotlight, but he was an independent being with his own individuality. He might literally reflect the spotlight if he wore, say, a suit of mirrors or spangles, which some clowns did. In that case, the reflection would not in any way be a metaphor and would carry no wider implication. Barry struggled to compose and insert that extra line about the mirrored suit. It seemed straightforward enough at first. He simply added the phrase *In my suit of mirrors* at the end of the verse.

And it was very apt when he thought about it. He had already described the clown as *ashen-faced* which could be explained by the sort of make-up that certain clowns used. Barry knew there were red-nosed clowns with baggy trousers and white-faced clowns with ice-cream cornet hats and white make-up who might very well wear suits of mirrors. The red-faced clowns fell about and had water poured over them while the white-faced clowns remained cool and immaculate under any circumstance. But that created problems. Which sort of clown did he want the clown in the poem to be? Surely he was more like the red-nosed clown than the white-faced clown? He had made a fool of himself over this girl whose name might be Alison and he was full of regret and misery and self-loathing. He wouldn't mind a bucket of cold water in the face – oh no, he would welcome it. What was it that John had written? *Hey Jude, don't play it cool...*

"No," said John in the seat next to Barry, "that was Paul. That was definitely Paul." He smoothed his Zapata moustache.

"Right," said Barry, "I'm sorry about that. But you did work together a long time, you and Paul."

"Vot is dis nonsense?" asked Erwin, sitting across from both of them, "Vot is dis clown to do mit real life?" He fingered his Iron Cross and his monocle glinted in the light from the fruit machine.

"It's love," Barry explained, "Love *is* real life. And it turns people into clowns. I know," he smiled the smile of the knowing. "I've had it happen to me. Occasionally." He went back to the poem.

"*All you need is love*," said John, "That's one of mine, as a matter of fact."

"Dis is not loff," said Erwin. He removed his cap and scratched the top of his head. "Dis circus stuff is not loff. Loff is big and strong and noble. It is the warfare of the emotions, the battleground of the senses. It is the stuff of opera, *Tristan und Isolde*."

"There are clowns in opera," said John, "There's *Rigoletto*." He pulled a face and waggled his ears in a way that Barry could imitate but Erwin could not. This failure annoyed Erwin.

"Good point," said Barry.

"Dere are no clowns in Vagner," said Erwin. He glanced purposefully around the room. "Hey, you better order yourself another Coke, Barry. Der barman is looking over here."

Barry nearly got to his feet but stopped himself in time. "It's only been 35 minutes since I bought this one, Erwin. I always allow myself three quarters of an hour."

"So you should," said John, "So you should, wack. Don't let the old Nazi git push you around."

Barry particularly liked it when John used Scouse words like *git* and *wack*. It created rapport between them. Erwin, on the other hand, with his occasional *ach* and his *Gott in Himmel* never seemed to overcome the social barriers that went with English being his second language.

"John, do you think it's a white-faced clown or a red-nosed one?"

"It's whatever," said John, lighting up a large spliff, "It's all and nothing. You can be anything you want to be." He leaned back, letting the smoke out through his mouth.

I will be anything I want to be, wrote Barry, red nose or white face. Just give me the word, my beloved.

It was good having John around at times like this. Barry drained his Coke and went across to the bar to order another. When you finished a poem, when you knew you had got it right, it was worth celebrating. He looked around at the other customers, seeing them for the first time. There was a girl in the corner nursing a *latte* and an old woman near the door with a pot of tea for one. A strange thought occurred to Barry. Surely these were the same people who had been in *Ali's Place* earlier?

He considered the idea while he paid for his Coke. On the one hand it seemed unlikely that the same two individuals should turn up in *The Turnstile*. And yet... At this very moment, perhaps, they were asking themselves the same question about him. And for him there *was* an explanation, involving the Poets, the library, the copying machine and the reasonable wish not to be seen twice in the same place on the same day. Perhaps it was the same for them. Not the Poets nor the copying machine, obviously, but the need to stay on the move, ring the changes. He sighed. Perhaps they were as sad beneath their outward show as he was beneath his.

Especially the girl. She seemed older than the last time he had seen her, nearer 17 than 13. And she had changed her clothes in the meantime, switching her tee-shirt for a polo-neck. Unfortunately the polo-neck did not allow him to see her midriff so there was no point walking across to check the tattoo. Just as well, really, because he could get into trouble looking at girl's navels.

But he could at least get close enough to the old woman to detect her smell. That wouldn't seem strange. Not with an old woman. He picked up his Coke and walked towards the door, passed behind the old woman and sniffed, though not noisily. He turned round, walked back to John and Erwin and sat down again.

The woman had smelt of carbolic. Well, maybe she had taken a bath since he last saw her. But he knew this explanation was unlikely. It was probably the case that this old woman was the double of the other one but had a more acceptable standard of hygiene. After all, everybody had a double. Barry had read this in his Dad's *Readers Digest*. We all of us have doubles – not just one double but probably lots. That was the most probable explanation.

But the girl in the corner was something he couldn't decide about. Was she the same one? He was almost sure. So what was she doing? Was she deliberately following him? Had she perhaps fancied him when she first saw him from across the room? Had she hurried home to change her clothes? But how had she known where he would be later on?

The one problem with changing his poem was that he would have to copy the changes on to all the other sheets. It would take a long time and would probably lead to more self-doubt. Each time he wrote in the new lines, they might offer themselves up for further change. Then a new thought occurred to him. Perhaps the girl and the old woman worked together. Perhaps they were investigators for the social security or some other branch of government who had been told to follow him around. It was true he had seen neither of them in the library but perhaps they were part of a bigger team. That would explain how they had been able to take time off to get a bath, change their clothes and assume new identities. The thought disturbed him. He decided to move on, to test the theory that the two would turn up again or that their colleagues would shadow him, and this time he would be aware and he would spot them.

He would go back to the art gallery. There was a room devoted entirely to Yorkshire artists with two Hockneys, a Henry Moore preparatory drawing for a statue of a man and a woman, and three landscapes by Louis Grimshaw.

He decided not to change his poem. After all, as John had said, you can be anything you want to be. Red nose or white face. He looked up from the page. John and Erwin had already gone. He shoved the poem copies and the ballpoint into his pocket and walked out, leaving his unfinished Coke. *You can be anything you want to be.* But he didn't want to be *watched.*

11 Harry Fountain

HARRY LEANED ON his spade. He looked round. It was a bright afternoon now, the rain had stopped two hours ago. He hitched up his trousers. He looked at the birch trees with their bits of supermarket bags hanging on branches. He looked at the grass covered in piles of broken chairs and mattresses. He looked at the dirty brown stream rushing over a rusted motorbike engine. He looked at Sunny. Sunny was working hard, digging away at the wet ground, panting. Harry leaned on his spade. He didn't know how he could make it more obvious, his feelings for Sunny, without actually spitting in the fucker's face. He grinned when Sunny looked up.

Sunny adjusted his glasses. He had taken off his jacket and rolled up his shirt sleeves. "You could do a bit more work, Harry," he said in between gasps.

"Somebody's got to keep watch."

"I don't think so, Harry. I don't think we're actually under police surveillance. I think it's OK to do a bit of digging."

So Sunny wanted to argue. Bad mistake was argument. It made the other bloke equal. Like saying: Hey, we'll have a debate and your opinion's as good as mine. *Fuck.* Sunny couldn't cut it. Sunny couldn't be like Daddy.

"I'm not dressed for it," said Harry. He waved a hand over his black leather Gucci shoes – annoyingly mud-stained anyway because of this stupid fuckin job – and his pinstripe trousers. He had put his raincoat in the car some time ago next to Sunny's jacket. Christ, Sunny must get his clothes from fuckin Safeways. Or Asda. No style at all. Christ.

"We're neither of us dressed for it," said Sunny, "Anyway, I think we've done enough. We're about through."

Harry looked at the hole Sunny had made. He'd chosen the wet earth near the stream, which was easier to dig, but wasn't too clever because anything that's easily buried can be easily found. Even so, it had taken them more than two hours to make a reasonable dent and Harry had started out matching Sunny dig for dig until boredom set in. Harry didn't like the thought of that soft earth and the stream running by it.

On the other hand, nobody was going to worry over the sudden demise of a shit like Charlie Pickett. Least of all West Yorkshire Police. They were too busy organising neighbourhood forums for pensioners and outings for young offenders, so they weren't going to shit bricks when a turd like Charlie bought it.

"Right, that's it," said Sunny, being the man now, being the boss. He carried his spade over to the Astra and leaned it against the back right wheel. He opened the boot. He grabbed hold of the thing inside and started to pull. "Give us a hand, Harry."

Harry smiled. "OK." He walked over to the car slowly, laid his own spade on the left back wheel, looked about him again to show he wasn't rushed. "OK. Which end you got?"

"I think it's the head."

"OK." This time Harry knew exactly what he was doing. He took a deep breath, made a grab for the legs, tugged them out of the boot. For a moment they both stood there, stock still, Harry and Sunny, pulling another breath into their lungs, ready to heave the thing across to the hole. Then Harry lurched towards Sunny and the body hinged in the middle – as he knew it would – and they fell into each other and Sunny nearly fell on his face. Harry dropped the legs and laughed. "Fuckin dead bodies," he said.

Sunny wouldn't look at Harry. "I think I can do it by myself." Sunny dragged the thing over to the hole. He dropped the body into the hole, but the legs stuck out a good foot or so. *The legs stuck out a foot.* That was a good one. Sunny grabbed hold of the legs and tried to concertina the whole body so it would fit. But the legs just stuck out at a different angle.

Sunny was gasping for breath again. Harry looked in the boot. There was the can of petrol he'd stowed earlier. He picked up the can and carried it across. He poured the petrol over the whole thing, legs included. He went back to the car, put the can back in the boot, walked back to the hole, took a box of matches from his pocket and lit one. He dropped the match into the hole. Charlie Pickett flared up like fuckin Guy Fawkes.

"Isn't that dangerous?" said Sunny. He was wiping his glasses and coughing a bit because he'd been standing too close.

"Old Charlie's not gonna feel it. Not in his condition."

"I mean won't people see it? The smoke…"

"Course they will. They'll think it's somebody burning rubbish. That's what people do up here."

They waited half an hour, then Harry used the fire extinguisher on what was left. Which wasn't much. At least the legs no longer stuck out.

"I don't think anybody could identify him now," said Sunny.

"Only the teeth. They can sometimes identify from teeth. But Charlie wore false ones, didn't he?"

Harry went round to the passenger door, opened it, put his hand in the glove compartment. He closed the door, checked there was no petrol on his hands, lit a Marlborough.

"You could still help," said Sunny. He had started shovelling earth on top of the charred heap. Again he adjusted his glasses. It was getting to be a habit that annoyed Harry.

"You're doing pretty good by yourself." Harry turned away and let the smoke drift out through his mouth. He was thinking: *well, that's the best part of the day gone, but at least I've got tonight.* He was pleased to be going on to Sheffield. It meant he'd be able to see Kim tonight. The thought of Kim gave him an erection and he grinned. *Come on Sunny, take a look at this,* he thought.

Sunny stopped shovelling. He put both spades in the boot and hurried for the driver's side. Harry let him. After all, it was public transport for both of them in a while. Harry thought about some prime places round Sheffield where he could burn the car and Charlie's clothes. Spoiled for choice, really. He threw away his cigarette and opened the passenger door, took out his raincoat and put it on. He sat next to Ray. He said: "Flaxton bus station's the best place. You can get a bus straight into Leeds and I can get the motorway down to Sheffield. You know Flaxton OK?"

"Sure."

Harry gave him directions anyway. "Why don't you just let me drive?"

"No," said Sunny, "it's no trouble."

Sunny started the car. It stalled because he wasn't used to it. Harry could have said something but didn't. A bit later he said: "Which one of you actually topped Charlie? You or your Dad? I mean, if you don't mind me asking?"

Sunny pretended to concentrate on the road for a bit. Harry waited in silence. Sunny said: "*I* did it."

"*You* did it?"

"I couldn't have done it without the old man, of course."

"You and your Dad. You're a team." Harry took out another Marlborough.

"I don't like people smoking in the car and I don't think my Dad likes it either."

Harry was looking for the turn to Flaxton. He put the cigarette back in the packet. "There. Go left. By that Jet garage."

"I see it." Sunny followed Harry's direction.

You and your Dad, thought Harry, *What a team.*

12 Raymond Dexter

RAYMOND DROVE INTO the car park next to the bus station. He got out of the car. He watched Harry drive off.

Raymond was glad to see him go. Still, Harry had been quiet the last half hour or so. Settled down a bit. Maybe he'd believed what Raymond had told him about the death of Charlie Pickett. Maybe Harry wasn't so bad after all. Maybe he – Raymond – could get some good work out of Harry once they got to know each other better.

"Don't forget," Harry had said, "your old man wanted you to phone him. Tell him where you are. Tell him I've gone on to Sheffield. Tell him I'll phone him when I've done *my* job."

Raymond felt in his jacket pocket for the mobile. It wasn't there. He tried his other jacket pockets. He tried his trouser pockets. He tried his jacket pockets again. He tried his trouser pockets again. OK, maybe he'd put it in the glove compartment. So in an hour or so it would be burned to the proverbial along with the Astra. Well, too bad.

What he needed was a payphone. He made his way through the automatic doors of the bus station. There was a woman's voice on the tannoy that told him the bus station was private property and that smoking was forbidden in any part. Good. He'd had enough of other people's smoke that afternoon with Harry. A few moments later the voice told him that CCTV cameras were in operation for his convenience and safety and that antisocial behaviour, including verbal or physical abuse of staff, would be followed inevitably by prosecution.

This was a new bus station and he only vaguely remembered the old one because he didn't come through Flaxton very often. What he did remember from the old one was cracked plaster, rusted ironwork, burger cartons, chip paper, vomit, pools of water. Now you had clean floors, automatic doors, a WH Smith, and a reassuring voice. People kept saying the country was getting worse, but one thing that was definitely improving was bus stations.

And the weather had improved too. The sky was turning orange with the dusk and it was going to be a nice evening. He even thought about going into WH Smith, with its sparkly stuff all over the windows, and looking at the books, though common sense told him they'd only have newspapers and magazines in their bus station branch. He looked for the sign that said **TELEPHONE**. When he saw it, it was pointing back the way he had come. Then he realised. They'd not got new phones yet. They'd still got the old phones outside the building on the brick-strewn concrete apron that until recently had been the site of the old station. He knew there were plans to build on the site, plans to develop the whole of Flaxton with a new covered market, department stores, a cinema, a bingo hall, and several fast food outlets.

When he was outside again, he saw the row of phone boxes. Not those huge red things that seemed now to be no more than a memory of childhood, but a sort of black post with a transparent plastic hood on top of it, almost invisible in the murk. He picked up the black receiver, shoved a 50p piece into the black coin box, dialled his Dad's number. Six rings and his Dad answered it.

"You know who this is?" said Raymond. There was a strict code for talking on the phone, even a public phone, and the first rule was no names. Raymond followed it to the letter.

"I know," said his Dad, "How did today's little job go?"

"It went OK."

"I take it your assistant got off OK?"

"Him? Yeah. Sure."

"OK. No need to talk any more, lad. See you at home."

"See you."

Raymond hung up. He started back again across the concrete apron, towards the lights of the bus station.

He was thinking about tonight. The Christmas Eve party. It wasn't much, just a few drinks round Bobby Nathan's house with a few of his old schoolmates and maybe a few girls. He thought maybe Cindy Newhall, whom he'd sort of fancied when they were in sixth form, might be there. Somebody had told him she'd got married but somebody else said she was divorced by now. Well, that was modern life for you. And it might mean she was available. If Bobby Nathan didn't have his eye on her already.

And then something happened to Raymond. First, he saw a fat, blond man about his own age, wearing a green anorak, walking towards him out of the dimness. Second, a firework went off – but it wasn't an ordinary firework. There were no flashes of light, no Roman candles, no wheeling Catherines. There was only an almighty bang. But it wasn't a bang you could hear, it was a bang you could see, even though that didn't seem logical. There it was – a red bang like a star that grew tentacles and reached out everywhere. And it seemed to Raymond that the bang was inside his head. If you drew a straight line from his left ear inward and drew another straight line from his left eye, also inward, then the centre of the red bang was almost certainly at the intersection of the two straight lines. Yes. And the bang was rapidly inflating to fill his skull and threatening to lift the skin from his face and the hair from his head like peeling the plastic top off a microwave curry.

Even while he was thinking these things, he knew they couldn't be true, that his senses couldn't be trusted, that his eyesight and his hearing and his power of thought had been suddenly, shockingly short-circuited. He didn't know how or why. But he knew he had to stay on top of it, this thing that was happening against all the natural laws, so he did what he always did in a crisis. He stayed calm and made notes. He could see himself doing this. Even as he fell, even as he fell into the arms of the fat blond man, he could see himself standing apart, looking on, making notes in an exercise book, the one he might have bought from WH Smith if he'd gone in and found there were no books.

Now he was looking through the eyes of the part of him that was making notes. He saw himself fall into the arms of the fat blond man. He wrote *Fat blond man* in his exercise book. He wondered briefly if letting himself fall into the arms of the fat blond man was a good idea. Maybe the man had been the one who caused the bang that he could see but not hear. But he had also seen that the fat man's eyes were startled, that he was completely unprepared for Raymond falling into him and almost let Raymond's slack body drop. That was reassuring then. Not as reassuring as the woman's voice on the tannoy in the bus station. But reassuring nonetheless.

Raymond thought hard about what to write next. If the fat blond man had not been responsible for the bang that could be seen but not heard, then somebody else must have been. But who? Raymond tried to identify the source of the problem, but his gaze remained fixed on the fat blond man. He wrote in the exercise book: *Can't move. Can't see much.* Instantly he understood why. The part of him that was making the notes was not the real Raymond. The real Raymond was the body now slumped in the arms of the fat blond man with his face in the fat blond man's anorak and he could only see what the real Raymond could see. He could only recall what the real Raymond could recall. He would have to take it from there then. He would have to work out what had happened from the data already available.

He wrote in the exercise book: *Bang. Red. Head.*
Suddenly it came to him. *Bang.* A gun. *Red.* Blood. *Head.*
Shot in the head.

God, thought Raymond, *I've been shot in the head.*
Then another thought occurred to him. *What if I'm dead?* And
this was followed by: *I don't want to be dead.* He nearly cried
at this point but stopped himself.

Why did he see the bang but not hear it? People
always *heard* bangs – that was what made them bangs. A
bang you couldn't hear couldn't really be a bang.

And he worked that out too. Light travelled faster
than sound. You saw it before you heard it. At least if you got
shot in the head, you did. That was logical. Which meant the
rest of the bang – the part you could hear – was probably still
on its way. As well as history A level, he'd got General
Science, though only a D.

And then it happened. The bang that could be heard.

BAAAAAAAAAAAAAAAAAAAAAAAAAAAAANG!!

And then he screamed. That filled his head too. But
he didn't feel so bad now.

At least he knew he was still alive.

13 Barry Oldham

FOR A MOMENT or two, Barry didn't know what to do. The
dark-haired young man who had fallen into his arms lay there,
slumped, heavy, and... demanding. Barry didn't like
demanding. He didn't like things that happened that
demanded he make decisions. Barry liked it when he could
walk across car parks without having this sort of
embarrassment. And mostly that's what happened. He just
walked across the car park. Then he just turned into Alderney
Street. Then he just walked along to *The Victoria* and went in
and ordered a half of shandy and waited until the Poets

arrived. Then he just went upstairs and sat down with the Poets. Then he read his poem. Then he went home. Why should tonight be different?

He thought the young man might be drunk. That's usually why people fell into you. That's why Barry confined himself to a half of shandy during his evenings with the Poets. He didn't want to be drunk and fall into people. Actually he didn't like touching people at all. Not most people. That was something he could only do with effort. *Screw your courage to the sticking place,* as it said in Macbeth. Women were different, of course – he could always do it with women if they let him. Also it was his medication. That was another reason why he confined himself to a half of shandy.

He could almost be there by now. He could almost be sipping his shandy sitting in the red plush chair in the far corner of the Edwardian-style lounge bar waiting for the others to arrive. Going over his poem. There was that line he still wasn't sure about. It was *I am a clod of lowly earth.* He knew what Fred Whittington would say: "It's tautological, old chum. How can earth be anything other than lowly anyway? It's under your feet all the time." And Barry had started preparing his defence. "Well, some bits of earth are higher than others, otherwise you wouldn't have hills and mountains." But he knew these arguments were mere sophistry. He sighed. If he changed that line now, it meant doing it on all the copies.

But suddenly he wasn't going to be changing anything. Not for a while. Not until he worked out what to do with the dark-haired young man who was slumped in his arms.

The young man didn't smell of drink and – Barry struggled for a moment to remember – he hadn't staggered about before he fell. Actually there were two other explanations apart from being drunk that meant people fell into each other or made similar physical contact. No, three. There were *three* reasons.

One was violence. They bumped into you to hurt you. But that didn't seem to be the explanation here. People who bumped into you to hurt you were a lot more... *lively.* They didn't just slump there.

The second reason was sex. But it clearly wasn't sex the dark-haired young man was after. Again, people who wanted sex didn't just slump. That left only one explanation.

The dark-haired young man was himself a user of the mental health services. He was someone like Barry. But how could Barry be sure? He had best ask a friend.

"What do I do?" he said, probably aloud.

"Take him with you on the journey of your soul," said John.

"Tek him vid you," said Erwin, "Never let der vounded fall into der hands of der enemy."

This was probably the first time during their long three-way friendship that John and Erwin had ever agreed. Barry had felt for some time that if only he could get John and Erwin to agree on a few things, life would get easier. Well, his mind was made up then. He couldn't simply drop the dark-haired young man and leave him supine on the concrete. Not if John and Erwin were urging him to action.

But there were problems. First, the dark haired young man was decidedly heavy. Barry knew he couldn't carry him any distance. And he knew from experience that John and Erwin would be pretty useless in this situation. So. He had to get the dark haired young man to help himself. That was just the sort of thing Dr Hardy often said to Barry: *Barry, you must help yourself.* And Barry knew Dr Hardy was right.

Barry took a deep breath. He peered down at the face of the young man and said in a forceful voice, the sort of voice Dr Hardy might have used: "Hello. Can you hear me?

You are going to have to help yourself." It was then that he noticed the bloody gash across the young man's forehead.

The young man had hurt himself. How? Barry made himself remember every moment leading up to the fall. He replayed the video in his mind, using freeze-frame or slo-mo wherever appropriate. He, Barry, had been walking across the car park in the growing dark of the evening after a third visit to the art gallery and the exhibition of Yorkshire artists. He had especially admired the Louis Grimshaws with their louring dusks and shrouding mists. The dark-haired young man had been walking in the opposite direction, towards him. Suddenly the dark-haired young man had fallen into him...

Barry thought: *Maybe it was me. Maybe I did something.* He couldn't remember doing anything. But he did remember – now he came to think of it – a sort of *bang*...

And then the young man opened his eyes and said: "Help me..."

It was a weak, hushed voice, but Barry knew it was a good sign. He said: "Don't worry." He said: "It's gonna be OK." He said: "You've got to help yourself." He said: "You've got to walk."

The young man said: "I don't think I can." He was still slumped in Barry's arms, gazing up at Barry's face. Barry suddenly felt how Dr Hardy must feel. Powerful. He began to compose a new poem:

> *I am the healer. Come to me.*
> *I am the healer at the still centre.*
> *I am...*

"I don't think I can," said the young man, then: "Yes. Maybe I can..."

Barry abandoned for a moment the poem in his head. He felt suddenly strong. He, the healer, had already brought about a change in the young man, given him the will to walk.

Like Jesus and the crippled youth lying on his bed who had to be lowered down into the street. Or was that St Peter? They must have helped a lot of crippled beggars, the both of them, so it didn't matter which one he was actually thinking of. But it was the first time Barry had helped a crippled beggar. What was it St Peter had said? (He was sure it *was* St Peter now.) *Take up your bed and walk.* Barry said: "Take up your bed and walk."

"What?" said the young man. He looked confused. But he put out a foot, leaned his weight on it and began to straighten up. Very slowly. Barry felt the young man's body tense. He felt the muscles take the weight. He watched as the young man's head came up level with his own and turn so he was now almost standing, facing front. His glasses were askew on his nose. He put his right arm round Barry's shoulders. Barry didn't mind now. He was the healer. He had to let people touch him now and again.

The young man said: "What happened?"

Barry said: "You've had an accident." It was what people said when things like this happened and it sounded alright. Barry said: "I'll help you walk" and he put his arm round the young man, with his left hand under the young man's left arm. Slowly, the two of them hobbled towards the bright lights of the bus station. Barry's poem was writing itself:

> *I am the healer. Come to me*
> *I am the healer at the still centre.*
> *I am the mender of limbs and minds.*
> *I am here at the bus station...*

Ah, thought Barry, *but I shouldn't be here at the bus station. I should be at the Victoria Hotel by now. I'm expected.* It was true. Of all The Victoria Poets, it was Barry who never missed a session. It was often commented on.

There were three rows of red-painted metal seats at Stand 13. Barry eased the young man into one of them. He looked down at his charge. The bloody gash didn't look so bad now. Maybe Barry could clean it up. He took out his handkerchief, licked a fairly clean part of it and applied it to the groove. Suddenly the young man jumped in his seat and swore.

People looked round. An old man in a tweed overcoat and a Sikh in a turban reading *The Sunday Times*. "He's had an accident," said Barry, "but he's alright." The old man looked away. The Sikh returned to his reading. Barry looked about him. There were about a dozen other people in earshot but they didn't seem interested. He sighed. What a judgment on our civilisation when people were so unconcerned about the fate of their fellow humans!

Barry turned back to the young man. "Well," he said, "I'm sure you'll be alright now. I've got to go." The poem continued in his head, but with amendments:

I am the mender of limbs and minds.
I am here at the interchange of life
Waiting
I am here to catch the fallen.
Waiting
For that someone
Knowing I forgive you...

"Don't go," said the young man, "Don't go." He held out a hand.

Barry thought about the poem. If he didn't write it down soon, he'd forget it. Lose it forever.

He sat down next to the young man. "I won't leave yet," he said. The young man looked at him with obvious gratitude. Barry searched in his pocket for his pen. He pulled out all his copies of *I Am the Clown at the Centre of My*

Stage. He could always write the *Healer* poem on the back of one of the copies. While it was fresh. He pulled out his pen. He wrote:

> *I am the healer. Come to me.*
> *I am the healer at the still centre.*
> *I am the mender of limbs and minds*
> *I am here at the interchange of life*
> *Waiting*
> *Let the transports of fate*
> *Reverse and drive away*
> *I am here to catch the fallen*
> *Waiting*
> *For all of humanity*
> *I can forgive the world*
> *Though they are unconcerned about their fellow man.*
> *For I am the healer.*

Not bad for a first draft. Barry looked at the young man again. He really looked a lot better now. "There's some colour coming back to your cheeks," he said, though he knew Dr Hardy would never say that kind of thing. But his mother would. The young man continued to slump in his seat but it was true: he did look decidedly better than ten minutes ago. "Sit up straight," said Barry. That was another thing his mother would say. To his surprise, the young man moved his hands, gripped the sides of the seat, pulled his legs in and pushed his body up into a straighter position. "How do you feel?" asked Barry and added: "Do you know who you are? Can you remember your name?"

"Raymond," said the young man without hesitation. Then he looked surprised. Then he smiled. "After Raymond Illingworth."

"Right," said Barry. He was wondering who Raymond Illingworth was. If he was a poet, he was one of those Barry hadn't read. "See," said Barry, "you're alright. I said you were. Just had a nasty turn, that's all." Oh yes, that was his mother talking now. But many mothers had a genuine folk wisdom that had grown up over the centuries. Medical science didn't know everything. What else would his mother say? Barry said: "I really have to go." Raymond's face dropped. Tears started in his eyes. Barry said: "It's not far. I'm not going far." That really *was* his mother. Then: "You can come if you want."

Then his heart leapt into his mouth. Why had he said that? That was stupid. But why not? The Poets were always complaining there weren't enough of them. *Bring along a friend*, they always said. But Barry never did. But this time... They might let him read both poems if he brought someone else along. He heard himself introducing the *Healer* poem. "I've only got one copy, I'm afraid. I wrote it on the way over. In the bus station as a matter of fact, in the Interchange. My friend Raymond helped me. Helped me a bit." That should be enough for them. They couldn't turn down his request to read a second poem when his new friend had a hand in it. "Can you walk, Raymond?"

Raymond blinked. After a while he said: "I think so." He put his hands back on the sides of the seat and began to lever himself to his feet. "OK. I'm OK." And he was. But slow. At least he was standing by himself now. When he tried to walk, he wobbled and Barry had to get up as well and give him support. But he wasn't the awful dead weight this time. Barry said to no-one in particular: "I can handle it." He said: "Of course I can." He began to manoeuvre Raymond towards the automatic doors. In his head the poem sang to him:

I am the healer. Come to me.
I am the healer at the still centre.

It occurred to Barry that the second *healer,* coming so fast on the heels of the first, might be considered repetitive by Fred Whittington. Well, he would just have to take the flak. *Der flak,* as Erwin would say.

John said: "Hey Barry, don't stand head in hand, turned your face to the wall." It was nice of John to be so encouraging.

14 Dockie Williams

DOCKIE WAS SICK. First he was hot, then he was cold. First he was sweating, then he shivered. He knew who was to blame for his feeling like this. Fuckin Dave Castle.

Dockie lay on the bed and considered the situation. He always liked to consider himself doing everyday things, ordinary things, things that made him seem almost ordinary himself. But coiled, aware, prepared, ready to show what he *could* do, what Dockie Williams could really do.

It had always been like that. When he worked on the docks on Merseyside. When he liked to be the first to handle the big stuff, no matter what or from where. Crates of this, boxes of that. Big and heavy, heavy and big. He knew he was stronger than the rest of them. Any lift, any tow, any haul. Pick it up, move it along, get it out of the way. In the end, they could see why he was doing it, the way his muscles formed and grew and shaped. OK, it wasn't just the work, it was the gym too. But he had to pay for the gym whereas the work paid *him.* Big joke.

Then he was a fighter. Prancing in the ring in his black and gold shorts with his head down, his fearsome fists working like pistons, regally unaware of the crowd, the smoke, the occasion. Only at the end would he look up, hands in the air, acknowledging the cheers. *Dockie Williams! Dockie Williams!*

For anybody who was looking – and nobody *was* looking now, which was a shame – here he was, in his tight black tee-shirt, tight black denims with the black belt and gold buckle, and gold-and-black Nike trainers, Dockie Williams, Dockie Williams, still quite something. Especially for a woman.

He imagined a woman in the room right now. Long blonde hair and big jugs – but well strapped up, jutting out, not hanging down. Trim waist. Long legs, high heels. He imagined the woman looking at him as he lay there. She was weighing him up, taking her time. Noting the hard eyes and heavy lips pulled back in a snarl over the perfect white teeth; scanning the heavy biceps, broad wrists and flat belly; remarking the strong thighs and lean calves; lingering on the bulge between his legs and wondering how good he was. Then, without warning, the woman turned into Dave Castle. *Fuck.*

Dave Bastard Castle. Find that bastard. Find that bastard fast, before... before some people, some people as shall not be named, come looking for Dockie and Teague.

Two million pounds. He'd held it in his hand. Held the sports bag anyway. Felt the power, the juice, the energy of all that cash shoot through the handles of the bag into his fingers wrapped around those very same handles, the fingers of his left hand, his jabbing hand, then up, into his palm, then up again along his left arm, felt it zap across his shoulder blades, down his right arm, into his hand, his uppercut hand, his knockout hand, his cut-the-crap-and-finish-it hand, into his fingers wrapped around the trigger of the Uzi.

He still had that Uzi. Not that it really belonged to him. It belonged to some people, some people as shall not be named. But he still had it. And Dave Castle still had that money, that two million. *Fuck.*

He put both hands behind his head and sighed. He looked up at the anonymous whitewashed ceiling in this anonymous whitewashed room in this anonymous fuckin motel and sighed. To think it had come down to this. Dockie Williams the Brown Brigand. Dockie Williams who was up to fight Nigel Benn, next but one contest, no doubt about it, contracts signed, ink just dried, all done and dusted. Who'd've thought that silly cunt Benn would've let himself get beat by a bloke with a monocle and a name like a fuckin vacuum cleaner? Where the fuck did that leave Dockie Williams? Fuckin nowhere, that's where.

That Uzi. It lay under the bed beside a little leather bag with the extra ammo. He took his hands from under his head, looked down at them, flexed his fingers. He made two fists. He still had it. Still had that punch, that weight, that speed, that killer instinct. Jeez, he'd been good. He thought again about the Uzi. He wanted to touch it, put the fearsome fist of the Brown Brigand round the taut trigger of the Awesome Uzi.

Dave Castle would feel the juice. Soon. Feel the fearsome fist smack his teeth down his throat. Feel the big bad barrel in the back of his mouth. Feel the stubby steel jackets take his head off.

Dockie hesitated then. There was always a limit to his imagining, to his considering things. Would Dave Castle really feel the bullets blow his head away? Wouldn't he be dead the instant the first bullet... Hell. *Fuck*. Who knew that kind of thing? Only somebody who'd had his head blown off in the first place and where do you go to listen to a bloke like that?

He swung his feet off the bed before he even knew why he'd moved. Then he realised. There was a sound outside. Feet on the gravel. Must be Teague. But you never knew. He started to reach for the Uzi, then thought better of it. It *was* Teague, that was all. And Teague was carrying. Maybe he'd get the wrong idea if he walked in on a Uzi. Maybe he'd start reaching for the Browning 9mm he kept in his jacket. Maybe…

A key turned in the lock.

Dockie's moment of indecision passed. It wasn't Teague's face that peered round the opening door – it was the face of a woman, young, painted, grinning. A lot like the woman in Dockie's daydream, in fact. Except she had red hair and wore a purple tee-shirt. But it was Teague's voice that wafted in after her. "You wanna see this black lad I've got for you, our Monica. He's got muscles where you wouldn't think muscles could grow." Then laughter, high-pitched, drunken, from the still unseen Monica. Maybe *she* was blonde then.

By now all three of them were spilling into the room. The redhead said: "You must be Dockie." She smiled, showing a gap where her right molar should have been. Teague carried a Safeways bag. He said: "You don't touch him, Glenys, you're all mine, you big-titted bitch!" Glenys laughed. She sounded just like Monica. Then Monica came all the way in so Dockie could get a good look. Hey, she *was* blonde. Though her eyes didn't seem to focus right and she had a bit of a beer gut. Still…

"I don't let you down, do I, lad?" Teague slumped on the bed next to Dockie. He was a fat lad with long black hair and tattoos on his arms – a blue dagger through a red heart on the left, and on the right a scroll that said *Mother of God Forgive Me.* He smelled of lager, as though he'd just taken a bath followed by a shower in the stuff. He said: "Dockie, your old mucker Teague doesn't let you down. Look what I've brought home, will you?" And to the girls: "Girls, this is Dockie." And to Dockie: "This is the girls." Then all three of them laughed again and this time Dockie joined in. Only then did he remember why Teague had gone out into the streets of Newcastle to begin with. Gone out and spent the whole fuckin day.

"You see Angelo?" Angelo was Teague's mate. Angelo knew things other people didn't. Not just about Newcastle neither.

"Did I see Angelo? Sure I saw Angelo. Angelo's a good boy, a good friend. Sure I saw him."

"And..." Dockie felt his fingers flexing, his nails digging into his palms.

"And... he's finding out. He's gonna find out the lie of the land. Certain persons..."

Who shall not be named, thought Dockie.

"Certain persons," said Teague, "and what they know and what they're thinking. And that cunt Castle. Where he is, how we can get our mitts on him, our arms round his lovely fuckin neck."

"I don't care for bad language," said Monica.

"Teague," said Dockie, "He *is* OK, isn't he? This Angelo? He's your mate, right? This is *your* town, right?"

"Right as rain," said Teague, "Right as fuckin rain. Hey, sorry, Monica!" He took a bottle of Napoleon Brandy out of the Safeways bag. He said: "There's some glasses in the bathroom if you wanna get them. Chance to get yourselves spruced up and ready."

"There better be more than a drink in this," said Glenys, "you told us you were flush."

"Ay, there's one o'them in there an' all," said Teague. He rolled over on the bed, clutching his sides. He said to Dockie: "What do you think of 'em? Bit of all right, eh?"

"I think you shoulda stayed cool. Not got pissed. Not brought tarts back." It wasn't often Dockie acted like his brother's keeper. But he had to say it. Suppose this Angelo gave them away, suppose... ?

He got all the way up off the bed before he even knew why he'd moved. By then it was too late. The two men in sharp suits stood in the open doorway. They pointed their guns at Dockie and Teague. One of them said: "There's women." The other one said: "Too fuckin bad."

Dockie stood there and considered. He considered himself standing there waiting. He felt coiled, aware, prepared, ready to show what he could do, what Dockie Williams could really do.

He made a dive for the Uzi.

15 Barry Oldham

"DO YOU WANT a shandy?" Barry asked Raymond.

Raymond shook his head. He looked round *The Victoria's* red-plush lounge – a little nonplussed, Barry thought. *Nonplussed in the red plush lounge. Nice line.* Barry ordered a shandy for himself.

"They've already come," the barman said, pouring the shandy.

"We'll go straight up then."

Barry and Raymond climbed the stairs. Raymond seemed a lot steadier now. The walk from the bus station had been a bit of a nightmare, with Raymond wobbling all over the place. "He's had a bit of an accident," Barry would tell the passers-by.

At the top, Barry went to the door marked **PRIVATE PARTY**, turned the handle, went in. Raymond followed.

It was a small room with cream wallpaper, a stained Berber carpet and sparse electric light. Next to the window, two red plastic-topped tables were pushed together. Around the tables sat – oh dear! – only *four* Poets. They had their poems laid out in front of them like place mats.

"Comrade Oldham! We thought you'd given us the slip this week," said Jim Wiggins, a ferret-faced man in a tweed sports jacket with leather pads at the elbows.

"Who's your friend?" asked Fred Whittington, a fat man in his sixties with grey hair, grey beard and grey bristles sprouting from his nostrils.

"It's Raymond," said Barry.

"Raymond, is it?" said Fred, sipping his Jack Daniels.

"Yes," said Barry. Then: "Raymond, I want you to meet..." And he introduced Jim and Fred. And Celia, a tall, thin, white-haired woman in a green velvet dress who stroked a glass of red wine. And Veronica, a plump, bespectacled woman in her mid-thirties wearing a pink cardigan and sipping a glass of tap water.

"Is there another name that goes with Raymond?" asked Jim, picking up his glass of stout.

"Yes," said Raymond, "Illingworth is one."

Fred said: "Damn right there. And what a man! What a sportsman! We won't see *his* like again."

"No," said Raymond, "that's what my Dad says."

"Tell your Dad he's a man who knows his cricket."

"I will."

Barry pulled up a chair, Raymond did the same. Barry saw everyone was looking at Raymond and he took a quick glance himself but could see nothing wrong. Well, nothing very wrong. The gash across Raymond's head had responded well to the spit-and-handkerchief treatment. There was only a small area of dried blood now and it was quite brown, which was a healthy sign. So. It was only what Dr Hardy would call a flesh wound then. On the downside, Raymond's hands were shaking. But Barry himself sometimes shook like that. Then another voice sounded a warning.

"Der volk don't like your friend, Barry."

"Now, now, I'm sure that's not true, Erwin." Barry spoke in what he hoped was an inaudible whisper.

"Don't listen to him, Barry. He's a just a Nazi tosser. He's crippled inside."

"Thank you, John. But I don't like to think ill of any person, if you don't mind. So be a bit more civilised. Both of you." After that, they shut up. Barry was surprised but pleased. He didn't often speak so sharply to them.

"I'll take the chair unless there are any other candidates," said Jim, "Since I understand Mr Peterkin is indisposed."

"Nothing serious, I hope?" asked Celia.

"Only the usual chronic alcoholism," said Jim, "I have also received apologies from young Heyford. I think he's staying in for Santa Claus. Now, have we all got poems to read tonight?" He glanced round the tables. "Raymond?"

Raymond looked back at Jim and blinked.

"Raymond hasn't brought a poem," said Barry.

"Getting acclimatised, are you?" asked Jim. "But you do write?"

"Oh yes, he writes," said Barry.

Raymond sat, smiling and trembling.

"That's fine then," said Jim, "I'll let the ladies go first."

Veronica leaned forward and giggled. "I'll go then. If nobody minds."

"Nobody minds," said Celia. She sniffed.

"Well then," said Veronica. She held a tiny handkerchief tightly in one hand. She picked up the sheaf of papers and began to hand out copies. "I've done ten so there should be enough."

"If mathematics means anything," said Jim.

"I wrote this one over the weekend. It was such a cold weekend but – you know – I've got two squirrels in my garden. Well, not really in *my* garden, but sort of in the trees at the back which are in my neighbour's garden – Mr Slingsby who grows vegetables. And they haven't hibernated this year. They're still running along the fence at the back. And they're so lively. And I thought: *Isn't it wonderful that even in the darkest days there is such life in nature?* And I just had to write about it." She coughed. *"Flashing Grey* by Veronica Adams," then:

> *"No dolphins could leap nor falcons fly*
> *with such a grace on this dark day*
> *as two grey squirrels passing by*
> *striding the fence along their way.*
>
> *"In foreign vales and sunnier climes*
> *nature's glory shines and shines*
> *but here upon this dreary day*
> *the brightest colour is flashing grey.*
>
> *"Oh flashing grey! Flashing grey!*
> *Thou hast thy glory too.*
> *Even on this dreary day*
> *I sing my song of praise to you."*

Silence followed. The others kept their eyes down, re-reading the verse from the pages she had given them. Only Raymond did not read from the page.

"That was good," said Raymond. A shiver ran through him. "Grey squirrels. Running along fences. I can see that."

Veronica giggled again. She took a gulp of her water. "Oh thank you. Yes, I wanted you to see it. I wanted to write a poem where you could really see what I saw. And feel what I felt."

Barry said: "It's very colourful." Right away he realised he'd said something stupid.

"For a dreary dark day," said Jim, a *grey* day."

"I don't know that I liked the word *striding*," said Fred, "That gives me a picture of these squirrels sort of...

well, sitting astride the fence. Which I don't think is what you're trying to convey, is it?"

"Well…" Veronica started.

"I liked it," said Raymond, "I could definitely see them running along the fence. Really running."

"And I notice the rhyme scheme changes in verse two," said Fred, but his voice trailed away.

Celia said nothing. She tapped her teeth with a fingernail. They were impressive teeth for a woman of her age.

"Well," said Jim, "thank you, Veronica. Who's next?"

Celia's poem – which was typed on purple paper – was a hymn to the beauty of ageing in which she swore to wear gold earrings and no bra until she was well into her nineties. She read it in a voice that reminded Barry of the heroines of pre-war British films. It caused some gallant comments from Fred, though he disliked a phrase about the moon shining, since "the moon always shines. It's in its nature to shine. We don't have to write that the moon shines."

"I liked that," said Raymond. Barry had watched Raymond throughout the reading and noticed him glancing round the room as though seeing everyday things like the tables, chairs, lamps and windows for the first time in his life. And suddenly it occurred to Barry – Raymond no longer had his glasses. They must have been lost on the walk from the bus station.

Now Raymond pressed his hands hard together – Barry thought this was intended to suppress the shaking, though it might have looked to the others like an expression of intense concentration. "I liked it a lot," said Raymond.

"Thank you, dear boy," said Celia and smiled at him. Barry suddenly realised she had false teeth, but they were obviously privately made.

Barry was next. He didn't bother handing a copy to Raymond. *I am a Clown at the Centre of My Own Stage* was quite well received, at least by Veronica who thought it spoke of "the ineffable nature of loneliness itself."

Jim, on the other hand, asked him why he always wrote about girls he couldn't get. "Can't you see you're allowing your immature desires to make you a puppet of the capitalist state? There's a huge military-industrial complex out there and it doesn't just use bombs and missiles to destroy people – oh no, it uses advertising, fear-mongering, body-fascism and brainwashing. Why can't you write about what's real for once instead of what you imagine?"

Barry said: "Human emotion is real, Jim." And then he blushed.

"You know what Chekhov said?" Jim was into his stride now, just as much as Veronica's grey squirrels had been. "Do you know what he said? He said realism isn't showing how *real* things are but showing how things *really* are. Can you honestly say your poems show how things really are? No, they glorify your subjective desires and adolescent emotions. They're *bourgeois*, Barry. I know that's an old-fashioned word to some people, but it's still a relevant word as far as I'm concerned, a word that comes from the people."

"From the *French* people," said Raymond.

"What?" said Jim.

"It's a *French* word," said Raymond.

"I know it's a French word," said Jim, "*I* didn't go to University, but I'm not stupid. I know it's French."

"I think," said Fred, "that Raymond is making a point. And I think it's a valid point. The word *bourgeois* used in English is largely the prerogative of intellectuals and middle-class thinkers. Nobody who's really working class uses a word like *bourgeois*."

"*I* do!" said Jim, "And the *French* working class use it. So it's a working class word. QED."

"*Quad erat demonstrandum*," said Raymond.

"What?" This time Jim's voice rose a little. The women broke into broad smiles.

"QED," said Raymond, "*That which was to be demonstrated*. It's Latin."

"Look, I know it's Latin," said Jim, "Just the way I knew *bourgeois* is French."

"I think," said Fred, "Raymond is making another point. And I think it's another good one. He's making a point that you would need to come from a middle class background to use a phrase like QED. If it *is* a phrase. If a set of three letters of the alphabet can claim to be a phrase. I don't know that it can, but I'm willing to take advice on that. Of course, in its full Latin form, it *is* a phrase. But then it's a *Latin* phrase."

"I know it's a Latin phrase, Fred. I've spent 25 years in the trade union movement and I know Latin when I hear it."

"I was in a union too, Jim."

"I'm sure you were, Fred. But *I* was an official. *I* was an activist. And I know what realism is and I know that *I am a Clown At the Centre of My Own Stage* is not realism. It's not about life. Not as working people know it."

"People *work* in circuses," said Raymond, "otherwise there wouldn't *be* circuses. *Clowns* are workers." He paused, then added: "Though not all workers are clowns."

"I think Raymond has yet another valid point," said Fred, "although there are certain things that must be said. First, clowns don't work on a stage. They work in a ring. So it really should be *I am a clown at the centre of my own ring*. Secondly, I wonder in what sense the stage – or the ring – is the *clown's* stage or ring. I mean, it doesn't belong to the clown in the legal sense. Not if he's just a worker, as has now been established. It belongs to the owner of the circus. Unless the clown is also the circus owner, which is possible but not very likely."

"No," said Barry, "It's the clown's stage or the clown's ring in the sense that he is *in* the ring or *on* the stage. It's *his* ring rather than another ring where..."

"Where some other clown might work instead of him," put in a helpful Veronica.

"At least we know it's a ring now and not a stage," said Fred, "but how can we say that it's the *clown's* ring just because he appears in it? He must surely appear in the company of other clowns. Especially if he's a white faced clown..."

Oh no, thought Barry, *he's picked up on the phrase ashen-faced*.

"...because then he's bound to be playing second fiddle to the red-nosed clown and so it's more proper to say that when they are in the ring and working as an ensemble, the ring belongs to them rather than to him."

"It could still be a stage," said Veronica, "if they do a special performance on a stage for a particular purpose – for instance, it could be a touring circus that visits orphanages and centres for young offenders and places like that, places where they might not have a ring of their own."

Raymond said: "I think it's a stage because the clown is singing in *Pagliacci*. And I think it's his stage because he's the star and he dominates it."

Barry looked at Raymond. "Yes. That's it. It's *Pagliacci*. I know Erwin doesn't think much of *Pagliacci* because it isn't German but..."

"Erwin?" asked Celia.

"Erwin Rommel," said Barry, "the German war hero."

"I never knew Rommel wrote about opera," said Fred, "that's a real eye-opener."

"Well," said Jim, "Time flies. Let's have one from you, Fred."

91

Barry wondered for a moment whether he should mention his second poem – *The Healer* – but thought better of it.

"I've been up in Cumbria in the past few weeks and I've come back with a whole swatch of nature poems," said Fred, "I can always find inspiration in the haunts of the Romantics."

"I'm a fan of the Romantics," said Raymond, "particularly Coleridge."

"Well," said Fred, "I'm more a Wordsworth man myself." He handed out copies of his poem. Raymond made no effort to pick up *his* copy. Barry saw he was now staring at the plaster cornice where little boy cupids shot darts at little girl cupids, if there were such things as little girl cupids, which Barry doubted. He would have to ask Fred some time.

"*Extracts from the Diary of a Poet*," Fred began, "*From the Vale of Grasmere, August 12, 2000,*" And then:

> "*The finest shade of colour on the hills,*
> *The sweetest shade of peace upon the valley,*
> *Is more beloved than urban thrills*
> *From tarmac street and fetid alley...*"

The poem had nine verses and Barry felt guilty that he lost interest in the poet's wandering in the Cumbrian fields at verse seven. Barry sighed. In many ways, Fred represented all that was best in the English poetic tradition: the open-hearted love of nature and humanity, the sensitivity of a soul who sought to be at one with the world. But Barry recognised in Jim's contempt a valid stance. Fred did not write about the real world, not even the real world of Lakeside greenery. He wrote in the dawn of the 21st century in the style and voice of a 19th century aesthete, even as Jim wrote in the spirit – but none of the style – of WH Auden in his Communist period.

There was some friendly praise at the end of Fred's effort but no real discussion from the Poets. They were tired, Barry knew, and the nine verses had underlined the fact.

Jim said: "As chairman I always leave myself till last." His poem was called *The Killing Machine*. It went:

> *"Fascist interrogator, your iron bar*
> *will not bloody this worker's head*
> *for you have lost your power*
> *of subjection, your ability to miasmate*
> *the working people of this world.*
>
> *"Yes, you who were so proud and bloody*
> *now your works are laid bare*
> *and justice with her iron claw*
> *will smite you down in your animal's lair*
> *as peace-loving peoples everywhere*
>
> *"Unite........................."*

"What," asked Fred as soon as Jim had finished, "does *miasmate* mean?"

"I would have thought that was obvious. It means to create a miasma, to make a mist, to confuse and blind the eyes. I would have thought a man of your linguistic ability would have worked that out."

"There's no such word," said Fred.

"Poetic licence," said Jim. And then, after the silence had gone on as long as the poem: "Well, if there's no more discussion, I'll close the meeting..."

"Wait," said Raymond. He stood up. Barry noticed the shaking had gone now.

"I thought," said Jim, "you didn't have a poem..."

"Not written," said Raymond, "but here, here in my head." He touched the small wound on his temple.

"What's it called?" asked Veronica.

"It's called *The Killing Machine*. Like Jim's."

Barry felt his heart thump. He didn't know what was going to happen and he didn't like the feeling.

All eyes were on Raymond. He raised his hands like a Baptist preacher abjuring his flock. He called out in a high, pained voice:

"*The Killing Machine* by Raymond Dexter:

"You go out there and bury the body.
You go in the car and bury it.
You go out there and bury the thing.
Go out, my son, and bury it..."

His head moved suddenly from side to side as though he were struggling with the pain of his own words.

"It won't bite.
It won't run away.
You just do it.
He was a shit.
You know he was a shit."

He paused, gazed round at the assembled Poets.

"But sometimes it does bite back.
And sometimes there's another biter.
Sometimes they come for you
Out in the car park."

His hands fell to his sides. His head lolled.

"And then you got to get it sorted.
And then you can't fool around any more."

He looked at Barry. And Barry laughed. He couldn't help it. Then they all laughed. Though some of them looked puzzled. And Raymond sat down.

"Was it free verse?" asked Veronica, "Only, I always have trouble with free verse."

"Me too," said Raymond, "Usually. But tonight I feel like a new person."

"That's because it's Christmas," said Barry. And everybody laughed again. And Barry blushed again.

But ten minutes later, when the meeting broke up to cries of *Merry Christmas*, his own was among the loudest.

Part Two: Christmas Day

"In first-class matches each innings starts with a new ball which is usually taken by the fast bowlers. Why is this? The two main reasons are shine and hardness. Shine affects the swing of the ball. Hardness makes it bounce more. But there will always be occasions when the pitch favours the spinners and then the captain must decide whether they should go first. Sometimes, whatever the situation, a captain has to trust his gut instinct."

– **Arthur Tetley, My Bat and Me, Pheasant Press, 1976**

16 Simone Dexter

SIMONE HAD A LITTLE day-dream. She was in *Hello* magazine, introducing the world to her lounge. Seven colour pictures over a three-page spread. Lots of people with wine glasses, old and distinguished or young and slightly drunk. Mrs Dexter with husband, businessman Bradley Dexter. The Lord Lieutenant of the County with his wife. Mrs Dexter with Sir Mick Jagger and his latest girlfriend, probably pregnant because she was on tonic water. Sometimes the pictures were so vivid they started to move and became a TV show with Carol Smillie or Jill Dando. Of course, Jill Dando was dead, some lowlife with a shooter, but that didn't matter in a dream. Camera zooms in on Mrs Dexter's cocktail cabinet with wine bottles, whisky bottles, liqueur bottles, bottle of Belgian beer and as many types of glasses as there were drinks. Christmas cards and paper streamers in background. Camera pans across to Edwardian *chaise longue*. Mrs Dexter, in white high heels by Gucci, wrap-around turquoise evening dress, silver buttons running high up the right, but a number of them daringly undone, is reclining on *chaise longue* as camera zooms in to reveal long slim legs and slender waist, moving up to encompass generous breasts with right amount of cleavage, nothing vulgar, long brown hair with ash blonde highlights, and natural peach complexion, the envy of much younger women. No, scrub the *much*.

It was only when Harry Fountain came in looking like a new recruit waiting on sergeant's orders that the spell was broken and she exchanged her welcoming TV smile for a scowl that meant yes, she knew what time it was, and she started looking through her handbag.

Harry had been late coming in this morning. Of all mornings! Offering some lame excuse about working late for Dexy the night before. *Well,* she thought, *Dexy's out working on Christmas Day, so there's no bloody reason the hired help can't turn in on time*. But then her thoughts turned to Raymond: he hadn't been in all night, though she knew he'd been due to see some old schoolfriends and she wasn't too worried. Just to be hoped he hadn't picked up some scrubber who used to sit behind him in geography class…

After a bit, she got worried about Harry, still standing there, saying nothing, doing nothing, and there were no notes in her handbag she needed to pass on right now.

"You nervous, Harry?" She got up from the *chaise longue*. "You *look* nervous. It's only a cocktail party. Just a few friends round at Christmas. Well, I say *friends*. I don't mean friends at all. Acquaintances. Contacts. My husband's good at meeting useful people. But that's the easy bit. Then you've got to entertain them. That's where *I* come in." She walked across to him, picked an imaginary piece of fluff off his lapel. She was glad she'd insisted on a black evening jacket for Harry. Lots of guests would come in casual, and there was nothing she could do about it, but it raised the tone to have the servant dressed properly.

Harry swallowed. Simone thought of him as not particularly good looking, but nothing really wrong. Neat hair going thin, small nose, good teeth, broad shoulders, flat belly, fit and strong. He clearly felt he had to say something. In the end, he said: "Yes."

"Yes what?"

"Yes, Mrs Dexter."

"I mean what does *yes* mean, Harry? Which part are you agreeing with? Mr Dexter being good at meeting people? Or me being good at entertaining?"

"Both, Mrs Dexter."

Simone sighed, patted the lapel and took her hand away. "You're a very agreeable young man, Harry Fountain. Tell me again –   how'd you ever get into this line of business?"

"I was an accountant. I got made redundant."

Simone smiled. "That's not the way a little dicky bird told it to me."

"I got caught."

"With your hand in the till."

"We don't have tills in accountancy. We don't even have ledgers any more, Mrs Dexter. Well, you can still get them in Woolworths. But that's not the way the work is done. Nowadays it's all computers. I keep telling Mr Dexter we ought to get more computers…"

"And he keeps telling *me* what a bright boy you are."

"I don't think Mr Dexter takes me seriously. Or…"

"Or he wouldn't give you all the shitty jobs. Is that it?" She paused just long enough for him not to say anything. "Well, you don't have to answer that, Harry. You don't have to agree with everything I say. You know, you're far more agreeable than most of the young men Mr Dexter employs. Most of them I wouldn't give house room to, I certainly wouldn't let them near my guests. Most of them… well, they don't have any conversation. That's their trouble. If it's not football or cars or women's arses, they've got nothing to say. And I don't take much interest in any of those subjects."

"No…"

"No what?"

"No, I don't suppose you do, Mrs Dexter."

"But you've got conversation, haven't you, Harry? I can usually tell a man who's got conversation. Though sometimes I have to bring it out of people." The next pause she let run on a bit because she knew he wouldn't say anything. "Do you like music, Harry?"

"Well…"

"Do you like classical? *I* like classical very much. I've got three Richard Clayderman CDs. Do you read much? *I* do. I read the *Daily Telegraph* from start to finish. Well, except for the sport. And you know what I like about the *Telegraph*?" She didn't wait for his answer. "It never has

99

pictures of tits. Except models in fashion shows, where you might expect it. No, it's not vulgar like some newspapers. Some newspapers I would never have in this house because, personally, I can't stand vulgarity. Well, Harry, what do you talk about then? What do you talk about with *women?*"

"I don't know."

"Have I embarrassed you? When I said *with women,* Harry, I didn't mean *in bed* with a woman. I just meant the normal day-to-day things that men and women talk about." She turned away. "Get us a drink, will you, Harry? A red wine. That St Emilion 75 at the back. I've already taken the cork out. I had one earlier. In the bath. And have one yourself. It's a good wine, that is. I read about it in the *Telegraph.*"

Harry went across and poured a glass of St Emilion. He didn't so much walk as glide across the room like an office chair on castors. He said: "I don't think..."

"I'm sure you *do* think, Harry. That's one of the things I like about you."

"I don't think I should be drinking..."

"...when you're on duty? When you're guarding the crown jewels? Pour one for yourself and come over here."

Harry did as he was told. But he had to grumble. "I just think Mr Dexter wouldn't like it if he knew I was drinking ..."

He glided back, a glass of St Emilion in either hand, and when he got within a foot, she grabbed him hard by the balls. "Careful, Harry! Don't spill anything!"

Harry said: "Aaaarggghhh!!" in a loud high voice.

Simone held on. "I don't think Mr Dexter would like it if you spilt red wine on my carpet."

Harry stood perfectly still, the discomfort etched into his whitening face. But he didn't spill a drop. "Please, Mrs Dexter..."

"You think about it, Harry. If you spill wine on my carpet, Mr Dexter is very likely to chastise you. And if you tell him why you happened to do it..."

"Please...!"

"If you tell him how it came about..."

"Ohhh...!!"

"If he doesn't believe you, he's going to cut these little chestnuts right off. And if he *does* believe you, then he's still going to cut them off. That's what's called a no-win situation." She took a deep breath. "I'm making a point, Harry. Do you see the point I'm making?" She pulled her hand away to let him speak.

His voice was quiet. "Yes. Yes, I see."

"I'm sure you do. But I'll spell it out anyway. My Mr Dexter is not a man for leaving well alone. That's why he regularly hires some nice young man like you to look after me, to drive the car, to carry the shopping, to answer the door. Some of these young men think they have power over me, that they can tell me what to do, then run back to Mr Dexter if I don't do it. So I make my point early on. *I do what I like.* And you keep your mouth shut. Because if you ever go back to my husband telling tales, *I* will tell tales about *you*. And even if Mr Dexter believes what you say, you can be sure he'll believe every word *I* tell him. And I wouldn't like to see you with your face burnt off. It's such a pretty face." She stroked his face just once before she took the glass out of his hand. "There. Now we've got that settled, what do you think about this dress? It's Versace, you know. It's the one he'd just finished when he got killed."

"Very nice, Mrs Dexter."

"And what about these knickers?" She pulled up her dress on the silver buttons side. "Do you think they go with the dress? They're only Marks & Sparks but they're comfortable and I do like my comfort. Only trouble with these slit dresses is matching your underwear. You think I should change them?"

"Maybe you could..." Harry struggled, "...button up some of them buttons..." He pointed awkwardly.

Simone let the dress fall back. "Oh, I don't think so, Harry, that's not my way at all. No, I'll go and change 'em. You sit down, make yourself comfortable, read a magazine. There's nothing more unsettling for a mature woman than seeing a young man standing to attention all the time."

17 Bradley Dexter

THE CARPET HAD been well cleaned in the few hours since Charlie Pickett met his end. Mrs Ndingu from the KWIKLEEN agency had been scathing about the side of Christmas beef Mr Dexter had inadvertently dropped on his carpet. She never ate red meat anyway and advised Dexy to buy a turkey from the supermarket in future where the packaging might cost as much as the bird itself but then it never burst, and if it did, there wasn't any blood. Dexy agreed it had been a silly thing to do. He even gave her a £10 Christmas box for such a fast and efficient job. Then he had phoned Marty Green, who ran KWIKLEEN and another organisation that Dexy frequented more often.

"I'm still waiting," he said.

"It *is* Christmas day," said Marty.

"I know that. I've only got a couple of hours. Then I'm due back home for a party. That's why I wanted prompt. Remember what I said?"

"Young, small, well built, not much in the talking department. I remember. Right you are, I know just the little lady. And she's on her way over. Even as we speak. Actually, you've met her already, round at Johnny's." He reminded Dexy with some personal details. Dexy remembered.

Her name was Chanelle. She was dark haired, olive skinned, pert breasts and buttocks, trim waist and well-turned legs, wearing a plunging black halter top and orange miniskirt under her mock sable coat. Half an hour after Dexy's phone call, the coat and skirt were lying on the floor along with her black platform shoes and the girl herself was lying across the desk next to the video player, holding an empty Champagne glass, staring hard at the Asti Spumante bottle on a silver coaster nearby.

"Now," said Dexy, "Pay a bit of attention because this bit is very interesting."

Dexy turned back to the video player. Men in white flannels were trooping out on to bottle green pitches under slate grey skies, smiling and generally having a good time. The voice of John Arlott was saying: "The last few years have not been kind to Yorkshire Cricket Club. But it is beyond belief that the historic team of Len Hutton, Johnny Wardle, Brian Close, Fred Trueman, Ray Illingworth and the incomparable Geoffrey Boycott should not once again rise like a phoenix from the ashes to bring about a new age of splendour and achievement as the next decade approaches...." Orchestral music swelled, then cut off.

"There," Dexy leaned forward and pressed the OFF switch. It should have happened like John Arlott said. But it didn't. Geoffrey Boycott. Eight thousand one hundred and fourteen runs in test cricket including 22 centuries. Thirty-two thousand seven hundred and fifty runs for Yorkshire including a hundred and three centuries. Geoffrey Boycott, the greatest living Yorkshireman. "And what did we do to him?" asked Dexy. Chanelle glanced across, as though she might have missed something. Dexy smiled. "We sacked him – twice. Chanelle, you can't ever predict the outcome of the Great Match of Life. One minute you're hitting boundaries all over the place. Next, you're leg before wicket and Dickie Bird is giving you your marching orders. But if you're a team, you've got to hold together, you've got to support the leader. And you've got to have a leader that knows what it's like to face a long hard innings, to fend off the spin bowlers and keep those runs coming. There's always a temptation to take chances, you see, to please the crowd, a little dig here, a little shot there, when what you really need is staying power..."

Chanelle said: "Oh yeah. I *like* watching old videos. I mean, it was really interesting. Baggy trousers. I like to see men in baggy trousers and white shirts. It's sort of a fashion statement, isn't it? It's like saying: *I don't give a shit.*"

Dexy leaned across and stroked her hair. "I'm glad you liked it, girl, because the game of cricket is just like the game of life. You can see that, can't you?"

"Oh yeah. I can see that. Because it's like in life when you..." she allowed herself a think, "when, when, when you have to stand about a lot and not do nothing, just like them fielders have to, and there's somebody down the far end like the batman..."

"*Bats*man."

"Yeah. And the bowler's so far away the *bats*man can't properly see what he's doing. You can't even see his face. But you know he's planning to do something to *you*. You got to be prepared for that. Yeah, I can see why it's like life..." she was gaining confidence now, "...you just wait around for a long time for something to happen, and when it does, it clips you round the head. Cos they're hard, them cricket balls. That's why those fellas wear armour nowadays, all wire round their faces. So you gotta look out. So yeah, that's a lot like real life." She laughed.

"How old are you, Chanelle?"

"Why? How old do I look?"

"Nineteen, twenty..."

"Yeah, that's right. Nineteen. Twenty."

"When you're 19, you've not seen a lot of life. But I'm glad you enjoyed my little video and I think it's been good for you." He stood up, took a roll of notes out of his pocket, counted them off. "I knew you were the kind of girl who'd get something out of it." He handed her the notes. "Let's do it again – sometime soon."

Chanelle also counted the notes and she grinned. "Is that it? Is that all I have to do then? I mean, well, I really enjoyed it. Yeah. Are there any more like that then?"

"The videos? Sure. I've got 15."

"Fifteen. Wow. That's, well, great. Well, I'd really like to come again." She put the cash down the front of her top just like he knew she would.

He was warming to his theme now. "Women play cricket too, though it's not the same. Women don't really have the patience. But it only goes to show the appeal of cricket is universal. And all those different races play it. Have you ever thought of that? Africans, Australians, Pakistanis, Indians..."

"The Chinese don't play cricket, Mr D. And the South Americans, they don't play cricket. And the *real* Americans play baseball." Then she caught herself. "Mind you, I expect everybody would play if they knew more about it."

Now it was Dexy's turn to be Devil's Advocate. "You're right about that. It's them Mongolian races, they're the ones that don't play cricket. That's your Chinese and your South American Indians, all descended from the same ancestors from the time when there was a bridge across the Bering Straits. In those days you could walk from China to America. One of the seven wonders of the ancient world, that was, until some bastard burned it down. But you're right – the Mongolian races don't have the cricketing gene. Nor the Arabs. Nor the Jews neither. It's because they don't understand discipline, team spirit."

Chanelle thought about that. "What about that chap in *Chariots of Fire*? He was a Jew, wasn't he? I thought he was."

"Harold Abrahams. Course he was a Jew with a name like that! But he wasn't a cricketer, was he? He didn't play team games. He was a runner. What do runners do? Get out in front and stay there. You've heard of *The Loneliness of the Long Distance Runner*?"

"No."

"Well, it's a medical fact. They get lonely. It's because they're always trying to get out in front, to suit themselves. That's the opposite of cricket. In cricket it's the team that matters. Batsmen, bowlers, fielders, wicket keeper, they've all got a part to play."

Chanelle allowed herself one more lingering look at the Asti bottle. "I've never been on a team. I was never good at sports when I was at school."

"That's one of the things that's wrong with our education system. They don't turn out team players any more because they don't know what team spirit is. That's why they get disruptive pupils in class. You know what my ambition is, Chanelle?"

Chanelle took her eyes off the Asti and gazed into his. "No, Mr D."

"My ambition is to put something back into this country because this country has made me. I'm a patriot. I'm proud to be British. And English. And a Yorkshireman. And what I'd like to do, when I'm retired from my profession, when I've got a bit of time on my hands, is put some money into sport. Into cricket. Train up some youngsters to be the new Boycotts, the new Len Huttons or Johnny Wardles. And it wouldn't matter to me where they come from, Pakis and Indians and Afro-whaddayacallits, except they'd have to live in Yorkshire of course. Because if it started up again in Yorkshire, these kids would soon be leading the country and then the world. And we wouldn't have those bloody Australians laughing at us, like they do now."

"Don't you like Australians?"

"They're too bloody cocky. Len Hutton used to say it. He used to say he got fed up being told how to play by

106

Australians. If I had my way, we wouldn't get all their TV programmes neither. What have they got on *Neighbours* or *Prisoner Cell Block H* that you can't get on *Emmerdale*? No, I stick by my own kind."

At that moment there was the sound of a key in the lock, then footsteps. In what seemed like an instant, Chanelle put down her glass, jumped off the desk, pulled on her skirt, dropped her coat over a chair. The door opened and Ray came in. Dexy hadn't expected Ray. And it was clear from his startled expression that Ray hadn't expected Chanelle.

Dexy said: "What you doin' here?" And then: "Come in, Ray. I thought you'd be at home with your mother by now."

"I had to pick up my Polo," said Ray, "took a taxi over."

"Oh yeah," said Dexy. He'd forgotten the car. Of course. Ray had to come to the office to pick up the car. "You have a good time then?"

"Good time?" Ray glanced again at Chanelle.

"With your mates. That party you were going to."

"Oh, it didn't work out. I met somebody. Stayed over with them." He was still looking at Chanelle.

Dexy said: "You're not interrupting anything, Ray. Chanelle here is a bit of a cricket fan, as it happens." And then he noticed the red mark on Ray's forehead. "What happened to you, lad?"

"Oh, nothing, Dad." Ray brushed a hank of hair across. "Fell over. Bad weather. Patch of ice. Hit me head."

"Right," said Dexy.

Chanelle said: "I've been watching some videos. Cricket videos."

"Yes, said Ray, "I know what you mean. Our Dad keeps all his videos here in the office. For when the work slackens off." He was still having a good look at Chanelle and she was having a good look back.

107

"Well, there's not a lot of room at home…" Dexy started.

"Our Mum doesn't let him keep them in the house any more," Ray cut in.

Dexy coughed. "She's not a cricket fan, not Simone. She has her own interests. We've got a modern marriage."

Chanelle looked back from Ray to Dexy. "Simone? That's French. *My* name's French. What's it mean – Simone?"

"It doesn't mean anything. My wife's mother saw *Room at the Top* when she was pregnant. She was named after that actress, Simone Siggnorette."

Ray corrected him. "You don't sound the *g* and *t* – it's not a bloody drink, Dad. *Sin-your-ay!* Not *Sigg-nor-ette*."

Dexy knew when youth had gone too far. "Well, listen to that! Listen to how French my lad can be. He parlays the France-ays. Maybe we should have called him Raymondo instead of Raymond."

Ray said to Chanelle: "What's *your* name mean then?"

"Chanelle. It means scent. *Scent* like *nice smell*, not *sent* like *sending a parcel*."

"That's what it means, does it?"

"Yeah. C-H-A-N-E-L-L-E. Like Chanel Number Five. That's a sort of scent."

"I suppose it is," said Ray, "Why did your Mum give you a name like that?"

"Well, she didn't actually. I just liked the sound of it so that's what I call myself."

"So what did your Mum call you?"

Chanelle giggled. "I don't like to say."

"Bet it wasn't French."

"No, it wasn't."

"Go on. Tell us."

Dexy, who had felt embarrassed for himself when Ray arrived, now felt embarrassed for Ray. "He's a real nosey parker, my lad, a real busy-body. That's what you get with education. You tell him only what you want to, love, don't put yourself out to do what *he* says."

"Doreen," said Chanelle.

"Doreen!" said Ray, "Well, that's not too bad. It's not like… Tara or Kanga or Tiggy Leggy Burk. It's not like those names you get in the *Telegraph*."

Chanelle said: "Oh, I think those names are glamorous. But Doreen's not. It's not … exciting, is it? It's not like the name you'd have if you was a model."

"Are you a model then?"

"Like I said, don't tell him any more than you really want to."

"I'm *trying* to be a model. I'm building up my portfolio."

"We could help, couldn't we, Dad? *I* could help. I know a few photographers. Hey Dad, what's the name of that chap down Roundhay that we use now and again? Trask, isn't it?"

"*Johnny* Trask. Yeah. That's right."

"That's where I met your Dad."

"I had some work needed doing, you see, Ray. Some pictures took of some property for sale. I always use Johnny when it comes to property."

"Well," said Chanelle, "he doesn't only do property for sale. He's done some pictures of me."

"What kind of pictures?" asked Ray.

"A bit of fashion, some swimsuit pictures, a bit of topless…"

"Are they any good?"

"Your Dad liked them."

Dexy said: "I thought they were very… *artistic* as a matter of fact. He's a good lad is Johnny Trask."

"Not just on property then?" said Ray, then: "Right, Dad! Mum'll want us back home early to get a shower and get our clothes changed for the party."

"Right, son. I didn't realise the time."

"You're going to a party?" Chanelle looked deep into Ray's eyes.

"Just a few drinks with a few influential people," said Dexy, "And a bit of food – nibbles and canapés and stuff like that. Though I don't think I'll be eating much myself. Got a touch of indigestion…"

"Two judges, a banker, three MPs and a bishop," said Ray to Chanelle, "Why don't *you* come?"

"No, no. It'd be boring for her. It's gonna be business talk."

"It's boring anyway, Dad, because your bishops and your judges are boring. She can talk to me. I won't be talking business." He turned back to her. "Anyway, *modelling's* a business, isn't it? Maybe we can introduce her to a few people."

"Oooh yeah!" said Chanelle. She jumped up and down in her bare feet.

"I don't think…"

"If she's with me, that should be OK. Right, Dad? Then there'd be nothing that Mum might ask to know about." He turned back to Chanelle. "You'd like to come, wouldn't you, Chanelle?

Chanelle smiled her full-colour 8x10 portrait smile "If it helps my modelling…"

"I'm sure it will," said Ray.

"OK. OK then," said Dexy. He knew he'd been outsmarted – it was just that he usually got the better of Ray. Something had happened to the boy. Maybe he'd been drinking. "Very pleased to have you come along, Chanelle. But maybe we could drop you off first for a change of clothes.

It's going to be a bit formal, you see. Nothing elaborate, just a few evening dresses on some of the ladies."

"She can borrow something from my Mum. You're about the same size, Chanelle. I mean in height. I'm sure our Mum's got something that'd fit you."

"Wouldn't your Mum mind about that?"

"How old are you?"

"Nineteen. I've already been asked that."

"Nineteen! Then I don't think my Mum would mind at all. Not if her dresses fit *you!* Right. It's settled then. You go down to the car, Chanelle. It's the red Polo. We'll lock up and follow you down."

Chanelle put on her shoes. Then she did a little twirl, ending up looking straight at Ray. "OK. See you down there." She went out the door and down the stairs.

Dexy said: "What the hell are you playing at?"

"I like her. She looks OK." Ray smirked. "Those pictures of Johnny Trask's... *artistic,* were they? He always did have a good eye for a bit of property."

Dexy took a deep breath. Maybe that knock on the head had sent Ray a bit daft. But with any luck it would wear off in a few hours. And it *was* Christmas and families ought not to fall out at Christmas. "OK. Now let's go see your Mum. We don't want to be late..." He went across to the pegs and put on his worsted overcoat. "But *you* do all the talking about this girl, right? I want no part of it. She was never here. You met her in a club. Or the well women clinic. I don't care. Just keep me out of it."

It didn't do any harm to be honest with the lad. Might even do him some good in the growing-up department.

And suddenly he knew why Ray looked so different – he wasn't wearing his glasses!

111

18 Simone Dexter

SIMONE LISTENED INTENTLY as the bell chimed a strident phrase from Vivaldi's *Spring* and Harry opened the front door. She heard the brief flurry of Geordie accents that told her it was Eddie and Gina. She raised herself to her full five-feet-nine, thrust her breasts forward as the footsteps in the hall got nearer. She smiled. She waited. Then the lounge door was pushed open. She rushed towards it, arms outstretched.

"Eddie! Gina! It's so nice to see you both!" she embraced Gina, offered her cheek to Eddie. "Oh, Gina, you do look nice!"

Gina slipped out of her pink leather coat and gave it to Harry. She did a little pirouette to show off her very short, tight, strapless black dress. "Do you like it then? It's my present from Eddie. Plus matching handbag." She held up the handbag.

"Oh," said Simone, "I *do*. I do think it's sexy." And she did. And she thought Gina was sexy anyway, with her small breasts, long legs, slender waist, urchin haircut and lean boyish face. If you liked that sort of thing.

Gina was still talking about the dress. "It's Alexander McQueen. Actually, it's very special. It's one Versace was working on when he got shot and they asked Alex to finish it for him." She took Simone's arm. "You know, I do take that as a compliment, coming from *you*, Sim. Because you are a good-looking woman. You are just the sort of middle-aged woman that I would want to grow into."

Eddie glanced across at them and laughed, showed his big, strong teeth, made the scars on his cheeks pucker up. He was in his late thirties, still had his thick curly hair and his belly was flat as an ironing board, but he looked older than his years. And he was ten years older than Gina anyway. He said to Simone: "I parked the Merc in the drive. I trust it's in

112

nobody's way." He said to Harry, indicating the sports bag in his left hand, "Can I just leave this by the bar, laddie?" He went across and plonked it down.

As though he owned the place, thought Simone. She said: "It's not a Kalashnikov, is it? Only we don't have a shooting permit." She laughed to show it was all in fun. "So what'll you two have to drink?"

"Eddie's on the tonic water tonight, Sim. Gin and Italian for me."

Simone shouted over: "Harry, when you're ready, a Frankie Detorri for Mrs P," and both women laughed.

Gina said: "And you're so witty too," in a little-girl voice that let her get away with it.

Eddie removed his charcoal grey coat. He was wearing a blue pin-stripe suit and mauve open-necked shirt. Yes, he was a smart dresser, was Eddie, if a bit old fashioned. Simone could see that Eddie and Gina were a pair. She said: "And a tonic water for *Mister* Patterson, Harry! Would you like a twist of lemon, Eddie?"

"No, I'll take it neat." Eddie put away his smile. "Is Dexy here? I've got a bit o' business I wanna talk out with him."

"He's on his way. Had a bit of stuff to sort out at the office."

"On Christmas Day?" Eddie tut-tutted. "The man's a workaholic. You'll have to do something about that, Simone."

"You can't tell my Dexy what to do, Eddie. He's not that sort of fella. You two are the first to arrive. Red wine for me, Harry, and remember the carpet."

"So," said Gina, "what did Dexy buy you this year?"

Simone exhibited her left wrist.

"Oh God, Sim, a gold Rolex! That's so modish. *Everyone's* got one this year." She took Simone by the arm again. "You and me should have a chat, Sim. Leave the men to talk about which one of the *The Spice Girls* they'd like to shag the hardest." When Harry had handed them the drinks, she shouted at Eddie: "Me and Simone are gan to powder our noses. You lads talk amongst yourselves. Don't start fighting, mind."

They walked along the hall and Simone opened the bathroom door. She was glad she'd asked Mrs Ndungu to pay special attention to the bathroom this week. It was always the one place that could show you up. As they got inside, Gina made a beeline for the teak chair in the corner by the bath. She said: "I hope you don't mind, Sim, but I think it's good that the women should get together now and again and talk some sense before the men start having sulky silences."

Simone parked herself on the lavatory seat. "Why should there be sulky silences, Gina?"

"Because of this thing that's happening. It's very big, Sim, maybe bigger than you think. Otherwise I wouldnae interfere. By the way, I meant it when I said how good you looked. Your Dexy is a lucky man. My Eddie always says so when we're on our own and he's making lists of good-looking women."

"He does that often, does he? Makes lists of women?"

"Oh ay. Kim Basinger, Melinda Messenger, Ulrika Johnson. It's one of his hobbies. I encourage him. I say I'd rather have him list them than fuck them."

"Wouldn't you trust him with Melinda Messenger then?"

"I wouldn't trust him with a hole in the wall." Then: "But that's enough about Eddie. No, it's this two million pound bank job that everybody's talking about."

Most things are undignified when you're sitting on a lavatory. That made an extra reason why Simone shouldn't show her ignorance. "Everybody's talking about it? Maybe they *shouldn't* talk about it. Maybe that's the way people get into trouble."

"Oh come on, Sim! Who's gonna hear us in the lav? What sort of pervert is gan to listen in on two women in the privacy of their own bathroom? I know there's been a lowering of standards since Mrs Thatcher's time but I don't think things have got quite that bad. I'm telling you, Sim, this bank job is bigger than you know."

"Bigger than two million?"

"It's the people involved, not the money. It's not just bankers. It's the people who bank with the bankers. People who like to sell Government surplus missiles that fell off the back of a truck in Vladivostok."

"You saying Russian Mafia?"

Gina took a sip of her drink. "I'm saying they're taking an interest. Breathing down Eddie's neck, as a matter of fact. Because two of these silly buggers that did the job were up in our backyard, see? Just outside of Newcastle. *The Cameron Arms*. Little motel with a bit of a pub attached. Nice little place that does a good roast dinner on Sundays. Seems one of them was a local lad and knew his way around. And Eddie was asked by these Russkis to have a word, like…"

Simone was suddenly nervous. But she had to ask: "What happened?"

"Sulky silences. I can always tell when something's gone wrong. He wouldn't answer any of my questions. Then I heard it on Radio Newcastle before we drove down here. *Massacre* they were calling it. Mind you, I think that's a bit much. I mean, 62 people in Egypt, that's what *I* call a massacre. This is only four. But that's the press for you. Sensationalise everything, even the BBC do it nowadays. Anyway, I had another go at Eddie. It turns out those silly buggers that did the bank job were *carrying*. Not just shotguns like most folk, but Browning automatics the same as *our* lads carry. And an Uzi under the bed. Course, these other blokes didn't know how to shoot properly. Bloody amateurs. But one of *our* lads, a nice young kid called Eric, got himself shot up. So now Eddie's got him down at the kennels, and it looks like he may need putting down. And the others, the ones that shot him, are no longer with us, cast off their mortal toil."

"You said four."

"Two lads, two lasses. I don't think anybody meant to kill the lasses. I think they just got in the way." Gina put her glass on the rim of the bath, took a tissue out of her handbag and blew her nose. "If they could only have got the bodies out...! Eddie's brother's got the contract for building a dogtrack outside Sunderland and we could have had them in concrete in half an hour. But the whole thing was too noisy. And with Eric under the weather, they decided not to stick around and chance it."

"Stupid bastards."

"Aren't they just? So now we still don't know where the bloody money is. But we know your Dexy is looking out for it as well."

"So you've come to parley? Get Eddie out of a hole with these Russians?"

"I don't think it's just Eddie that's in trouble. I think it's Dexy too. And anybody else who's English. These Russkis, see, they think anybody that's got territory over here must be working together to do them down. It's what I call their Cold War mentality."

"They want their money."

"They want *something!* I don't know. I can't exactly figure it out. Neither can Eddie, but that's nothing new."

There was a knock on the door, it opened a little way and Eddie poked his head round, grinning. "Somebody mention my name, was it? Hope I'm not interrupting you ladies when you're doing something private..." Simone got up quickly off the lavatory seat. She could see he had the sports bag in his hand.

Gina said: "If it *was* something private, we'd've locked the door."

Eddie went on: "I was having a right old chat with that barman of yours, Sim, that flash Harry. And then the other guests started coming in. I just met a bloody vicar, I did! So it wasn't like I was bored. But... it's just that somebody very special has now arrived."

At this point Eddie pushed the door open all the way and Dexy was there in the hall, standing awkwardly. He said: "Hello, my angel. Hello, Gina. Funny place to find you two."

Simone said: "Where's Ray? Did he come back with you?"

"He's in the lounge. Mingling."

Eddie laughed again, a dirty one this time. "Mingling with a nice little raver. Skirt up to her collarbone. Wouldn't mind a bit of mingling with that one myself."

"Don't be coarse," said Gina, "Not in company."

"Dexy, who is this girl?" asked Simone, "What's she got to do with Ray?"

Dexy smiled briefly. "Nobody important. Just a girl. He's a normal lad, isn't he?"

"I just hope she's a fit person to talk to our guests, that's all."

Eddie was in his element now. "Fit? She's got *them* in fits. That vicar fella..."

"Bishop," said Dexy quickly.

"Well, whatever. Couldn't take his eyes off her arse. Kept asking her if she wanted a *7-Up*."

"I told you, Eddie..." Gina got up off the chair.

"Oh come on, Gina mon, lighten up. We're among friends. And I've brought our friends a gift. A Christmas present." He handed the sports bag to Dexy.

Dexy took it. "It's not gonna go off in my hand, is it, Eddie?"

"If it was, would I be staying around to see it?"

"You've got a funny sense of humour, you geordies. I mean, funny *strange*." Dexy began to unzip the bag. "Well,

117

alright then, let's see..." He put his hand in the bag and felt around. When it came out again, it was holding a cricket bat. "Ey up, it's a cricket bat!"

"Got it in one!" Eddie guffawed, "Nobody can fool you, eh, Dex?"

"It's just what we need," said Simone, "Thanks, Eddie."

Eddie held up his hands. "It's not just any old cricket bat, Dex. Take a good look." He pointed. "The names."

At that point, Dexy changed. His awkwardness vanished. His face beamed. "It's autographed!" He studied it. "John Hampshire, Tony Nicholson, Richard Hutton, Don Wilson!" He began to speak more quickly and loudly. "Padgett, Sharpe, Binks, Trueman, Close, Illingworth, Taylor! It's... it's..."

"The whole 1968 team!" put in Eddie. His face was as radiant as Dexy's.

Simone looked across at Gina and noticed a brown stain on the tiling below the shower head. That bloody Ndungu! She'd never use *her* again! She looked back at Dexy. "What's 1968?"

Dexy could hardly get the words out. "It's the last time Yorkshire won the championship! It's... it's the best present I've ever had, Eddie mate! Oh yes!" He tapped the bat on the bathroom floor, taking up a position that Simone recognized as the sort of thing cricketers did. He raised the bat.

"You mind that cabinet," warned Simone, "And the mirror. And the picture."

But Dexy was too wrapped up in it. "Oh, this is nice, Eddie. This has taken you a lot of time and trouble. But where'd you get it? It's a real collector's piece."

Eddie had been staring at the picture on the wall, a naked woman stepping out of a bath. But it wasn't up to much, it hardly showed anything. He turned away. "You

118

know how it is. Some old lad falls on hard times. He sells his medals from the war, his first edition King James Bible, his autographed *Beatles* programmes from 1962, you know, the tour with Helen Shapiro. People sell everything in the end. And I'm the sort of lad that *buys* everything in the end. Especially when I've got a good mate like Dexy here who I know is panting for this sort of stuff. I'm a football man myself. More Magpies than Dickie Birds."

Dexy said: "What can I ever do to repay you, Eddie?"

"I'm sure he'll think of something," said Simone. She thought: *As long as it isn't me.*

"Ahh…" Eddie allowed himself a sigh, "Well, Dexy mon, we do need to talk…"

Gina got up from the chair. "Leave it till afterwards, Eddie. I mean after the party. Simone here has gone to such a lot of trouble with all those drinks − and I saw some cheese and pineapple chunks on sticks, which you know you like."

"It's not just cheese and pineapple chunks," said Simone, "I've got smoked salmon as well. *And* garlic mushrooms. I've got *canapés.*"

"Ay," said Eddie, "let's get at it."

"And," said Simone, "I want to see this girl Ray's brought back. If she's some little tart…"

Dexy waved the bat, wriggling his wrists the way Simone had seen cricketers do on TV. "Oh, don't spoil the party, my angel. We should all be enjoying ourselves tonight." Then: "I've not got much of an appetite, actually. Bit of heartburn."

Simone felt it was no time to give Dexy sympathy. She was still annoyed about this girl of Ray's and still fearful about her cabinet. She said: "You can put that bat in the conservatory, Dexy. I'm not having you wave it at the Bishop. And you're the last one out of the bathroom − see you put the light out."

It was party time.

119

19 Dave Castle

DAVE WASN'T EXPECTING Lorraine. He should've been. She was always coming round anyway.

She was running on the stairs. She came bursting in. "Dave, Dave!" she shouted. She jumped on the bed where he was lying. She said: "Oh Dave, I'm sorry! And I'm so scared. Scared for the both of us!" She hugged him. "It's them, isn't it? I met them at that Christmas party Aunt Sylvia gave. I remember the black one. He was lovely, such nice teeth he'd got." She gave him a shake, but he didn't need it. He was wide awake. He'd already seen it on telly.

"Dave, it *is* them, isn't it?

"Yeah, it's them."

"They're the ones that went on the job with you."

"Yeah. They're the ones."

"And they're dead!"

"And the women. I didn't think they'd kill the women." Dave wanted to cry.

"It's all true, isn't it? Four people dead. There wouldn't be four people dead if it wasn't true. It really was a million pounds."

"Two million. That's what they told us. They knew what they was doing. They knew the alarm system. They knew the closed circuit video. They knew the people in the bank. It went smooth as clockwork. Smooth as cream."

"Who set it up, Dave? Who's killed Dockie and Teague?"

"I don't know. I mean, I know names, but they won't be real. Nobody'd give their real names." He had a think. "Wait. I know somebody who'll know. Somebody who gives out stuff like this." He swallowed. He said: "We had an arrangement. For giving them the money, splitting the take. Meeting up with the fellas that set it up."

"But you didn't turn up."

"I ended up with the bag. And we got separated. And I thought: *why not?* Why not take the whole bloody thing? Two million. I saw them put it in. Saw the little bags of notes. All of them labelled. *£10,000 in £10 notes, £50,000 in £20 notes.* Like bags of tea. Them bags is like European regulations now. That's what they said. Nobody put up a fight, them fellas who worked at the bank. They were all gonna get their cut. That's what they thought. And that's what Teague thought. And Dockie. But I fooled them all."

"You ran out on them? *All* of them?"

"I thought: *two million pounds.* I've never seen that much money. I couldn't imagine it. I didn't believe you could get so much money in a sports bag. I ran and ran and when I looked back, there was nobody running after me. I thought: *OK, I'll phone them, I'll tell them where I am. I'll square it with them, Dockie and Teague. We can still do the dirty on the others, the lads that set it up, but I'll square it with Dockie and Teague.* But then..."

"You ran out on all of them."

"In a way it wasn't the money, it was the number. I thought about the money, I thought what I could get for it. I tried to think of all the crack I could get, all the heroin, all the coke, all the Es, all the speed, all the purple hearts. I started thinking all the whisky and the brandy and the vodka. And then I started thinking all the hash and the cigarettes – ordinary cigarettes that've got a proper health warning. And then I thought of all the lemonade and the cream soda and the sherbet bombs and the liquorice sticks and the gobstoppers and Rolos and Polos and Kit-Kats and Penguins. And the fish fingers and the baked beans and the corn flakes and the Opal Fruits made to make your mouth water. But I had to give up because I couldn't think of where it would end. It scared me, Loz. I couldn't see it ending. It was like I'd be on this supermarket trolley for the rest of my life. I could never get off. And I hadn't even started thinking about jackets and chinos and jeans and rugby tops and Reebok trainers and Doc Martens."

"You're mad. You've gone daft. You're funny in the head."

"And I was scared. I came back here and I stuck it under the bed and I never opened it. I never even had the key. They never trusted me to have a key. I told you: *The fellas in the bank was in on it and they never trusted me. Not properly.* So they kept the key."

"You could rip it open. You could use a breadknife!"

"I didn't like to. Not till I split it with Dockie and Teague. I wanted them to know I'd not touched it. Anyway, I was scared to look at that money. It wasn't the money any more that mattered. It was the *number*. Think about it, Loz! The number!"

"I *did* think about it! How can I *not* think about it?"

"It's such a nice number. I saw that number, Loz, I saw it in front of my eyes when I was awake and when I was asleep and it seemed like a perfect number and I didn't want to lose it and I didn't want to break it up and I didn't want to spoil my perfect number. Do you understand that, Loz? Do you think I'm mad?"

"No, no, Dave! I don't think you're mad! I can see it too! *Our* perfect number! I can see it!"

"That's why we've got to keep it safe. Keep it perfect. Not let anybody else get at it."

Lorraine broke away from him, put her feet on the floor. "It's really in the bag, all of it? And you've not even broken the padlock on the zip? Get it out, Dave, show me!"

Dave rummaged under the bed and brought out the blue sports bag.

"It's beautiful, Dave! It's lovely! But you've got to come back with me. Now this thing's happened, now these people are dead, this Ironmonger isn't going to protect you.

He won't protect the perfect number. You and me, Dave, we can protect it." She grabbed the bag and stroked it.

" OK, sis, I'll come back. I'll stay with you. I've got my gun." He pulled it out of his waistband.

Lorraine got up off the bed, took a step backward. "Keep your gun, Dave, keep it by us. But hide it. Don't let people see it. We won't let people see the bag neither. We won't open it until you're ready, I promise. Just take it out and look at it when we're on us own. Come on, Dave."

"I know somebody who gives out information. A copper. But I still don't want that Joby licking my face, not with his stinky breath."

Lorraine said: "I won't let him, Dave. I'll tie him up in the kitchen."

"Are we leaving the teabags then? Are we leaving the powdered milk?"

"You don't like powdered milk. *Nobody* likes powdered milk."

"I was getting used to it." He put the gun back in his waistband. "That copper. He'll know who killed Dockie and Teague. Rankin. That's it. Rankin will know."

"We can buy some more powdered milk. When we get sorted. We can afford it. Come on." She started out of the room, clutching the bag to her extravagant chest.

Dave trailed after her. "I'm not sorry to leave here. I've not been able to flush the bog at all today." Then he remembered what day it was.

"Oh yeah," he said, "Merry Crimble, Loz."

20 *Det Sgt Derek Rankin*

DET SGT DEREK Rankin was pissed off. What a way to spend Christmas Day!

He could've been with his kids. He could've been with his wife Melanie. He could've been with Josie, the bottle blonde 36D-cup life therapist and manicurist that he'd met at the *Oh-Zone!* Club last Saturday night while on undercover drug surveillance duties. But no. Things hadn't worked out that way.

Despite everything, despite all the regulations in place to ensure that married men with families got priority for leave on the Great Festive Day, he'd still ended up sat in the God-forsaken office, making phone calls to people too busy mixing sherry into the sage and onion to want to talk to him, he'd still ended up typing the useless reports on his computer screen, he'd still ended up smoking the left-over fags from other people's desk drawers because he'd left his own at home and now the shops were shut. (At least he could smoke in the office on this Very Special Day because there was nobody else to observe him breaking the rules).

And whose fault was it? Whose fuckin fault was it?

Step forward, Det Sgt Derek Rankin. Or just stay sat in the standard issue office swivel chair.

Because he, Derek Rankin, tall, good-looking, thirty-something, cool dresser, fashionable gelled haircut, he, Det Sgt Derek Rankin, smart arse that he was, had slipped the info to Dexy and his Midnight Runners, and they'd obviously had a word with one Charlie Pickett and they'd obviously passed the word on to some bastard on Tyneside who'd made the sort of connection in the space of an hour or two that Rankin's superiors – that was ferret-faced Det Insp Wainwright and fat-bellied Supt Mackintosh – couldn't make in a fortnight. And they'd gone down to the Bates Motel, or whatever, and blown away two villains and a couple of girls and left the Newcastle Police feeling pissed off and wanting to know what the fuck was going on that the West Yorkshire boys couldn't tell them these arse-holes were in Gateshead on the run, and Rankin's superiors had hummed and harrumphed and said well, actually, it was all news to them too, but they'd get their smartest team on it right away and follow up clues and get statements and generally help the Geordie lads out of their hole. And that was why Derek Rankin was pissed off. With Christmas. With life. And with himself.

But it didn't last long. No man is an island, as Jim Morrison used to say. Laugh and the world laughs with you, scream and no-one can hear you in space. After a couple of hours of telephone chat and keyboard skills, Det Sgt Derek Rankin found the unlocked drawer in Det Insp Wainwright's desk and the bunch of keys that led him into Supt Mackintosh's locked office and into the equally locked filing cabinet and to the discovery of a bottle of Tomatin single malt whisky, opened but not much diminished. He used the polystyrene coffee machine cup rather than risk breaking one of the chief's Woolworths glasses. And he salvaged a yellow paper crown from the waste bin, not emptied since the office party, to complete the illusion of seasonal joy.

He was just settling down in the swivel chair again when the call came through on his mobile.

"Sgt Rankin?" It was a young man's voice.

"Who's this?"

"I was told to say it's been a good day for the cricket."

"Oh yeah." Rankin relaxed. He took a sip of the Tomatin. "But not at Headingley."

"We have a delivery for you. A Christmas present. But it's got to be a personal delivery. Face to face. No post on Christmas Day."

"Won't it wait?"

"I'm told things are moving quickly. I'm told there's a regular place you use…"

"Yeah, yeah." Rankin told him the place. There was a brief silence. Rankin looked at his watch. Give it maybe another hour in the office. The people he was trying to talk to, the people whose names were on Det Insp Wainwright's list, would all be pissed as newts in another hour so he could reasonably withdraw his services. They fixed the time. Rankin took another sip. "How will I know you?"

"I'll be carrying a copy of yesterday's *Telegraph*."

Rankin burst out laughing. He spat whisky on his trousers. He put down the polystyrene cup and started to rub at the stain.

"Is that funny?"

"Everything's funny at Christmas."

The young man rang off. Rankin checked the number on his own phone. He wrote it on a slip of paper and put it in his pocket.

Rankin made two more calls on the office phone. That brought his total to ten. A respectable sum, he thought, as anything in double figures is always impressive.

And what had he got? Fuck all. Thank God. It meant nobody knew anything. And if anybody did know anything, they weren't going to tell. Not when four people just had their guts blown out with heavy artillery.

He allowed himself another drink then looked back at the screen. Ten names. Ten stupid statements from petty criminals and hangers-on. Ten terse judgements from Yours Truly. *Information sparse. Information unreliable. Informant unco-operative.*

He phoned Josie on his mobile. To his surprise, she answered straightaway. "Dennis?" she asked.

"Derek," he corrected her. "Look, babe, how about us hooking up later today? I thought I might come round..."

Silence.

"Look, I know a place I can get some Champagne. Yeah, even at Christmas. Yeah, of course I got some more of the happy powder." He knew there was still a small pile of reasonable quality coke stashed in his car, squeezed out of some low-lifes during his club duties. "That is, unless you're busy, family and that?"

"I'm an orphan," she said. And then: "Champagne? I could do us something out of the fridge to go with it."

"I'm an orphan too. Now there's a coincidence."

When he put his mobile away, he dialled Mel on the office phone. "Sorry, my love," he said, then repeated *sorry* some six or eight times while she rabbited on about the turkey. "Cold leftovers? Don't worry. I'll settle for that, Angel Face, as long as it's made by your own loving hands. I'll be back for seven. Honest. You know what it's like being a copper. Yes, and I *do* know what it's like being a copper's wife. No, I don't like it much either. Yes, I *will* complain to Wainwright. We'll have the evening together anyway, Angel." It was one o'clock now, he'd allowed an hour for meeting the young man with the interest in cricket, four hours for fish fingers with Josie, then... "Put the boys on," he said, and that put her in a better mood. He wished Jamie and Oliver a *Very* Merry Christmas, asked them how they'd liked their presents, especially the Gameboy and the radio-controlled miniature Aston Martin, said he'd be home before they went to bed if Mummy let them stay up, and asked for Mummy again. "See you then," he said, "Merry Christmas, angel. Love you lots." When he put the phone down, he wondered idly what was on telly. Must be *Only Fools and Horses*, or was that tomorrow?

And then a nasty thought struck. Maybe there really was a Dennis. Maybe Josie hadn't just got his name wrong after all.

It unsettled him and he drank another whisky before logging off.

127

21 Barry Oldham

BARRY WORE A GOLD paper crown. His brother Andy wore a red one. His other brother Richard wore a purple dunce's cap. Mum wore a green pirate's hat which was just a triangle with a skull-and-crossbones printed on it. Ursula, Andy's girlfriend, wore another dunce's cap, only this one was orange. It went well with her red-blonde hair, Barry decided. Dad was bare-headed and showing his bald spot. Barry wondered if *he'd* go bald like his Dad.

"It was a good bird this year," said Mum, "though I thought the legs were a bit tough. Maybe I should have taken it out at twelve instead of adding the sausages."

No, no, said Richard and Andy and Ursula, *it was just right*.

"Even better than last year," said Richard.

"But it was a good bird last year. I remember," said Mum.

"I'm not saying it wasn't," said Richard.

"He wasn't saying it wasn't," said Andy. He and Ursula exchanged glances.

"There'll be lots of sandwiches later on," said Mum, "We won't run out of sandwiches this year."

"We never do," said Dad.

Earlier, the presents had been fine. Money, of course, for each of the boys from Mum and Dad. A big box of Cadbury's Dairy Milk for Ursula from the Family. (Andy's present had not been described in detail but Ursula had offered the clue that it was something to wear, that not many people would be allowed to see her in it, and that she would probably take it back and get it exchanged anyway.)

But it had been a poor box of crackers this year. Apart from the hats, the family had extricated one plastic ring, one pyramid puzzle that Dad failed to put together, one magnet which failed to attract anything, one miniature plastic knife and fork and a number of jokes on little slips of paper which now littered the table.

Barry had memorised the jokes. Everything was grist to the mill of a poet.

What did the girl say to the elephant? Can I make a trunk call?

What's the difference between a jeweller and a jailer? One sells watches, the other watches cells.

Why should we be careful crossing the road? Because Jesus died on a crossing.

Barry particularly liked that last one. But Dad had objected. It wasn't the sort of joke you expected to find in a Christmas cracker, he said. But Barry argued it wasn't the sort of joke you expected to find anywhere. That was what he liked. After a while, Mum told Barry to bring in more sage and onion from the kitchen and she punched Dad on the arm.

Barry's Mum was a slight, dark woman who moved very quickly and whose small bright eyes glanced about nervously, except when she was watching telly. "Well, this is very nice," she said when Barry came back. "Nice to have us all here round the table."

That was what Mum said every year. Even when one of the family failed to turn up. In any case, she would always save a piece of Christmas cake for the absentee, parcel it up and make sure it was sent first class.

Dad always scoffed at this. He was a big man, running to fat, with thick wrists, bulging biceps and the motto *Born to Raise Hell* tattooed just beneath his left elbow. "It's only bought," he would say, "it's only M&S. If you made your own like you used to, I could understand it."

Actually, there were very few things that Barry's Dad *did* understand. He once admitted he'd never heard of Simon Armitage. He never read books of any kind. Not even the *Guinness Book of Records* which the boys had bought him one year knowing of his love of sport. "No good getting me this," he'd said as soon as he'd opened it, and all their arguments about how easy it was to look things up had gone by the board. So this year they'd clubbed together to buy him a set of Bruce Lee videos. Mum was a lot easier – another cookery book to add to her life-long collection.

At least *Richard* knew who Simon Armitage was. Barry's older brother was a dark-haired man in his late thirties whose sharp features and darting eyes echoed those of their Mum. He was a schoolteacher – head of English and Literacy Development at a comprehensive school in Gloucester. Only it wasn't called a school any more. It was called a Language College. Richard was married but his wife Andrea had to stay home this year. "She's going through a difficult period," Richard explained, "she needs some space." Barry wondered about that. Why would Andrea need space? It wasn't as if they lived in a small house or had children. Maybe Andrea needed more storage for her sculptures. Although Andrea had been a primary school teacher when Richard first met her, she had some sort of breakdown – Richard called it a *mental episode* – and had finally turned to sculpture as therapy. Barry had never seen any of her works, not even a photograph, so he was unable to make any judgment on their merit. But he guessed from the titles she sometimes mentioned in conversation – *The Evil of Man, Woman at the Crossroads of Destiny, The Soul of the Destroyer* – that they were probably of an abstract and indignant nature.

Andy also had his mother's dark looks but none of the nervousness. He was his father's equal in height and reach and Barry knew that Dad had once entertained hopes of Andy going into professional boxing as Dad himself had done before becoming a plumber. In the event, Andy had opted for computer studies, saying something about repetitive strain injury being less damaging to his looks than repetitive punch injury. Now he was a commercial software adviser. And Dad had settled for the career decision without much complaint.

But then Andy had charm – Barry recognised this without understanding what it was. Andy also had a succession of girlfriends, most of them beautiful, a few quite intelligent, one or two who actually liked poetry and were pleased when Barry read them some of his verse. Barry considered Ursula in the light of those previous girlfriends. He imagined her in the shower or using the toilet. The result was OK but not exceptional. She was not half as beautiful as Elizabeth, the one who had looked like Kate Moss, but she was a lot more friendly. She wasn't as clever as Hermione, who had admired Barry's *Ode to the Nature of Love and Losing Things*, but she laughed more. She had especially laughed at the Jesus joke. So she was probably OK and would last Andy for another three to six months.

Barry was the last of the sons still at home, so he never missed Christmas dinner. Sometimes he wished he could find an excuse. Like having a girlfriend or something.

At that point, John came in through the kitchen door. He was grinning. He said: "Pull a wishbone with me, Barry, you long-faced git."

"Piss off," said Barry, but quietly. He hadn't specifically invited John to Christmas dinner and wasn't sure how he felt about the intrusion. At least Erwin knew better than to gate-crash an intimate family occasion like Christmas.

"Go on," said John, holding out the bone, "it's Christmas."

"Piss off," said Barry, a little louder this time.

"Well," said John, "Not much Christmas spirit here, is there? Unless it's *me*, the Spirit of Christmas Future. I know what it's like to be dead, Barry. Remember that." And he walked out through the hall, slamming the front door after him.

"What happened to your friend?" asked Mum.

Barry started. He wasn't used to other people reacting to John. "He had to go somewhere suddenly," said Barry.

Mum looked puzzled. "Well, it's not often you bring your friends back. I was hoping he'd at least stay for breakfast. And he didn't look at all well last night. Not that I got much of a look at him, what with it being so late when you came home. I could see you'd been drinking. I hope you made him a coffee or a tea."

Barry realised she wasn't talking about John. Barry said: "We had a couple of beers after the Poets. Well, it *is* Christmas." He had recognised the disapproval in his mother's tone. "He couldn't stay, Mum. He'd got to get back to his family." That was something she would understand. "He phoned for a taxi."

"What's his name?"

"Raymond."

"Where did you meet him? The Poets?"

"He was *at* The Poets."

"I could have given him a lift," said Dad. Barry was suddenly aware that the whole table was listening in. Not literally the whole table, of course. He meant that all the *people* sitting at the table were listening. That was just the sort of quibble Fred Whittington would bring up. But it was as well to acknowledge the correctness of the observation. Self-criticism was important.

"Where did he sleep?" asked Mum.

"In my room," said Barry. And quite quickly: "On the floor."

"He could have had my folding bed," said Richard, "I always bring a folding bed. It's in the car."

"We've never asked you to bring a folding bed," said Dad, "we've always got enough beds."

"I know. It's just that I keep a folding bed in the boot of the car. I always do. Just in case..." Richard trailed off lamely.

"We've even bought that double bed for when Andy..." Dad began. Mum reached out suddenly and put her hand on Dad's hand. Ursula, who had shared that particular bed with Andy for the first time last night, looked away.

"It's not that he often needs a double bed," said Mum in her reassuring voice to Ursula. And then to Barry: "He seemed such a nice young man. Does he live round here?"

"Not far," said Barry. He realised he had no idea where Raymond lived. But it sounded strange to say that.

"How did he get that cut on his head?" asked Mum, "Did he fall?"

So she noticed *that*. Barry said: "Yes." Again, that was quite true. Raymond had fallen into him when the ...

When the *what*?

Barry thought about Raymond putting on his trousers that morning, at half past five, putting on his jacket, putting on his shoes, looking for his glasses, not finding them, glancing into Barry's bedroom mirror and gently touching the red weal on his forehead with his fingertips. He thought about Raymond saying: "I bet you don't get *many* people shot round here. Not in the bus station."

Barry, sat up in bed in his striped pyjamas, was about to say that the car park wasn't strictly the bus station. But something stopped him: the sudden realisation of what Raymond was saying.

Somebody had shot Raymond.

In those circumstances, it made little difference whether it had happened in the bus station or the car park. He felt sure of that.

"It's been really something," said Raymond as he combed his hair over the mark, "I'm never gonna forget last night." He grinned at Barry. "Poetry! It's great, isn't it? How'd you get into it?"

"Oh, I've always written poems. When I was a kid even."

"You know something? I'm gonna come to the Poets next time as well."

He certainly *sounded* enthusiastic. Barry had to ask him to drop his voice a little so as not to wake the rest of the family. "Great," whispered Barry. He felt calmed. This was proof indeed that poetry had healing powers, just as he'd always felt. If Raymond could come through a thing like that... Still, there were things that had to be cleared up.

"Shouldn't you tell the police about getting shot?"

Raymond laughed. "It was probably one of the police that did it!"

"Surely not...?"

"OK, maybe not. They got too much respect. But it's no good going to the Boys in Blue because they'll want to know things. Want to know too much. You get my meaning?"

"Er... no."

"Well, it's like to do with my Dad. He's a good man, my Dad, he looks after us. He's an ODC. You know what that means?"

Barry didn't.

"In Northern Ireland, where they have to fight terrorists and scum like that, any proper criminal that they got respect for, they call an ODC – Ordinary Decent Criminal. That's like my Dad."

"Are you one too?"

"Well, yeah, I suppose I am."

Suddenly Barry began to feel excited about Raymond. Just as excited, he guessed, as Raymond had become about poetry.

"Anyway," said Raymond, "I've got to be off. I've got to collect my car and go to a very boring party with my Mum and Dad. I'm gonna have to phone for a taxi. Is that alright? I'll leave some change."

"You don't have to do that. You don't have to leave any change."

When Raymond came back, he pointed to his forehead and said: "All it did was make a little groove. In the skin. Look. I was bloody lucky."

Barry didn't want to look. He said: "It's a shame about your glasses. Glasses are very expensive these days."

"The funny thing is," said Raymond, "I can see OK without them now. You wouldn't believe it, would you? First time in ten years. Bloody miracle." He said: "I'll give you a bell later in the week. We can have a jar or two like last night. OK?"

"OK."

When Raymond had gone outside the house to wait for the taxi, taking pains to be as quiet as Barry had admonished him, Barry got out of bed and ambled over to the rolltop writing desk in the corner of the room, the desk his parents had bought him for getting Grade B in his English A level when it briefly looked as though he might go to University. He pulled open the collapsible wooden chair and sat down on it. He took out writing paper and ballpoint pen. He licked the blunt end of the pen as he usually did at such moments. He wrote the title:

Friendship. Then he sat and thought and sat and thought. For once no words leapt out at him begging to be included in his composition. *Friendship,* he thought. There was a problem. It was like the problem with sex. He would have to get some experience before he could write it properly.

22 Chanelle Braithwaite

CHANELLE STOOD IN a corner of the Bradley Dexters' lounge with a glass of something called St Emilion in her hand. She wasn't actually drinking it. She had temporarily lost her appetite for drink. She was a stranger in a strange land and she knew enough not to drink red wine among people who might not, after all, be as friendly as they made out.

That was her first reason for caution: that she didn't know the people who swarmed noisily around her.

The second reason was the house. Coming in along the drive in Raymond's Polo was like travelling along one of those tree-lined avenues you see in old paintings. The house itself was mock Tudor, or *mock turtle* as Chanelle liked to think of it. It had a central porch and decorated chimney stacks but no open fires. The windows had leaded panes and the high ceilings had fake beams stained to look like wood. I'm a low-ceiling person, she thought. I couldn't stand all this space.

The third reason was that she was now wearing a dress that Ray's Mum had been surprisingly eager to lend her. It was a long, floaty, green silk dress with a sort of lacy collar. Like Chanelle, Simone had a French name; but unlike Chanelle, she seemed to have been born with it. She also had a lot of slit-up-the-side, plunging-neckline dresses that didn't really suit a woman of her age but would have looked well on Chanelle. Simone hadn't offered any of these stylish little numbers to Chanelle but had palmed her off with what looked like an old bridesmaid's dress.

The fourth and biggest reason Chanelle was unhappy was that Raymond had left the party. In fact, *left the party* hardly summed it up – Raymond had gone before the party got started.

"Sorry, sweetheart," he said, "I really like you and I really want to be with you but I've got this job to do for my Dad."

"On Christmas Day?"

"My Dad doesn't believe in public holidays. Listen – you stick around, look pretty, have a few drinks, and I'll be back in no time."

"Look pretty? You think I'm pretty then?" Compliments were commonplace to Chanelle, mostly from clients and mostly a lot more intimate and more to do with specific parts of the body. So she was surprised she should be so easily pleased by the fact that Raymond found her pretty and was bothered enough to mention the fact. But it still didn't make up for his going off.

It was nearly an hour since she had put on the green silk dress and been brought down to the party room and given the glass of wine by Harry Somebody, the slimy little gopher with greasy hair. What sort of man was it that worked in a job like that?

Then Simone had gone swanning off, putting herself about with the important guests, the *real* guests, leaving Chanelle in the corner next to a tall chrome standard lamp.

It was second nature to Chanelle to study the lie of the land, suss out the prime suspects, whenever she felt lost and out of her depth. And she usually started with the women. Because, on the whole, she felt more confident that she could handle the men. But this time she was really adrift – and the formula for when you're really adrift is to study the couples and guess what they liked doing to each other, or what the one who liked doing some particular thing could actually get away with when it came to doing it with the other one. One thing she had guessed right about Simone was that Raymond's Mum was a list-maker. And *there* was her list of guests, hand-written on Basildon Bond, lying on a small silver tray on the drinks cabinet. Chanelle picked it up. She had always known knowledge was power, or at least protection, and she wanted to know who was who and remember it afterwards.

Chanelle looked over at the woman they called Gina, the one who came from Geordieland and talked like a scrubber, but dressed like a scrubber that had done well for herself. She checked the names on the list. *Eddie and Gina Patterson*. Truth to tell, Chanelle envied Gina her straight

137

boyish figure, flat stomach and equally flat chest. Chanelle herself would not have done half so well in her chosen career if she'd not had what she thought of as grown-up tits, because the men she got to know liked a bit up there to grab hold of when they were at their peak, so to speak. On the other hand, it was a mark of Gina's class that she had got on in the trade without bothering about tits. It meant she must have had a superior clientele – fellas who were too intelligent maybe, or too well educated, to care about tits. The kind of people who thought Kate Moss was gorgeous. Chanelle had always hoped to graduate to that sort of client because it meant better manners and probably bigger money. Still, she was still young and surgery was getting cheaper and less time-consuming every day. Lunch-hour tit reduction couldn't be far away. Never once did it occur to Chanelle that maybe Gina *hadn't* been on The Game.

That Eddie who was with her. Same name, so husband obviously. Look at him. A body-builder's waist and shoulders but a whisky-drinker's skin. Where else would he go looking for his women except in the disco or the knocking shop? He didn't seem like a bloke with wide interests. Business was his interest and his business wasn't anything legal, was it? Of all the men there tonight, she knew that only two of them might be dangerous and only one of them could ever be dangerous to *her*. If he got the chance. That was Eddie. Well, Gina mon, you're welcome to him.

Next Chanelle looked round for Simone. Raymond's mother was now talking animatedly to a man in a vicar's collar and a purple shirt. Chanelle shook her head. Gina she could pigeon-hole rightaway, but Simone was different. Simone was a fit piece, or had been in her day. But she wasn't the kind to ever be doing it for straight cash. She didn't fit the two main types that dominated Chanelle's view of women: mothers, like her own Mum; or tarts, like herself. It was all down to temperament really, all down to who you were

138

beneath the No 7 foundation and the Rimmel cream eye-shadow. But Simone didn't fit the categories.

So where did that leave Bradley Dexter, Raymond's old man? That question was always going to be the interesting one because every man turned out like his Dad if he was a real man and like his Mum if he was a poofter. And she didn't think Raymond was a poofter, though she might have had some doubts at first. Bradley, she saw, was sat on the sofa talking to a mousey woman in a dress that was even more bridesmaidy than Chanelle's. She guessed he was having his troubles, most of them six inches down from his bulging waistband. That was what all this cricket stuff was about, all this rabbiting on about *did she enjoy his videos*? And Chanelle knew Bradley didn't want a *Mastermind* winner. Even if she'd known anything about cricket – which she didn't. He only really wanted her for one thing. And if he couldn't do that, then the second best was that she should be so dumb that he had to treat her like a child and then he could say to himself: *I couldn't fuck her because she's just a stupid kid. It would be like fucking the daughter I never had.* Instead of: *I couldn't fuck her because I couldn't fuck her.*

And what did Simone see in all that? Probably the man she married, the man she'd grown so used to in the first few years that she couldn't see how he'd changed. Marriage. Look what it did to people. *Good job my Mum missed out on it then.*

There were several other women of various ages and various stages of flouncy dress in the room, and Chanelle quickly dismissed them as non-threatening. They were all mothers, she decided. Or mothers-in-waiting, which was a kind of sub-category of her system. Mothers-in-waiting didn't mean pregnant. It meant mothers who were going to be mothers whatever, and didn't mind in the last analysis who the fathers were. But they *were* prepared to hide their true nature for a while if it meant that by doing so they could actually hook a better class of father-to-be. So mothers-in-waiting wasn't a third type of woman: it was just a mother with a tiny bit of self-control.

At this point Harry Nobody had come across from the bar to stand in front of her. His little eyes looked her over. He pointed at her glass. "Can I get you another?"

"I haven't finished this one." She put the list in the top of her dress. She said: "I must be a slow drinker."

"I bet," he said, "you're not so slow at *some* things."

Oh Christ, thought Chanelle, *he's coming on to me.* The nerve of the bastard! In Raymond's own house, for God's sake!

But it wasn't that. Harry went on talking but his little eyes now seemed to scurry all round the room rather than look in hers. "It's a shame Ray couldn't stay," he said, "Me and him are good friends, you know?" Finally he looked back at her. "I could see you two were close." He paused. "Last night, were you with him? I mean, do you know where he was?"

She said: "If you and him are such good mates..."

"I've just not had chance to talk to him. Not today. Not so far. He's such a busy boy."

"No," she said, "I don't know where he was last night." And straightaway she regretted it. She'd given something away. That wasn't like her. She took a sip of the St Emilion.

"Are you sure about that drink?" Harry was smiling now. "Alright then, I'll see to the other guests." And he was gone.

So Chanelle took out the list and went on with her game, and now she turned to the men. That Harry for a kick-off. She'd had clients like him. And the trick was: not to let them take you by surprise. But that's just what she'd let him do. She cursed herself. He was shit, but shit sometimes stuck to your boot and stunk and you couldn't get rid of it without getting it on your fingers. Yet Harry wasn't dangerous by himself. He was only dangerous when used by other men. And she wondered who was actually using him, although it was clearly Raymond's old man who paid his wages. And she wondered if Bradley's bollocks might not be the only part of him that was losing its liveliness.

After Harry, the other men seemed a pointless lot, just there for scenery. The vicar in the purple shirt turned out to be a bishop. That's what it said on the list: Miles Knox-Porter, Bishop of Hallam and Matlock. Anyway, she'd heard Simone call him *Bishop* and he'd corrected her in a flirty, comic way, saying the correct address was "Your Grace" but that she could call him Miles. That's when he and Simone started dancing to Boyzone. When she saw the way he danced to *Love Me For a Reason*, with his mouth open and twisted to one side, she suddenly recognised him from the Parky Show or Des O'Connor. He'd been telling Parky or Des about *grey areas of sexuality*, which had made Chanelle prick up her ears for half a minute, thinking it might be educational, but it wasn't.

Over in the corner, pointedly avoiding dancing, was another one she recognised. She glanced at the list. It was the fat sweaty face of Marcus Critchett, Labour MP for Swanfields and Summerdean, the place where her aunt Bessie still lived. He had actually kissed her once – when she was eight or nine – at a protest rally against incinerating waste on the site of an old pit near Bessie's home. She wondered if she should go over and remind him about the kiss but decided the joke wasn't worth the risk. Anyway, he was useless. Every time she went back to see Aunt Bessie, the washing on the line was filthy with the smoke.

One of the men Marcus Critchett was talking to was burly and balding, wearing an Amani suit and jewellery. It had to be *Lucas Bernstein, entrepreneur*. He and Critchett were in a three-way conversation with a long-haired man in a sweater and brown corduroy trousers they called Darius. They

141

were discussing the government's latest green paper on funding the arts and Darius was clearly complaining. Chanelle checked her list. *Darius Goodrow.* God! He was a painter and she'd actually seen some of his stuff at an exhibition a pretentious punter had taken her to in Leeds, lots of arrowhead patterns and circles with splotches of primary colour. Chanelle knew a bit about painting and she knew a bit about crap. And Darius Goodrow was crap.

Just at that moment, the mousey woman got up from the settee and went over to Marcus Critchett. She took his arm and said something that clearly had to do with leaving. Chanelle looked at the list. She must be *Christine Ploughman, parliamentary researcher.* And the thought struck her: *God, he's an MP. Can't he get something better?*

And then Chanelle looked back to the settee where Bradley Dexter still sat, nursing a half of lager. And the realisation came to her. In a moment, she had put it all together: the gay bishop, the well-suited entrepreneur, the crap artist, the has-been MP, the Plain Jane from the researchers' department. And all those mothers-in-waiting.

And the realisation was: *This is just a crap party!*

She thought: Bradley and Simone Dexter have invited all these people to show them how important Bradley Dexter is. But Bradley can't get up off the settee and the people they've managed to get to come are all nobodies anyway.

And who the hell put Boyzone on?

And then she thought: Bradley hasn't just lost it in his trousers. He's lost it full stop. And what makes it worse is that he's invited these big shots from Geordieland to show off to and all he's done is show what a pushover he is.

Chanelle had known from the first that Eddie Patterson was a dangerous man and now she wondered if Raymond knew, if he maybe even guessed, how far things had gone. And she suddenly wanted to warn him.

She screwed up the list and dropped it on the floor. She took a gulp of St Emilion. At least her appetite for drink had come back.

23 Det Sgt Derek Rankin

FOR A GENTS' BOG, it was not a good example of the breed. Not exactly an advertisement for Leeds City Council and all who sail in her. That's what Rankin thought when he went in. Water on the floor. Locks broken off the stalls. Graffiti above the urinals. *Dial 09077-600378 for a wild wank* and *Sexy Ian has a big cock just for you.*

He unzipped his fly and took a leak. Then this sickly looking bloke in a brown leather bomber jacket and a pair of green chinos walked in. The messenger boy? Rankin kept his eyes on his cock. But he sensed what the other man was doing. Saw it all, if you like, through the hairs on the back of his neck. That was all part of being a detective.

The newcomer had walked in quickly, stopped suddenly. He'd looked round nervously and seen there was only one man at the trough. Saw the man was big, well-muscled, fit, could take care of himself in any bit of bother. He'd hesitated then. Rankin *felt* him hesitate. This *was* the messenger boy. Rankin could feel him standing, worried, scared of making a fool of himself in front of a stranger in a piss-house.

Rankin felt the messenger boy sidle up, then back off a little. The messenger boy cleared his throat. He said: "The weather isn't so bad for the time of the year, is it?"

Rankin nearly burst out laughing. He thought: *I'd piss myself if I wasn't already.* He said: "I hear it's a lot worse in Birmingham."

The other took a deep breath. He said: "But, according to Teletext, it's very sunny in Lanzarote."

Rankin turned round, grinning. "Really? I heard it was pissing it down. Like me. You must be Ray. You know who *I* am."

The other started to put out his hand, then thought better of it, as Rankin shook himself and put his cock away. Instead, he wiped the hand on his trouser leg. He said: "My principal has sent you a package."

Rankin zipped his fly and went across to the wash basins. He swilled his hands under the tap, then stuck them under the dryer. He looked at the messenger. Yeah. Everything was exactly what the hairs on his neck had told him. He grinned again, let him have the teeth. "A Christmas present from your boss, eh? Give it here then."

The other clearly had to think about it first. "Just a minute." He looked round. Rankin followed his gaze. Rankin thought: I know what he's thinking. Would they have CCTV in a place like this? Wasn't that against the European Convention on Human Rights?

In the end, when he obviously couldn't see anything, the messenger said: "You never know who's watching you these days." He took the package out of his jacket pocket. "I've brought the cash. As you requested. But in future we prefer to do business in a more discreet way. You should give me your bank account number and your sorting code."

Rankin snatched the package out his hand and tore open the brown paper wrapping. He showed his teeth again as he counted the money. "OK," he said, satisfied. He shoved the money into his pockets: right inside jacket, left inside jacket, right trouser, left trouser, a little in each, less obtrusive. Then: "Are you mad? You think I was born last Friday? Your boss must think I'm still wet if he expects I'll give you that sort of info."

"We're only doing it for safety." The messenger didn't sound convincing. Well, it was his boss's dialogue, wasn't it? Poor little nipper. Better stick to it for now.

"*Whose* safety? Not *mine*. Oh, if I want to be Dexy's errand boy for the next 30 years, or his sex slave, or clean his car, I might consider it. Or why don't I just sit down when I've got half an hour to spare and write a list of all the favours I'm doing him and sign it in front of witnesses and post it to him registered delivery? Then he's got me where he wants me. You must be stupid."

"Please!" the other said, and: "Don't call me stupid!"

Rankin said: "Why not? You gonna get your boss onto me? You gonna rush home after school and tell him? Get smart, junior. I can do your boss a lot *more* favours and he knows it."

Suddenly Rankin lunged at the other, grabbed his arm and twisted it, rather neatly he thought, up behind the boy, knuckles on spine, nothing to it really. The other clearly hadn't been expecting this. But then Rankin always had been good at taking people by surprise. *Well*, thought Rankin, *you stay calm, nipper, and maybe you'll learn something. You stay calm with your face all cold against the cold, cold tiles.*

Then, as suddenly as his anger started, it subsided. He let go. He laughed as the messenger straightened up. He said: "OK. That's it. Nice to have met you. Nice to do business. Bank accounts! Sorting codes! Oh, you have to laugh sometimes! Life's not all bleak, is it, my son?" He sauntered away, out of the gents' and into the sunshine. He knew he didn't have to look back.

Rankin suddenly felt sick when he got back to his Ford Focus. Maybe he shouldn't have had that third polyester cup of Tomatin. Or maybe it was just the bad air in the bog. Or the smell of the company he had to keep. Oh, you didn't need telly with people like that around!

24 Lydia Oldham

LYDIA OLDHAM LOOKED at her husband Ted. He was sitting in his chair in the lounge reading yesterday's *Daily Mirror*, still wearing his Father Christmas cracker hat. Picking his teeth with his nails. He reached out and touched the miniature image of Father Christmas, made from a hollow chocolate mould, dressed in gold and red foil, hanging by a silken thread from the Christmas tree. What was he thinking? Ted worried about being fat, she knew. He'd lost the athletic figure he'd spent so much time perfecting in his youth. He'd been middleweight champion of his regiment, the Second Kings Own Yorkshire Light Infantry.

She had met him in a dance hall in Hull where him and his mate Corporal Slammer Green were visiting Slammer's married sister Amy, and Amy brought her friend along, and it was Lydia. And they did the locomotion or the watusi together and they fell in love. *Love!* She liked it when he said he loved her, though she was wise enough to know the reasons men said things like that. But she said it back to him anyway. She was pretty in those days, with her slim, small-breasted figure and her black-as-raven hair. And *he* wasn't bad looking. And he'd got his qualifications, his certificate in plumbing. And he soon gave up thinking about boxing without any help from her.

Lydia sighed. Looking at Ted, remembering, was the deliberate start of a new sequence, a new stirring to action. She looked at Ted to see that he was alright, that he wasn't doing anything that would require her attention. So she could get on with the other things. So she could do the things she always did on Christmas Day.

Lydia wondered if everybody had this sort of timetable for Christmas – every *woman*, anyway. Of course every woman had the shopping and the meal and the cleaning and the rest. Every woman made a list and calculated the timings and pre-heated the cooker. But she wondered whether every woman had the second half, the painful part, the check, the balance, the running total.

Because Christmas was the natural time for calculating how far you'd got in life. It was the one time you had all the family together – if you were lucky – and it was kind of symbolic anyway, being so close to New Year.

Lydia got to her feet, cleared out the teacups on the tray, carried them into the kitchen. Andy and Ursula were in the kitchen, leaning against the stainless steel sink, their arms around each other. "Ah, there you are," said Lydia and they broke apart, a little embarrassed. She looked away and smiled. In any case, it wasn't Andy she wanted to talk to right now. She had her own timetable.

She found Richard in the garden, standing on the patio by the lawn, smoking a cigarette, wearing his brown suede car coat, the one she and Ted had bought him this year. "You're trying out your new coat," she said.

"Yes," he said. Lydia thought of their hopes when he'd married Andrea. *At least we'll get some grandchildren now*, Ted had said to her, meaning: *About bloody time.*

Lydia said to Richard: "What do you think about the winter jasmine?" She knew he could barely recognise a tea rose, let alone a winter jasmine, even though she and Ted were keen gardeners and had been cultivating the same plants for 20 years.

"They're coming on well."

"I'll give you some to take back. For Andrea."

"Yes. That would be nice. She'd appreciate that."

Yes, thought Lydia, *like she'd appreciate a Chinese burn*. "We were so sorry she couldn't come."

"Yes. Well, she's sorry too. You know how it is."

Lydia thought: *No, actually I don't know. That's what I need to find out.* "What does the doctor say?"

"Well, you know doctors."

147

Yes, she knew doctors. She knew nurses. But she didn't know Andrea, not really. "What do the doctors say?"

"Acute depression." Richard relaxed as soon as he'd said it, as though naming Andrea's affliction gave him hope of containing it. He rubbed the end of his dying cigarette, carried it over to the dustbin and returned. "I told them: that's alright then. We all get depressed now and then." There was another silence but this time Lydia made Richard fill it up. "You know about the miscarriage? The second one?"

Yes, she said, she did. But really she couldn't remember. Maybe she was getting past it, the running total, the family audit. Who would do it if she couldn't? She still remembered the first miscarriage though. She hadn't even known Andrea was pregnant at the time. But Andrea told her all about the miscarriage. All the detail. Blood and guts. Well, blood anyway.

"You're both young," she now said to Richard.

"Andrea doesn't know," said Richard, meaning Andrea might not want to try again, perhaps that he might not want to try if it led to acute depression and doctors thinking he was stupid.

"How is she in herself?" She had to ask these things, tick them off her list.

"As well as can be expected."

"And you?"

"Nothing wrong with me. Strong as a horse."

"That's good. And the job?"

"It goes OK. I only do four hours a week teaching now."

"Good. And Andrea's sculptures?"

"She had an exhibition at the local library. Didn't sell anything. But it's a start."

"Yes, it is," Lydia began to unwind. She had asked the necessary questions. Andrea's depression was unfortunate but it was explainable: the woman had suffered two miscarriages. As Richard had told the doctors: *We all get depressed now and then.* So she, Lydia, had now done her bit with Richard, whom she loved, and who could now be placed properly on the family list of priorities which Lydia kept in her head at all times.

Lydia left Richard gazing in the general direction of the winter jasmine, hung her anorak up in the hall, went back into the kitchen. Andy was putting a new batch of crockery into the dishwasher. But then he'd do anything to avoid sitting in the lounge with Ted. Ursula was no longer with him. The sudden sound of the upstairs toilet flushing indicated where she must be.

"I've got a computer problem," said Lydia, "Come up and I'll show you."

They passed Ursula on the stairs going down. "I won't be a minute," Andy said. Ursula smiled the smile of the guest who was not yet privy to family rituals and went on down. Lydia took Andy into the spare room they called the office. She switched on the computer. She said: "It doesn't happen all the time. But sometimes the screen looks very blurred. The writing looks strange. "

"Intermittent fault." He nodded.

Intermittent fault, thought Lydia. Well, that was a good way of describing a lot of things.

He sat down on the typist's chair that had lost one of its castors. He picked up the mouse. "It's OK at the moment, isn't it? What do you think?"

"I told you. It's not there all the time."

"I'll start a new document." The document sprang on the screen. He began typing a line of characters: *nnnnn mmmmm wwwww bbbbb.*

"Type something sensible."

"Like what?"

"Like *Ursula.*"

He turned and looked at her, turned back and did as he was told.

"She seems like a nice girl." When Andy said nothing, Lydia said: "How long have you been going together?"

"Oh, three months now." He typed *OK mother OK* on the next line. Lydia pretended not to notice.

"Are you serious about her?"

"Ho hum," he said, "You know there are certain questions you don't ask." He typed:

AAAAARRRGGGHHHH!!

Lydia smiled at that. "At least you're happy. What does she do for a living?"

"She told you. She's in PR."

"Oh. PR." He might as well have said *interplanetary travel*. "Does that mean she earns a lot?"

"No more than me. So I won't be marrying her for her money."

"So you've thought about it?"

"Not until just now. Not until you made me."

Well, that was honest. And it was true that Andy had always been the sort to play the field. All those girls. Lovely girls. Picked up and then... Changed like he changed his car when the new number plate came out.

And maybe there was another reason for Andy's inability to settle down. Maybe Ted was right. Maybe Andy didn't want children because he was afraid of them turning out like Barry.

She asked Andy about his health, the job, the latest car. Everything was running OK. Another box ticked. She put her hands on his shoulders. "It's good to know you're happy."

"As much as anyone ever is." He said: "I can't find anything wrong with this machine."

"It's an intermittent fault," she said. "Now you go down and talk to Ursula. She'll be wondering what's keeping you."

When he had gone down the stairs, she turned off the computer and walked across the landing to Barry's room. She knocked. "Hello, Barry." There was no reply. She knocked again. "Hello, Barry." Silence. "I'm coming in." She thought: *What's the worst that can happen? That he's hanging from the light flex? That he's taken off his underpants?*

He was lying on the bed, fully clothed, eating a piece of Christmas cake. He didn't look up when she came in.

"You're very quiet. You were very quiet at dinner as well."

"No, I wasn't." His face took on a sullen expression. He had cake crumbs round his mouth.

"Well, maybe I'm wrong." She glanced at the painting on his wall. It was a new one, rather charming and child-like. It was Dr Hardy who had got him to paint in poster colours once a week at the drop-in centre. At first the pictures had contained a strangeness that had made her afraid. Fields of grass with huge cogwheels beneath. Trees with claws at the ends of their branches. Now they were just fields and trees and walls. That was progress. Dr Hardy seemed to think so.

"How are you?" Then she caught herself. She hadn't meant to say it like that, as if she had just bumped into him for the first time in six months, as if the fact that she had been talking to him only half an hour ago, swopping cracker jokes and making herself laugh at them, had disappeared from her memory. But she was resigned to the fact that most of her conversations with Barry were empty rituals, trivia leavened with awkward politenesses. Except the Christmas conversation, the one where she always asked him what he planned to do with his life. She asked the question now.

He finished the cake, listened to the questions, looked hard in her face. At such times she couldn't read his

151

expression at all. "I don't fuckin know. I've got to think." He didn't say it in an angry voice. It was as if the *f-word* meant nothing. And he turned over on his side with his back to her.

At one time Barry might have turned out just like Richard. He'd got the brains, that's what his teachers said. And it seemed he was running on greased rails until he was 18, until he'd got his A levels behind him and was all set for University, for an English course at Loughborough. Then, one day, he came home looking pale and gasping for breath. Ted and Lydia questioned him. "I've thrown them away," he said, "I've thrown them all away."

"What have you thrown away?" asked Ted.

"My poems," said Barry. He began to sob. He fell backwards on the settee and curled up.

They knew Barry wrote poems. Barry had been writing them ever since he went to high school. Some of the other sixth-form kids laughed at him. They called him Homer. The Greek poet, not the Simpsons. Barry had often read his poems to Ted and Lydia. Ted had said "very good" though he'd looked a bit blank. Lydia had been more positive. "You ought to send those in," she had told him. Then she'd said: "The *Flaxton Gazette* have poems, don't they?" And they did. On the women's page. So Barry sent in three of his poems and the *Gazette* actually published one of them with a headline that Lydia saved and pasted on the fridge: *Rhymes of our times – Flaxton schoolboy's poem about modern life.* Though the poem didn't actually rhyme at all, as Barry pointed out. And they never offered any payment, which Ted said he thought was a bit off. But Barry was pleased as punch and Lydia was too. Then Barry sent in three more poems but they didn't publish these. And three more. And maybe a few more after that.

Now the 18-year-old Barry had thrown away all his poems, every single one, thrown an Asda bag full of them off the bridge that ran across the River Aire at Puddlegood and watched them float away.

"Why did you do that?" asked Ted.

"I thought," explained Barry, "they were my A-level history notes. I always hated history." He was crying softly now.

"Why did you hate history?" asked Ted.

"How did you get them mixed up?" asked Lydia.

"My history notes were in my *other* Tesco bag. I made a mistake."

"Can't you just write some more?" asked Ted.

"No, he can't," said Lydia.

At this point, Barry had buried his face in his hands and begun to scream.

Their local GP, Dr Rainsford, wasn't too worried at first. Lydia had explained the symptoms: Barry was withdrawn, refused to speak, cried a lot, slept a lot, didn't wash or eat or get dressed without being told to. Lydia and Ted didn't mention the poems because they believed there was no known illness with the symptom *threw away his poems*. Dr Rainsford suggested a virus and told them to let things take their course. When asked whether Barry was likely to be well enough to start the term at Loughborough, he said he didn't see why not.

But it wasn't a virus and Barry wasn't well enough. Not that September and not the following September. It was 18 months before someone suggested a psychiatrist. Ted was against it. He didn't believe in shrinks any more than he believed in priests – or vampires for that matter.

But then there was that Louise, the girl from Grimbles the newsagent. Sometimes she and Barry would go down to the coffee shop when Barry was doing his temporary job at Boots the Chemist next door. And when she broke it off – if there was anything to break off – that was the worst time for Barry, the worst time for them all. One night he got out of bed and walked in his pyjamas and slippers all the way to Flaxton Town Centre and they found him outside Grimbles, waiting for it to open; waiting, he said, to buy *The Sun*. Ted was horrified. Even he knew Barry would never really read *The Sun*. That was when Lydia insisted about the psychiatrist.

What Dr Hardy told them was that there was no cure as such because nobody understood what caused the condition. But there were some new drugs that might control the symptoms, might allow Barry a fairly normal life.

"What's *fairly normal* mean?" asked Ted.

Lydia said: "We'll do everything that's needed."

And she always did. At least she'd asked the questions. At least she'd gone through the list. She hadn't expected proper answers anyway.

On the way out of his room now, she noticed another painting lying on the floor. The trees were just trees, no claws this time. But she recognised them straightaway as the copse by the stream where he had built his wigwam. It was the first time she had recognised a specific scene in any of his paintings. Her heart filled with terror at the memory of that night. When he ran away naked, to live in the woods. Though they'd got him back within a day and the extra medication had seemed to put a stop to that one.

She went out and closed the door behind her. *Intermittent fault*, she thought.

25 Barry Oldham

WHEN HIS MUM had gone, Barry cried. It was a soft crying, but it was a real cry, not a put-on thing, not poetic emotion recollected in tranquillity.

"Why did you do it, John?" he said.

John said: "Gimme some truth, Barry. That's what I give you."

"Why did you have to swear at my Mum?"

"It's just truth, man. Fuck is truth."

"Der fuck is not necessarily der truth," said Erwin.

"It is where *I* come from," said John, "It is down Lime Street." He began to sing "*Dirty Maggie May, they have taken her away...*"

"You didn't have to say fuck to my Mum."

John stopped singing. "Barry," he said, "don't be boring. You're getting to be very boring. I've noticed it. I'm trying to do something about it, that's all."

"I am *not* boring."

"Oh," said John, "tell me more. So the clown at the centre of his stage isn't really boring. So I just made that up, did I?"

"I just asked you why you had to say *fuck* to my Mum."

"He can't answer," said Erwin, "yust look at him. Vot's der matter, Yon? Are you yust a yealous guy maybe?"

"Don't you get stroppy with me, wack. Don't you get brutal with me, you fuckin Nazi gas chamber shit head."

"I did not do der gas chambers, yon. As I tink you know. I vos a *general* in der German army." Barry noticed that Erwin pronounced the word *general* with a hard *g*, as a German probably would. But he pronounced *German* with a soft *g*. Barry wondered why this was so. Perhaps it was because German was not actually a German word, but an English one. If Erwin had used the German word, he would have had to say *Deutsch*. Barry was reassured.

"Don't you ever say *fuck* to my mother again."

John turned away, tapped his foot, gazed out of the window.

"And also," said Erwin to Barry, "I never liked der vay he treated Paul."

"You weren't even fuckin alive when Paul and me was going," said John.

"But I read about it," said Erwin.

"*I* never liked the way he treated Paul either," said Barry to Erwin. He was surprised at himself for saying this.

"And so this is Christmas!" said John.

"I don't see what that's got to do with it," said Barry. Then: "Actually saying *fuck* to my Mum at Christmas *is* probably worse than saying it at any other time of year."

"Because it is der family day," said Erwin. Then: "I tink dot Yon should say sorry. I tink dot is der only vay forvard now."

"Oh, so I'm the one that's got to say sorry! That's rich coming from a Nazi, that is. I'm supposed to say sorry for saying *fuck* to Barry's Mum. Why don't you say sorry for burning down Warsaw then, eh? I happen to think burning down Warsaw is a slightly bigger crime than saying *fuck* to Barry's Mum."

"No, it's not," said Erwin.

"Well, maybe I'm just fuckin strange," said John, "but I still think it is."

Barry felt suddenly disturbed by the way the argument was going. "Actually, Erwin, I think John's got a point. I think destroying the capital city of Poland is a bigger crime than saying *fuck* to my Mum. Even though," he went on, "it happened in the last century."

"Und I vos never actually fighting in der Poland," said Erwin, "I vos fighting in Africa mit der Afrika Corps. That's vy dey *called* it der Afrika corps. If ve had fought in der Poland dey vod hef called it der Polish corps, vod dey hev not?" Erwin slapped his thigh with his glove. "You're a silly boy, Yon."

Barry said: "Erwin does also have a point there, John. If he wasn't fighting in Poland, then you can't blame him for burning down Warsaw, can you? It's very unfair."

"Yes, I can," said John, "It was all the same gang, right? It was all the fuckin German Nazis, wasn't it? So what

156

does it matter if he was never there? He was still on the same side. He was still on the side of the people who burned down Warsaw, wasn't he?"

There was a silence. It was John who broke it. "One thing I've never understood about you, Barry, is that you pick Erwin to be your second best friend after me. I just don't see it. I mean, you go around acting like some great fuckin poet so I can see why you pick me as a friend. I can see you'd look up to me. And you're so full of love for fuckin humanity..."

"..und girls," said Erwin.

"Girls are part of humanity," said Barry.

"But mit a specialist function," said Erwin.

"But," said John, "I don't see what fuckin Field Marshall Erwin Rommel has got to do with either of us."

Another silence. This time Barry knew he had to be the one to break it. Yes, it was logical that he should have picked John to be his friend. But where was the logic in choosing a second world war German military leader?

Suddenly: "Barry didn't pick me," said Erwin.

"Yes I did," said Barry. He was annoyed that Erwin should interrupt at this point. Didn't he think Barry could fight his own battles?

"*I* picked *him*," said Erwin.

"No, you didn't," said Barry.

"Why?" John asked Erwin. He had perked up suddenly – possibly because the argument had moved decisively away from his use of the word *fuck* – and he seemed to be enjoying it at last.

"Becos he is like me," said Erwin, "becos he is a ..." Erwin paused , "I don't know vot is der phrase... ya, I tink... Barry is a congenial spirit." He spoke the word *congenial* with a hard *g*.

"Congenial," corrected John, using the soft *g*.

"I am not a congenial spirit and you didn't choose me," said Barry to Erwin. Erwin smiled.

"Come on," said John, "let's give peace a chance." He turned to Barry. "That's something you never hear that bastard say. You never hear your second best friend say that."

"Also," said Erwin, "I am not his second best friend, Yon. I am his *very* best friend. Isn't dot so, Barry?"

But Barry couldn't answer. For once the words wouldn't come.

26 Lorraine Castle

THE CAR WOULDN'T start. It was a white Fiesta, bought second hand, or maybe that wasn't quite the phrase, from a bloke in a pub. The bloke was wearing a Beanz Meanz Fartz t-shirt so Lorraine had trusted him because he was clearly a man with a sense of humour. And he was fat. Well, *cuddly*. Lorraine preferred the word *cuddly*. Like in the lonely hearts ads – *Soul Mates* it was called – that she was now re-reading: *Cuddly young-looking 35-year-old seeks sincere gentleman for friendship maybe more.*

Dave had tried to help with the car but he was useless. At first she didn't know what to do so she let him get on with it. She sat on the settee in the sitting room of her two-bedroom council flat in Pendle Heights, reading the free newspaper and stroking Joby who lay across her knees asleep. Every so often she would look out of the window to the grey tarmac courtyard below to watch Dave put his head under the bonnet for a couple of minutes, pull himself upright again, wipe his hands on the piece of rag she had brought out from under the sink, take a swig of the sweet tea she had taken down in one of her Leeds United official mugs, and stick his head back under again.

That was the second cup of tea Lorraine had made him this afternoon and she knew he would be back up the stairs in a minute or two to use the toilet again. When he did, she would have to talk to him about getting somebody out to fix things. It was Christmas Day and she wasn't a member of Green Flag or the AA or anything like that, but she knew a couple of men who were handy in that area and who didn't have too much to do on Christmas Day, not having close family or owt, and who would maybe come round and help her for the usual reward. The only thing that had stopped her so far was the fear they might want to take their reward while Dave was around. It would have to be part of the bargain that they delayed their satisfaction for a while.

Thoughts about men made her turn back to the paper. The *Women seeking men* ads were pretty good this week, interesting. Some of them a bit daft too, mind. Like the one that said: *Polite female, 22, WLTM older man.* Why would an older man want to meet a polite female, for God's sake? Or a younger man, come to that? Honestly, some of these women had no idea. Then there was the one from *attractive professional black woman* which began: *Are you a chocolate lover?* Well, fancy them letting that one through! It was racist, wasn't it? Lorraine couldn't imagine what sort of bloke would reply.

If she ever put an ad in the paper – and she wasn't that hard up, not yet – she couldn't imagine asking for a *gentleman* because that was bound to attract the namby-pamby men whose mothers had made them take elocution lessons. She couldn't imagine asking for a *genuine* man because that would just be like some big magnet that attracted every phoney bastard in the world. She knew she wasn't *petite* but she wouldn't be describing herself as *medium build* like some because that made you sound like a description on *Crimewatch.*

If she ever put one in the paper, it would say something *real* about her. Her star sign, for instance. She was a Scorpio and that meant she was sensuous. A sensuous man would know that because he would probably be a Scorpio too, or at least someone who knew a lot of women who were Scorpios.

Some of these women went on about being *intelligent*. Well, Lorraine knew *she* was intelligent but, being intelligent, she knew it wasn't intelligence that men looked out for.

On the other hand, some of the women called themselves *fun-loving* and they might as well have said *cheap*. Men liked fun in a woman but they didn't like it boasted about in newspapers.

Quiet nights in and fun nights out. Yeh. Lorraine liked that as soon as she saw it. That got the balance right. Told the customers you were serious and had real heart but you didn't sit around sobbing over *Coronation Street.* Should she say she had a GSOH? Because she *did.* Anybody who could put up with Dave and that droopy old Joby, who was the only greyhound in the world that couldn't stand running, needed a sense of humour alright.

Then she noticed one that nearly brought tears to her eyes. *Heart for sale, two previous owners.* Now. That was good. That was like telling them you'd lived a little but not been spoilt by it. That was OK.

Or was it? What kind of men would be wanting to reply to it? What kind of men used the ads anyway? Lorraine turned to the *Men wanting women* part. One man was seeking *a fun-filled r/ship*, another – who didn't give his age but described himself as *young at heart* – wanted a female for *socialising.* God, they did try it on! And some of them were dead cocky – lots more ego than the women. One described himself as *hunky* and another one as a *Grant Mitchell look-a-like*, which had to mean *bald.* And then there were a couple of really pathetic ones, the kind you wouldn't touch with surgical gloves. One was 47 and offering a share of his tin of beans on Christmas Day. Well, today was Christmas Day, but at least she and Dave had managed some chicken and baked Alaska. No bloody baked beans for them!

The thought of ever having to make do with baked beans made her think of the money again, made her get up again, shoving Joby off the settee so he moaned and barked before padding over to the hearthrug and slumping down there like the lump he was. Lorraine walked across to the front bedroom, to the wardrobe with the mirrored doors, now reflecting cheerfully the holly sprigs and fairy lights she had hung over the TV and sound system. She slid one of the doors open and looked once more on the sports bag. She touched its handle, its zip, its padlock. She stroked it. But she didn't pick it up. She didn't move it. She didn't *want* to move it. She didn't want to open it.

At first she *had* wanted to open it. Badly. At first, when reality dawned but she didn't quite believe it, when she couldn't connect that sort of money with anything her brother might get up to, she had been keen to check it out, make sure she wasn't falling for one of Dave's fantasies. But the killings had changed all that. Now she believed.

In fact, it scared her to think she would at some time have to look at all that money, at that unimaginable, uncountable array of banknotes. She couldn't get her head round it. She didn't think she ever would. And she was terrified about the killers who had done for Dave's friends. But there was also a kind of superstition involved, a feeling that if she put off touching the notes, put off opening the bag even, she would somehow stay uncommitted, untainted, safe from the revengers who haunted them both. Only when she actually got to touch the notes, got to help Dave count them and divvy up the spoils would she really become part of it. For now it was just a blue and white sports bag with a greyhound – a bit like Joby, only clearly more active – on the side. It could be full of old clothes, newspapers or lavatory brushes. The money still wasn't quite real. And as long as the money wasn't real, so the danger wasn't real.

And then there was that other thing. That thing Dave had tried to convey to her in Old Ironmonger's flat. She hadn't understood it then but she did now. That sense of something quite perfect, that overwhelming number with its six noughts. To open it up, to divide it, seemed a stain, a sacrilege. Even to look at it seemed to strip a veil from the mystery. She patted the side of the bag, touched the handles for luck, closed the mirrored door, went back into the sitting room. When she fell on the settee and picked up the paper again, Joby got up, climbed on top of her and settled back to sleep. Good dog, she thought, good old Joby, good old Dave.

Just then she heard Dave coming up the stairs. It didn't have to be Dave, of course. It could be the police. Or half the gangsters north of Watford. Whoever it was, it made no difference to Joby, who had started snoring.

But it was Dave. And yes, he did want the toilet. When he came out, he was grinning from ear to ear. "No more worries, Loz."

"You don't mean," she said, "you've fixed it?"

"No way," he said, spitting it out as though success in car maintenance was very much below him. "Truth is, it's too far gone, kid. Engine's completely dead if you ask me." Pause. "No. Tell you what. I've been thinking. I need to get to this Rankin bloke and find out what he knows. I need to pump him good, don't I? So. He might want to do things back to me, mightn't he?"

"So...?"

"I don't want to go after him in my *own* car, do I? I mean, in *your* car. That would be daft. He'd just read the number plate and track me down. Right?"

"Right."

"So. I'll just go out and nick a car, that's what I'll do. Makes a lot of sense, that does. I've made me phone call OK. I know where him and me are gonna meet. If I go out now, still light, I can come back early for some turkey sarnies and Morecombe & Wise."

27 Det Sgt Derek Rankin

HE'D GOT THE MESSAGE on his mobile. Now who the hell would have that number? Well, a lot of people. People who passed it on for a few quid to every Tom, Dickhead and Harry. Rankin didn't know the voice. But they'd mentioned Dockie and Teague.

Useful information, said the voice. Better come and see me then. The usual place. You know.

Rankin was mad. He'd been down the bog once today already. And it was Christmas Day for chrissake! And anyway, he'd just arrived at a crucial moment with Josie when the phone rang. But he was a professional, wasn't he? He knew what he had to do. He pulled on his clothes, ignored Josie's whining, lurched down to the car and started off.

He was reading about *sexy Ian's big cock* for the second time today and shaking his own, when he felt something in the small of his back and nearly shit himself. Still, years of training stood him in good stead.

The voice behind him said: "Hands up. Don't turn round." Then: "Do you know what I've got in my hand?"

Rankin heard his own voice say: "What?"

"More than *you've* got. Now turn round."

Rankin turned. He only opened his eyes when he'd done 180 degrees. It was Dave Castle. The gun was real. A Browning 9mm. In Castle's left hand. Was Dave Castle left-handed? He couldn't remember.

"You see this?" Castle waved the gun. Rankin's eyes followed it.

Rankin made himself say: "I must warn you that you are talking to a police officer..."

"I bet you've seen a lot of these down the station..."
Castle was smiling like a man who doesn't know how to do a
serious face.

"I must warn you that anything you say..."

"But I bet you've not seen one as big as this. Not up
close." Castle giggled. He was sweating. But it wasn't a hot
day, it was bloody cold. Rankin's cock felt cold where it
dangled out of his trousers.

"...will be taken down..."

Castle raised the gun to Rankin's face. "And it's
loaded. Sometimes I tell people it *isn't* just so they keep calm.
But it *is*. It *always* is. Loaded."

"You're never gonna shoot a police officer? You
know what happens if you kill a copper. We never rest. We
never stop till we get the bastard that's done it."

Castle stuck the gun right up against the end of
Rankin's nose and kept it there, pressing on his left nostril.
Rankin wanted to sneeze.

Castle said: "I don't know why you're saying *we* all
the time. *You're* not gonna be there. Not if I kill you, you're
not. It's gonna be *they*. *They* never rest till *they* get the bastard
that's done it. It won't be *we*. It won't ever be *wee* down your
trouser leg like you're doing it now."

"Don't kill me *please!*"

"It wouldn't look good on *Crimewatch*, would it?
Undignified. Shot while pissing himself in a public bog.
Members of the public, let's have your phone calls now."

Rankin heard a voice, high-pitched with terror. It was
his voice. It was loud too. "Oh please! Please, Castle, don't!
You've got no call..."

"You remember who I am then?" Castle lowered the
gun till it touched the end of Rankin's cock.

Rankin felt his cock dribble some more. He made a
great effort to bring his voice down. He said: "You was
always a good lad, Castle. I mean a *likable rogue*. That's what

we always thought of you down the nick. Not like some of the bastards we get nowadays, beating up on old ladies and raping schoolgirls. Not the sort of lad to go killing people. Not with malice aforethought."

"But if I was pushed…" Castle moved the gun back to Rankin's face.

"If you was pushed…"

"If I was provoked…"

"If you was provoked…" *Oh no*, thought Rankin, *he's got the bloody initiative.* Rankin had once been on a course in dealing with a hostage taker. So he knew: *you never let the other bloke take the initiative.* Somehow, he'd got to change all that. Maybe somebody would come in… some civilian, somebody who'd disturb Castle, put him off his stride… But then he might panic and pull the trigger.

"If I was provoked, then I'd be capable, wouldn't I, Sergeant? I'd be well capable."

Make him feel strong, make him the centre of attention. That's what they used to say on the course. "Yeah. Sure, Castle. Everybody knows that. You've got the bottle. Nobody doubts it. If you was pushed. If you was provoked…"

"Then I'd do it soon as winking. I'd do it soon as pissing."

"You've got no call, Castle. None at all. I've never provoked you. I've never pushed you. I always *liked* you. I've always said to the others: *that Dave Castle is a decent bloke…*"

"That's funny now, Sergeant Rankin. That's not what I hear when I meet one of your fellas normally. All I hear is: *Turn out your pockets for illegal substances.* Now I call that harassment."

"But not from *me*, Castle. Not from me. When have you ever had that from me?"

"It might not have been you, Sergeant. It might have been some of your mates. Maybe I'm just getting back at the lot of you. Maybe I'm making an example. Maybe it's just your bad luck you needed a piss right now."

"If it's any of them others, Castle, tell me his name and his number and I'll see he gets a bollocking. That's official." Rankin's voice was now in *official complaints* mode, a mode he had used often enough in the past so it ran automatically on a kind of tape inside his head. "You're a likable rogue, Castle, that's what I always tell them down the nick. Look, you don't even have to tell me his number. Just his name. And I'll have a word meself. I'll take him round the back of Hawthorne Street nick and have a private word. I *will*."

Castle made a deep sigh. It seemed to take a long time. Finally Castle said: "Maybe I'm *not* a likable rogue. Maybe I really *am* a bastard. Have you ever thought of that?"

Rankin shook his head. "No, Castle, I don't think so." But he didn't sound convincing.

Castle's voice was angry now and loud. "*Don't think so!* Who are you to say what sort of lad I am? You coppers are all the bloody same. Like teachers, probation officers, social workers. Put a label on some bastard and it sticks. But *they're* the bastards, really!"

"Not me, Castle. I'm not like them. I'm not like teachers or probation officers or social workers. I've no time for any of them. *Bastards*, that's what I say, same as you."

"But you're still a copper. You must like coppers."

Rankin's arms ached from holding his hands in the air and he wondered again if he dared take them down. Maybe even put his cock back. But no. "I'm thinking of getting out. Out of the police. It doesn't suit me."

"Racists, that's what coppers are. Racists and fascists and queerbashers."

Rankin nodded, vigorous in agreement. "That's why I'm going to quit. I can't stand it. Not any more. Not people like that."

Castle stepped back. He looked a little calmer. Or maybe he was stepping back to aim the gun. *That was the sort of bloke he was, wasn't he?* thought Rankin, *The sort of bloke who'd have to aim the fuckin gun when he was only two feet away.* Castle said: "You think I'm gay, don't you?" His voice seemed distant and calm, languid almost.

Languid. Now there was a word. Rankin couldn't remember the last time he'd used it. Maybe, if he got out of this one, he'd use it a lot more. There were tens of thousands of words in the fuckin English language and most people only used a few hundred. He'd *do* more things as well. See his Melanie more often. Spend more quality time with the kids, take Jamie in particular to some United matches. After all, the kid was a big fan of Harry Kewell. Rankin made a great effort to remove the picture of Harry Kewell scoring a goal against Manchester City from his mind and concentrate on what Castle was saying. *Had* said. "Gay? No, I never thought that. Not that there's anything wrong with it if you was. But I never…"

Castle interrupted. "I might be. I don't know. I don't know a lot of things. But I know this gun's loaded. How you gonna get out then? You're a bit too young for early retirement."

Rankin nodded furiously as the picture of Harry Kewell kept invading his mind. "I've been saving up."

Castle laughed. *Was that a good sign?* Rankin wondered. "Saving up, Sergeant? From a copper's pay? Enough to buy a country mansion when you quit the force? Enough to buy a country house like Michael Caine's?"

"No, no!" Rankin joined in the laughter. "Just pay off the mortgage. You haven't seen my house. It's small but it's OK for me and the wife and kids. A semi. Three bedroom. Bit of a garden. You could come round and visit if you want. Do you *like* gardens, Castle?"

Castle stopped laughing. "I can't stand the bugger. I hate plants. I want all plants to die. If I had all the money in the world, I'd buy poison and I'd poison all the plants. I hate the countryside and going for walks. I hate *Last of the Summer Wine* and Thora Hird! I hate the colour green. I hate all them green bastards that go on about saving bits of waste ground instead of building car parks. I hate all them bastards that want to save the tiger and the whale and the dolphin and the royal corgis. They're bastards and wankers and I can't stand them."

"Me neither, Castle." Rankin was talking very fast now, he couldn't help himself. "I know what you mean. But there's ways to stop them, Castle. There's legal ways. There's democracy. There's going on demos. You don't have to kill anybody."

That seemed to get through to Castle. Calm him down. He looked sad all of a sudden, like nothing was working out. *Like it wasn't worth...* He said: "Maybe I won't then, Sergeant. Maybe I'll let you live. But you've got to tell me something first."

"Sure. If I can. Anything."

"No lies now, Sergeant. No shit. Because I'll know. I can smell genuine shit a mile away even in here."

"Just ask. Honest. Just..."

"Who's after me?"

"I don't know..." Aagh! That was too sudden. He should've said: *Why should anybody be after you, Castle?* That's what he *should* have said.

Castle pressed the gun to the point of Rankin's nose again. *This time he was forced to sneeze, he couldn't help it, he was...* "Open your mouth, Sarge! Now!" Rankin did as he was told. Somehow the sneeze held off. Castle pushed the gun into his mouth, under his tongue. It tasted of oil and metal. The way you'd expect. "Now, I'm going to count to ten, you bastard, and when I get to ten I'm going to take the gun out of your mouth and you're going to tell me a name. This gun is going to come out of your mouth with a lovely little pop like a cork from a bottle and a word will come out after it, just one word and it will be a name. And it will be a true name or I will shoot you in the mouth. Understand? Nod if you understand." Rankin nodded. "OK, Sarge. One... two... three... four... five... six... seven... eight... nine... ten!" Castle pulled the gun away, out of Rankin's mouth, waved it in the air. "Name! Name!" he shouted.

"Dexter!" Rankin was shouting too.

"Dexter!" Castle stepped back even more now. He didn't look at Rankin, he didn't seem to look at anything. "The captain of the bleedin' team!"

Rankin was struggling for breath now. He thought: I'm gonna have a heart attack. Fuckin cardiac arrest.

Castle spoke in a quiet voice. "OK, Sergeant, emergency's over. Well, I've put *my* weapon away. I think *you* should do the same." And he walked out of the gents. *Sort of flounced*, Rankin thought afterwards. *Flounced* was the word.

That was another word he didn't use often.

Part Three: Boxing Day

"A spin bowler has a special skill. Energy used for developing speed in the fast bowler is converted by grip and action into spin instead of speed. The arm should be extremely high; the body swinging forward, up and over. The ball must go up from the hand and travel a curve on to a good length. So it's got a bit of a surprise then, always a bit of a surprise, for the batsman".

– Arthur Tetley, My Bat and Me, Pheasant
Press, 1976

28 Chanelle Braithwaite

CHANELLE LAY ON the floor of the bathroom. She was naked except for one of Simone's bathrobes, a white one, which was wide open now, and a pair of Simone's flip-flops, blue, which were half-on, half-off her small, red-nailed feet. She looked down, admiring her breasts, belly and legs. She wasn't being vain, she was just trying out some telepathy. She was planting an idea in Ray's mind. The idea was simple enough: the first word was *gorgeous* and the second was *Chanelle.*

Ray said: "How was that then?" He was naked too, leaning on one arm next to her. His red and blue dressing gown lay across the lavatory seat. He was no hunk but then she never went for that type. She liked them thin and boyish.

Chanelle thought what she should say. "A lot better than last night." She was referring to their abortive session in the single bed in Ray's room.

Ray sat up. A frown crossed his forehead. "It's my Dad's friends. Having them in the house. They give me the creeps and then I can't... do anything."

"What about that Eddie then? Don't you like him?"

Ray frowned some more. "*You* like him, do you?"

Chanelle hesitated. "I don't know about that. But he kept looking at me. I was embarrassed."

Ray grinned. "Embarrassed? You? I didn't think *you* could be embarrassed. I didn't think you knew what the word meant."

Chanelle pulled the left half of the bathrobe over her body. "Of course I know what the word means. I'm not stupid. It's like when somebody farts in a lift and people think it's you. That's *embarrassed*. Everybody knows that. Now why do you think that Eddie was looking at me?"

"He likes you. He thinks you're sexy."

Chanelle thought about the way Ray said it. He seemed pleased. "Do *you* think I'm sexy?"

"Do you have to ask? After everything we've just done?"

Chanelle pulled the other half of the bathrobe over her and sat up. "But men do it anyway. They do it with anyone. They do it with any*thing*. It doesn't mean they think the girl they do it with is sexy. It just means she's *there*."

"OK, I think you're sexy."

"Do you really?" Most men never said they liked her or found her sexy or even said *thank you*. Most men sort of grunted and put their trousers back on.

"I wouldn't say it if I didn't mean it." He looked as if he meant it.

That was amazing. *Ray* was amazing. She was pleased with what had just happened. She said: "You might. You might say that. Most men say anything that comes into their heads. It could be *yes, no*, or *Nicaragua*."

"OK, it's *Nicaragua*."

Chanelle let the robe fall open a bit, just to show off her left breast again. "Do you think I'm sexy enough to be a model?"

Ray snorted. "Is that what you're thinking about all the time? Is that why you had sex with me?"

Chanelle decided to look offended. She pouted a bit. "I *like* you."

"As much as you like Eddie?" What was the matter with Ray? Was he just testing her? "He's stayed over, you know. He's having breakfast with my Mum and Dad. You could share a kipper with him."

"I never like fish unless it's with chips. And he's married. His wife stayed over too. She's a funny one, isn't she?"

"She doesn't make *me* laugh."

"I know what you mean, Ray. She scares me."

"Does she scare you off Eddie?"

Now why would he say a thing like that? To tease her? Or because he was really worried? "She scares me off *everything*. She'd stick a knife in you soon as look at you, that one, that Gina."

"There's a lot of people like that who are friends with my Mum and Dad. My Mum and Dad are like that too. *I'm* like that."

This time it was Chanelle's turn to laugh. "Gerraway!"

Ray looked very serious, as much as a man can who's sitting on the bathroom floor naked. "I am. I'm like that. I'm my father's son, though nobody thinks I am. He killed a man this week. Charlie Pickett, a druggie, a nonce, a grass. My Dad did it and I watched."

Chanelle gazed into his eyes. "How did he do it?"

"A bit of wire round the neck, very quick, very quiet. Piano wire. Like Hitler used with the bomb plotters. You need to be confident. If you hesitate, the bloke gets his hands under the wire."

"Does he get away then?"

"No. The wire just cuts through his fingers. But it's messy. Bits of fingers everywhere."

"You're kidding me. You're having me on."

"No, I'm not. He did it. Tommy Cooper. Just like that."

"Tommy who?"

"He's in *Heroes of Comedy*. On the telly."

"Oh right." *Tommy Hooper. She'd remember that.* "Where'd he get the wire?"

"Greene's the ironmongers down Windhill Road. He always has a piece of wire in his pocket. Never knows when it'll come in handy."

"Bet he doesn't *always* carry it."

"Yes, he does."

"Bet he's not got it now."

"Of course he has. I've got one too. I made up my mind. I decided I should have one."

Chanelle heard her voice came fast and breathy now. She was a little bit scared, but that was part of the enjoyment. "Bet you've not got it now." She clambered to her feet. "Bet you don't *always* carry it. Where are you hiding it then? You've got no pockets." She reached down and touched his cock.

He got to his feet. "Bet I have. Bet I do." He went across to the lavatory seat and put his hand in his dressing gown pocket. He pulled something out. It was a handkerchief.

Chanelle shouted: "Liar! Liar! You've not got it!"

Ray felt around in the pocket and brought out his Rolex. "Now why did I take that off? Oh yes, you said it was scratching you in a tender place."

Chanelle's voice had run away from her. "You've not got it! You've not! Lies! Liar! Fish fryer!" She giggled.

Ray felt around in the top pocket. He was very unhurried. Very sure of himself, the bastard! The fuckin bastard! Oh, but he did look good, did look handsome, did look quite a bit like Tom Cruise. If you screwed up your eyes and looked at him from a certain angle. He took out a nine-inch piece of wire wrapped round two plastic clothes pegs at either end. "Believe what you see."

Chanelle was a bit subdued now. "It's just a bit of wire."

"That's what I said."

"You couldn't kill anybody with that!"

"If you don't think so..." Ray unwound the piece of wire and ran his finger along it. She saw he had an erection and that added to her own excitement.

"Show me!" she shouted, "Show me!" Her breasts felt heavy all of a sudden.

"It's just a bit of wire..."

Chanelle started jumping from foot to foot. She was afraid she'd wet herself. "Show me, show me!"

Ray stepped across to her. He was very close now, his mouth almost on hers. "The way my Dad showed Charlie Pickett? Are you sure? *Really* sure?"

Her legs were trembling. "Yes, oh yes!"

Ray stepped behind her. "Here we go then!" He wrapped the wire around her neck, one quick movement, one complete circle.

The terror rose inside her. She hooked her fingers under the wire. "No, no!" She had meant it to be a shout but her voice came out weak and breathy. She thought: *Bits of finger everywhere.*

"There. You knew it was coming. That spoiled it. Usually people don't know. Charlie didn't know. Still, it won't help. Just makes it messy." He pulled on the wire. She felt it tighten on her throat. *Bits, bits, bits.* The moment stretched out to fill her lifetime. "There," said Ray. He pulled the wire from round her neck in a sudden jerky movement.

She felt the warm wetness on her legs and pulled the bathrobe tight around her. "I thought you were going to do it. I really thought…" She rubbed her throat.

"You liked it though, didn't you?"

She smiled. Only a little. "A bit. I liked it a *bit*."

"I'll do it again sometime." He put the wire in the top pocket of his dressing gown and put the dressing gown on.

Chanelle stood still for a few seconds. Her breathing was steadier now and her voice was normal. "Yes," she said, suddenly getting an idea, "We could take a picture. For my portfolio."

"For your modelling?" Ray's tone had changed. She could tell he didn't like it.

"For Johnny Trask. It's different. He could sell it, I know he could. I could be naked, like stepping out of the shower. And then you come up behind me like Anthony Perkins..."

He laughed. "You're sick. You're funny in the head. You're as scary as that Gina."

She opened the dressing gown and touched him on his right nipple. "So are you."

"I'm not going on any photograph with this in my hand. I'm not doing stuff like that."

"You could wear a mask. A balaclava..."

"But somebody would still know it was me."

"Who?"

"Johnny Trask. The lab man. *You.*"

Chanelle allowed herself a pout. "I could get somebody else to do it then."

"No." Ray's voice had a sudden edge to it.

Chanelle felt warm and happy. She felt the wetness again. She'd have to have a piss soon. Should she do it in front of him? She said: "No?"

He pressed his face close to hers. "If anybody does it with you, ever again, it'll be me. It'll always be me. Nobody else."

Chanelle grinned. She *would* have a piss in front of him. It didn't matter. "That's settled then," she said, and: "What about some breakfast?"

"With that Eddie?"

"Don't be silly. With you. *Always* with you. And after that..." she made to kiss him but pulled away, "we could go into town. Do some shopping. Get me a party dress so I wouldn't have to borrow from your Mum next time. After all, it's a week to New Year. Still lots of parties."

"We'll see about dresses," he said, then: "You know what I told you? About the wire? I'm going to learn. Now I've got my own wire. Just like my Dad's. I'm going to learn how to do it. Kill people."

She nodded. "You do that."

They made sure their cords were tied really tight. Ray unlocked the door. As they were going out, he turned suddenly and said: "Hey, what's that?" He went over to the lavatory and pulled something out from behind it. It was a cricket bat.

Chanelle said: "What's that doing there?"

Ray shook his head. "Some people read *Playboy* on the bog. But not my Dad. He practises his cricket strokes." He took a closer look. "It's got names on. It's that bat Eddie and Gina gave him. Look at these names: Hampshire, Hutton, Trueman, Close, Illingworth... It's the 1968 team, the champions." He licked his finger and rubbed it on the bat.

"Are they real? They're not printed or anything?"

"They're not printed – the ink comes off. It's like that rollerball stuff. Now I never knew they had pens like that. Not in 1968."

"There's lots of things you don't know."

Ray looked bothered. "And there's lots of things my Dad doesn't know. I'd better put this somewhere safe. Somewhere more dignified. You know what *dignified* is, don't you? It's when somebody farts in a lift and nobody would ever *dream* it was you."

29 Barry Oldham

BARRY WOKE UP. He felt OK.

Erwin said: "Rise and shine! *Komm, schweinhundt!*" He laughed. Barry laughed too. He wondered where John was. He decided to get up. "I think I'll get up," he said.

Erwin nodded, still laughing. He clearly felt just as good as Barry. It was a strange sensation for early in the morning. Barry looked at his alarm clock which had not been set to go off. It was 10.30, and he'd come awake without the alarm! Of course, he recognised that 10.30 was not early for a lot of people. But it was certainly early for him.

"That's early for me," he said.

"*Jawohl*," said Erwin. Barry threw back the bedclothes and put his feet on the floor. Only then did he realise how strange it all was. The words hit him suddenly. *Threw back the bedclothes.* When had he last thrown back the bedclothes? When had he last demonstrated eagerness for the start of a new day? Not since high school. Maybe even before that. Anyway, not since Mrs Richardson made him stand in the corner for pouring milk over Janice Waterstone. Or was she called Janet Winstone? Or was that the author of *Oranges Are Not the Only Fruit*? He would have to think about it.

He looked down at his bare feet on the blue furry rug. It suddenly struck him they were dirty. Certainly a lot dirtier than the rug, which his mother cleaned regularly. There had been a time when she had cleaned *him* regularly, but that was long ago now. It suddenly came to him he hadn't washed his feet for several weeks. And it struck him that his green pyjamas with the dragon design and the elastic-topped trousers were sweaty and smelly. He pulled the top over his head, stood up and pulled off the trousers. It didn't do much good. He was just as smelly as his pyjamas. Now he recalled that his mother had complained about his smell... when was it? Christmas Eve, before he went out. Before the Poets' meeting. The Poets meeting! So much had happened since then! And he knew suddenly why he felt OK. It was because he had a new friend. It was because of Raymond.

He became aware that Erwin's manner was suddenly changed. He was looking hard at Barry. Barry was also suddenly aware of his nakedness. "Honestly," he said, picking up his trousers and holding them in front of his groin, "Honestly, Erwin, I get no bloody privacy!"

Erwin said nothing. He continued to gaze at Barry. But his gaze was fixed on Barry's face, not his now covered groin. There was something... *Jealousy*! That was it. As though Erwin could read his every thought. Erwin didn't like it that Barry had a new friend. Well, he could just lump it then! Barry threw the pyjama trousers on the floor and marched over to the door where his blue towelling dressing gown was hanging. That would show the old Nazi pervert! Barry put on the dressing gown, tied the cord in a reassuring knot, opened the door and marched towards the bathroom. *Marched!* That was another word he seldom used. Maybe thoughts of Erwin's militaristic background had put the word into his mind. It was a very decisive word, was *marched*. It had purpose.

He began a poem in his head: "The march of time, no, the march of life, de-dah-de-dah, is carrying me along, de-dah, *pitching* me along, de-dah, in its..." Well, he would work on it later. It would be the first poem of a new style, a new Barry Oldham. It would be a radical development from the romantic/sensitive Barry Oldham that various members of the Poets – like Jim Wiggins for instance and even Celia Simmons occasionally – had commented on with a sense of *dejà vu* that Barry could not altogether ignore. Well, the new Barry Oldham would be more life-affirming, life-enhancing, life-supportive.... No, *life-supportive* sounded too medical.

The words he wanted were words like: *bon viveur*, larger-than-life, take-life-as-it-comes, buccaneering. His readers would say: *That Barry Oldham! He's really got something. More your Ted Hughes these days than your TS Eliot.* Women especially would say things like that. Women always liked Ted Hughes. Look at Sylvia Plath for God's sake! OK, so some of the feminists started carping later on, but they were probably lesbians anyway. The reason they didn't like him was because he had lots of women. Barry tried to see himself having lots of women like Ted Hughes. He was starting late but he was a lot younger than Ted in his hey day. And it certainly didn't mean you were insensitive if you had lots of women. It didn't stop Ted Hughes being sensitive to the tragic implications of life. *Now is the globe shrunk tight/Round the mouse's dull wintering heart.* You don't write stuff like that if you're insensitive!

Barry turned the knob on the bathroom door. It was locked. There was a moment's silence, then voices from inside, one a man's, one a woman's, the woman's voice high and giggly, then more silence, then the drawing back of the bolt and a head through the opening door. "Hello, hello," said a smiling Andy. His hair was tousled and he looked even more boyish than usual.

Andy said: "I think we're finished." There was another giggle from inside. Then Andy opened the door all the way and came out. He was dressed in a short red and black dressing gown with his initials embroidered on the breast pocket. Behind him, Ursula wore a very short, white, lace-trimmed nightdress. Andy grinned at Barry. Ursula looked away, her still wet hair hanging over her face. Both had bare legs and feet.

"See you for breakfast," said Andy, and Ursula hastened into a run back to Andy's bedroom.

Barry stepped into the bathroom. The windows had been opened but everywhere was still steamy. *Steamy!* That said it all, that did. He locked the door, sat down on the lavatory seat and held his head in his hands.

"You don't look much like a working class hero," said John.

"I've just been complaining about the lack of privacy. I've just been saying..."

"Yes," said John, "Yes, I know. Erwin was telling me."

The thought of John and Erwin having conversations without him was disturbing to Barry. It nagged at him that they might have their secrets, that they might whisper in corners and make fun of him, like everybody else did.

"Not feeling so good, are we, wack? We were the life and soul of the universe two ticks ago. We were full of the joys. What happened to us, Bazza?"

"I don't know." Barry didn't usually like being called *Bazza* but this time it sounded strangely comforting as though it might betoken a change of personality.

"One minute we're up in the air, flying high, Barry in the sky with diamonds. Now we're down again. All because we've seen the real thing. Brother Andy and the love of his life. Flesh and blood. And we don't like it, do we?"

"I don't know." But he *did* know. He stood up, turned, began to urinate.

"Oh, go on! Don't mind me. Piss away. Fart and shit as well if you want. Who am I to be troubled? I'm nobody. Only one of your two best mates. Or is it your three best mates now?"

Barry stopped urinating. They *had* been talking together, they *had* been making fun of him. Now they had no respect for his bodily functions. They followed him everywhere. He had visions of a repeat performance every morning. Not being able to... *go*. Because John or Erwin would always be standing there, never leaving him alone... Actually, it would be John, not Erwin. He now realised that Erwin had been embarrassed, seeing him nude in the bedroom. That had been Barry's fault then. Erwin was too much of a gentleman to enjoy the sight of a man taking off his pyjama trousers. But John was just a nuisance, a scouser, a scally.

"That's right," said John, "write a poem about me."

How much they knew! It wasn't just a matter of following him on the outside, they followed him on the inside too. But now... Something had changed. Now he didn't like it at all.

"Let's get things straight," said John, "I'm not a jealous guy, not usually. So what I'm telling you is for your own good. You've got a new friend. It happens. Right now he thinks you're great and you think you're great too. And then you think maybe you're not."

Barry nodded. It was John's voice but it could almost be himself saying these things.

"And then you think maybe he doesn't really think you're so great, maybe he's just pretending, maybe he's part of the Bunch, the Bunch that run the world. You think maybe he's been sent to make fun of you some more."

Barry nodded again.

"Sometimes you get high and you think you can do anything. And sometimes you feel you're just at the bottom of the heap, crashed down again, like before, like it's always been."

Barry began to cry. "What do I do?"

John produced a Les Paul guitar. He put one foot on the edge of the bath and rested the guitar on his knee. He strummed and sang: *"I am the healer. Come to me./ I am the healer at the still centre./ I am the mender of limbs and minds/ I am here at the interchange of life/ Waiting/ Let the transports of fate/ Reverse and drive away/ I am here to catch the fallen/ Waiting/ For all of humanity/ I can forgive the world/ Though they are unconcerned about their fellow man/ For I am the healer."*

He sang it to the tune of *Imagine.* Somehow the words didn't fit. Barry reprised it in his head all through the shower, but he had to change part of the lyric to make it work. Afterwards, he donned his dressing gown and started back to his room. He heard Richard's voice from the hallway.

"I can't rouse her. I've dialled three times already."

"I'm sure it's nothing," said Barry's Mum.

"But why's she not answering?"

"Maybe she's gone out."

"On Boxing Day? Where would she go on Boxing Day?"

"To friends. Dropped in on the neighbours."

"She doesn't have friends."

"For a walk. She'll have gone for a walk."

"In the snow?"

"Some people like snow."

"*She* doesn't like snow."

Barry went back to his room, found clean underwear, put it on, searched for a sweater he knew his mother had washed last month but which he'd not worn since. And all the time he puzzled about it: *What sort of people didn't like snow?*

30 Raymond Dexter

FRESH AIR. RAYMOND needed fresh air.

Chanelle was getting dressed. Also raiding his Mum's underwear drawer. Ray was surprised. He hadn't thought Chanelle would have been interested in the kind of thing his Mum wore, either inside or outside. But she seemed to have taken a strange liking to Simone.

Women took an age to get dressed, didn't they? That was actually a nice thing about them, Ray decided. Any other time, he'd stick around and watch and make comments on her best parts. But he needed to be outside, alone, thinking.

Men weren't anything like women. Men just threw clothes on. He threw on his sweater and jeans. He didn't even glance in the bedroom mirror. He liked to do things the way a man should. It was a new feeling to him to be aware of himself like that. As a man, not as a boy. As Chanelle's, not his father's.

He didn't want to be away from her. But he still needed that fresh air. It was as though his mind was in hibernation, had been ever since the shooting. He'd been looking at the world like a video, and now he had to put the tape in reverse and press the slo-mo button on his memory.

The Polo was parked at the top of the drive, ten yards away from the front door. Ray enjoyed the sudden cold, seeing the smoke of his breath as he walked across to it. It wasn't locked. Ray got in. He adjusted the driver's seat and the wing mirror slightly, out of nervousness more than anything. He said to himself: *As a motor, this isn't so great. Just a box, that's all. But it gets you places. So it's OK for now.*

He thought: *I could have any motor I liked really. I could have a BMW, a Ferrari. I could have...* He stopped. He thought: *It's a box. It's a box that gets you places. That's all any car is.* Maybe it wasn't so clever having the sort of car that stood out. Might get it pinched. He laughed. Nobody was going to steal his car, the car of the son of Bradley Dexter. At least nobody was going to do it knowing who he was. And if they didn't know who he was so they did it anyway, his Dad would reach out and swot them. Splat.

It was like *The Godfather*. Nobody stole Don Corleone's car. No, it *wasn't* like *The Godfather*, it *was* the bloody *Godfather*. Nobody stole Don Corleone's car. But somebody shot him. And he thought: *Like somebody shot me.* He rubbed his forehead where the scar still throbbed. Flesh fuckin wound. He'd been lucky. One in a million. Hadn't even left much of a mark. His hair covered it up. He thought: *God, I thought I was Michael Corleone and now I'm bloody Harry Potter.*

Might end up carjacked though. Carjacked by some violent cretin that's never heard of the Dexters. But that only happened to people with *nice* cars. That's what happened to people with anti-burglar plexiglass windows and central locking and an immobiliser and all the gear.

He thought: *Might get carjacked by somebody who wants to shoot me again. Then it doesn't matter what kind of*

184

car. They've tried it once and they missed. More or less. They'll try it again. Whoever they are. Persons unknown.

He thought: *I'm lucky to be alive. I'm lucky to be fuckin alive.* He smacked the steering wheel with the palm of his hand. What to do? *He could tell his Dad...*

He thought: *Why didn't I tell my Dad when it happened?* He thought: *Because my Dad's past it.*

The thought sent a shudder through him. His buttocks clenched and his hands gripped the steering wheel. He thought: *If they didn't think my Dad was past it, they'd never have tried it on.* And they were right. Right now, they'd be thinking about the next move. But they'd also be thinking: *Old Man Dexter knows. Old Man Dexter will be watching out.* But of course Old Man Dexter wasn't watching out because Old Man Dexter *didn't* know.

Raymond smacked the Polo's steering wheel again. He *should* tell his Dad. He couldn't think why he'd kept quiet about it. But...

If his Dad was past it, he'd have to see to things himself. *Him.* Raymond Dexter. He blew air out of his mouth, not quite a whistle. What could he do? He'd need help. Somebody. *Harry Fountain.* He'd ask Harry...

And then the penny dropped. Harry Fountain! Harry saying: *Don't forget. Your old man wanted you to phone him.*

Raymond getting out of the Astra. Harry driving away to burn it. *Like they'd agreed.*

Raymond checking his pockets. No mobile. What happened to the mobile? It was there when they set out.

Raymond walking across to the phone box. As he would need to if he didn't have his mobile. As he would need to, to let his Dad know everything was OK. As Harry knew he would.

Raymond phoning his Dad. Raymond's Dad asking: *I take it your assistant got off OK?* Raymond saying: *Him? Yeah. Sure.* Raymond giving Harry an alibi.

Raymond smacked the Polo's steering wheel with his palm yet again. Once, twice, three times, four times, five times... He looked at his palm. It was red and angry. He thought: *I'm red and angry too.* He thought: *Harry Fountain! Harry fuckin Fountain!*

Harry set him up. Harry never expected Ray would come home. Now Harry must be sweating. Shitting bricks. *Well, I'll make him sweat, I'll...*

What? Make Harry talk. That was it! He'd make Harry talk. He'd...

What? Take him out somewhere. Take the piano wire.

What? Big tough Harry? Little Raymond, the A level boy? It didn't make sense. It wasn't going to work.

Shit. Raymond put his thumb in his mouth and bit it. There was a taste of blood, group O. A voice said: *Tell your Dad. He'll know what to do. He's got friends. He's got...*

He's got Eddie and Gina. Suddenly the full picture jumped out from the playback, from the slo-mo. Eddie and Gina. What the fuck were Eddie and Gina doing with his Dad? Answer: Using him. Coming down here to his Dad's territory, to the Corleone stockade. Chestnuts roasting on an open fire, Jack Frost nipping at your nose.

He remembered the bat. The names. Hampshire, Hutton, Trueman, Close, Illingworth... The 1968 team, the champions. He thought: *Beware Geordies bearing gifts.* He was glad now that he'd left it on the toilet seat after all.

He put his head in his hands. Up to then, he realised, he had considered his Dad safe. At least until after Christmas. What could happen to him in his own home, surrounded by his own people?

Now, he realised, that was bollocks. He thought: *I need a shooter. I need...*

Then what? He'd have to get to Harry Fountain. Not in the house, though. Not near his Old Man, not near his Mum. What about Eddie then? What about Gina? Sweat started up on his forehead. He'd have to take a chance. He didn't think Eddie would want to do the dirty work himself or be anywhere near when it happened. So his Dad was safe, after all, as long as he stayed home. Maybe.

And Chanelle? How safe was she? Probably a lot safer if he, Ray, wasn't around.

He thought: *I'm lucky to be alive.* And then: *I'm lucky anyway. I'm just plain lucky.* This was a new thought to him. It wasn't the kind of thought that had played much part in the life of A level Raymond up to now. He hadn't *felt* lucky. But now he knew he was. Lucky to be alive. Lucky to have a girl like Chanelle. Lucky to have a friend like Barry.

Barry! That's where he would go. Barry had saved him, stood between himself and the gunman – even if he didn't know he was doing it. Raymond would get the gun and go and see Barry. Barry was a poet, an outsider, he knew about life, he could help. What had he said in his poem? Something like:

> *I am a piece of the earth*
> *And da-dee-da your imprint.*
> *It hurts but shapes me.*

Hurts but shapes me. How true that was. And then... Raymond was amazed how much of it he remembered, just from hearing it the once. He continued to run the poem through his head:

> *I always knew it would be like this,*
> *De-dah-de-dah can change*
> *In an instant*
> *And you can change*
> *Me.*
> *Dee-dah.*

And you can change me! Barry knew people could change. Raymond thought: Like *I've* changed!

He would get a gun and phone Barry. And he would tell Chanelle what had happened. He would say: *Don't worry. No point in worrying. If I can get shot in the fuckin head and come out with a headache, I can get away with fuckin anything.*

Harry fuckin Fountain!

31 Simone Dexter

WHEN SIMONE WALKED into the bathroom, Dexy was stood by the shower with a big orange towel wrapped round his waist and a smaller orange towel in his hands, rubbing his soaking hair. She thought: *He's put on weight alright.*

She took the cricket bat off the toilet seat – it wouldn't do for Eddie and Gina to find it there. She'd best put it back in the lounge.

She pulled up her white lace Baby Doll nightie, pulled down her plain white night-time knickers, squatted on the seat and pissed. When she'd finished, Dexy said: "These towels aren't warm. I like *warm* towels."

She sighed and stood up, dropped her knickers in the Ali Baba linen basket. "You've not put the heating on. The radiators are cold. You can't expect warm towels if you don't change the setting."

"I *like* warm towels."

"You're getting soft."

"No, I'm not."

He threw away the smaller towel and glanced at his reflection in the mirror on the bathroom cabinet. "The very opposite, as a matter of fact." He combed his hair with his fingernails. "I've got to keep in trim. A lot of men my age don't. Warm towels help me keep my muscles toned. They keep me supple. Right now, I don't feel supple. I feel stiff. It's cold towels." He paused. "Brian Close was my age when he was called back for England to take on the West Indies. That was 1976. Them black bastards was just bowling high as they could, to knock people's heads off. Bloody coconut shy. But he feared nothing, did Brian Close."

"And he always had warm towels, did he? You could just take more exercise if it's *supple* you want."

"I *do* take exercise."

"Yeah. You *lift* beer glasses. You *throw* parties..."

"I socialise. That's a big part of my life – making contacts, keeping them sweet, fixing things. It's not as if I spend all my time in bed. There's plenty of fellas my age nodding off in front of the telly."

"I wish you did spend more time in bed."

"Just what does that mean?"

"If it's supple you want, there's ways of staying supple that you used to enjoy. We both used to enjoy. We don't seem to do much of that nowadays."

Dexy looked down at his feet. "I'm a lot busier. I get tired easier. Like last night at the party. The more you do, the more you need to take on. It's the business."

"Business!"

"Yes, business! You know how hard I've worked to make a success, to be somebody, to make *you* somebody. We've had some hard times, girl. I remember when the Crossley Brothers used to run this manor and nobody else could get a look in..."

"Phil and Don. I haven't forgotten them, Dex. I haven't forgotten what you did to them."

"They had it coming. They were well out of order. It got so the clubs, the pubs, the newsagents even, couldn't invest in the future, couldn't even stay in business, what with paying out premiums to the Crossley Brothers. They started squeezing the little man. Now that's one thing you never do if

189

you want to keep your market. And that's what gave me my chance."

"You put them out of business, Dex."

"I simply offered a better deal, more value for money. Cost-effective insurance with savings potential. The business community responded."

"They liked to see the Crossley brothers' heads in a very large biscuit tin. And that's what you gave them. It was one of those Christmas assorted, wasn't it? Savouries on the top, sweet ones on the bottom."

"You was very helpful then. Very supportive." Dexy had finished with the mirror now. She could see he was wanting serious talk.

She said: "Well, I'm not a great one for sweet biscuits anyway."

"But it doesn't stop when you've made it because then you've got to keep it. There's always new people coming up, causing bother. Remember Billy Stiles and Charlie Schofield?" He detached the big orange towel and started to rub his back with it. His belly was like a pillow these days and his breasts were like Melinda Messenger's.

"I remember Charlie Schofield alright, Dex. He came back to our house one time and started feeling me up..."

Dexy stopped rubbing his back. "I never knew that."

"I never told you. I knew what you'd do to him if you ever found out. I knew you'd cut him into little pieces and make him eat them one by one. And I knew you was going to do that anyway, so there was no point."

Dexy resumed the rubbing. "He was getting in the way, undercutting my profit margins."

"I'm not criticising, Dex, I'm not defending him. Like I said, he groped me..." Simone allowed herself to rub up against him, but the towel was still in the way. "And now this Eddie from Newcastle? This likely lad we've got staying in our house this morning? Is he gonna be like Billy Stiles and Charlie Schofield?"

Dexy clenched his right hand into a fist. *"He'd* better not lay a finger on you. Because if he does….!'"

Simone shook her head. She pulled the Baby Doll over her head and went across to the white towelling robe hanging next to the bidet. "That's not what I mean. He wouldn't be interested in *me* with a wife like he's got! What I mean is… are you gonna end up cutting him into pieces? Is it war, Dex?"

"War? No, eck as like! He's gonna be useful to me, is Eddie. He's got contacts. In Europe. And that's the way we've got to go. Expand. Diversify. Eddie could help me diversify. I need allies. I need friends who can look after theirselves. I do get a bit tired now and then. Like last night. When I went to bed early…"

"Left me to handle the party, look after the guests."

"You do alright. You're good at that. There's times when I depend on you, Simone, when I look for encouragement …"

"And that's what I give you. Here!" She pulled open the robe and pressed her right breast up against his arm. Then she wrapped the robe across her breasts and tied the cord in a double knot. "Well, then, if that's not encouragement, I don't know what is. And what are you going to do about it?" She allowed herself to pout. "I can see what you're going to do. Nothing. As usual It's a good job you've got a beer belly because there's nothing else would keep your towel up."

He turned away, hung the towel on the rail, put on his navy blue stripy dressing gown. He said: "We can't just do it in the bathroom. We could have people knocking on the door."

"Oh, that *would* be embarrassing! We can't have Eddie banging on the door wanting a widdle. We can't have Gina dying for a crap. That would give us all a bad name.

191

Mind you, we've already showed them where the second bathroom is. And the third."

"Not now. Not before breakfast. It's not that I don't fancy you. You know I still love you."

"I know you still *tell* me, Dexy. But I don't see a lot of evidence."

"I do everything for *you*!"

"You surround me with yobbos that think I'm only good for shopping and getting my hair bleached. Why do you do that, Dexy? Are you testing me, seeing if I'm going to drape my leg over one of them?"

"Don't be disgusting." He picked up the cricket bat and ran his finger along the black-taped handle. "Diversify. Don't get tied down in one line of business because nothing lasts. Two hundred years ago we used to have craftsmen. If they made you a doorknocker, say, with a lion's head on, you knew it would last. But that way of life is dead. People don't want the same bloody doorknocker all their lives. One day it's a lion's head, then they want Mickey Mouse or the Tellytubbies. So – if you're making things to last, you're killing the market. Now I've got to get some new things into focus. I know that. I know we should have more computers. People keep telling me. And I'll get there. But in my own time. There's always a temptation, you see, to please the crowd, to have a little dig here, a little shot there, when what you really need is staying power."

Simone tried to cuddle up to him again, "Oh Dexy, you used to have a vision. Like Margaret Thatcher. You had a vision and you made that vision come true. A Rolls. A BMW. A hundred-and-twenty-foot yacht. Stereo system. Colour TV…"

"That's what I mean by *change*, Simone. As you get more things, you learn that there's more things to get. You get a sound system for your tapes and CDs come along…"

192

"A ten-bedroom house with Elizabethan front and implanted oak beams, Dex. Three bathrooms..." She rubbed her face into his shoulder.

"Then a Jacuzzi, Simone..."

"Holidays in Ibiza..."

"Now it's Caribbean cruises..."

Simone stopped the rubbing. She was getting blue fibres in her mouth from the dressing gown. "That was one of the things we shared, that vision. We knew where we were going in those days, Dex. Now I don't know any more."

"If only..." Dexy's hair was still too wet. A drop of water ran into his eye and he had to rub it. "If only Ray had turned out different..."

Simone broke away, upset now. "Stop that. Mind what you say about Raymond. He's got brains, that boy!"

"He was good at school. OK. I'm not saying he wasn't good at school. But he's not like me, Simone. And he's not like Eddie."

"He's not foul-mouthed if that's what you mean."

"This Eddie, he's got something about him. He's a leader. Our Ray's not a leader. He's too bloody quiet."

"He thinks a lot. We could do with a few more thinkers in the world."

"I'm not saying we couldn't. But he's not like Eddie. I'm ready for expansion. And Eddie's somebody who could work with me, somebody I could delegate to."

"So that means our Raymond's out then?" Simone couldn't believe she was hearing this.

"Ray's not even interested. He never listens to me. That's what *educated* does for some people."

Simone knew she had to find a way to talk Dex out of this. Maybe a bit of sympathy wouldn't go amiss. "Kids! The way they hurt you is by hurting themselves. Haven't you learned that by now?" Then the anger took over again as she remembered. "Which reminds me. I suppose he's still in bed with that scrubber he brought over…"

Dexy was suddenly defensive. "She's not a scrubber. She's a nice girl."

"Don't make me laugh, Dex. I know nice girls – I used to be one myself."

"What you gonna do?"

"Well, I'm not going in there to demand my dress back. She wouldn't even be wearing it right now anyway. But I'm furious about the whole thing. At least *I* know how to behave…." She realised then how she'd let herself be detoured. She sank into Dexy's arms. "Are we friends again?"

Dexy hugged her. "Things will change, you know. Diversify, that's the answer. Find a new lifestyle that'll help me relax, give me more time with you and Ray. Banking. I've been thinking a lot about banking lately. And it would impress a lot of people in the banking trade if I could get hold of that two million."

"It would please me as well. We could have some more beams put in."

"Don't waste your time on beams, girl. We don't have to be Elizabethan all our lives. I thought we might try Georgian next."

And Simone was suddenly impressed. "Georgian? Is that like Jane Austen?"

"Georgian came *after* Elizabethan and it was very popular. So it's got to be an improvement, hasn't it? Whatever you say about Elizabethan, if people changed over, moved away from it, it's got to mean there was something better. Personally, I wouldn't mind Georgian. They made bigger houses for a start. If I get into banking, I reckon we're in line for a bigger house. I could even have a room for my videos."

32 Raymond Dexter

RAY PICKED UP Barry in the street outside the Oldham home. The weather was holding, the sun bright but weak, the snow starting to melt.

"I think," said Barry, "*The Turk's Head* is open on Boxing Day. I used to go there a lot."

"Right," said Ray. He followed Barry's instructions and they were there within minutes. *The Turk's Head* was the kind of pub Ray liked, the kind his Dad liked. Oak double doors with frosted glass and gilt-framed mirrors, long bar with hand pumps, little alcoves with wooden partitions, dim lights and no music. It should have been full on Boxing Day but for some reason it was empty except for the barman – a smirking effeminate boy in a white tee-shirt and black tracksuit bottoms – and a man sitting at the bar wearing a black suit and striped tie, black leather shoes duly polished, wisps of grey hair protruding from a grey trilby hat, a pint of best bitter in front of him.

"I bet it's never changed," said Ray.

"What?"

"Since you and your Dad came."

Barry looked round. "Yeah." He smiled. "You're right. At least," doubt had started to creep into his voice, "I *think* you're right."

Ray bought himself a whisky and bought Barry a pint of bitter shandy. They sat on a worn upholstered bench at a wooden table cracked with age and long-term erosion from wet beermats.

"A pint," said Barry.

"It's only shandy," said Ray. He said: "Are you taking your medication?"

"Yeah. I don't need it. But I take it."

Ray sipped his whisky.

"I'm not a schizo. They think I am but I'm not." Barry stared at the glass. "Fuckin doctors."

"Yeah, I'll drink to that." Ray had never heard Barry swear before and it surprised him. He was aware that *he* had started swearing lately, if only in his head. "I'm in a bit of trouble. I thought you might help out. Advise me, like."

Barry grinned. He took a sip of his shandy, licking his lips with exaggerated relish.

"It's my Dad. He's in a bit of trouble. So am I."

Barry put down the glass and leaned forward. His eyes shone with light reflected from one of the mirrors, his moustache looked more luxuriant than usual in the shadows of the alcove.

"It's friends of ours." Ray picked his words carefully. "It's friends of my Dad. They're not really friends at all. Do you know what I mean?"

"Once," said Barry, "I wrote a poem about friends who weren't really friends." He stitched his eyebrows together in a look of concentration. He began to quote:

> *"Oh you who were close to me*
> *And are now far away*
> *Will you listen? Will you hear?*
> *There is nothing to join our souls once more*
> *If ever there was…"*

"You're good at remembering, Barry," Ray interrupted, "I've started to be good at remembering too. I think it's from knowing you. I think things rub off on people. Do *you* think that? That people grow into each other and their minds sort of melt together?"

"That's right, Raymond. People talk to each other through their minds. Sometimes it's not nice, sometimes they think they can say anything they want even when it hurts you."

"I won't hurt you, Barry."

"I know you won't, Raymond. I knew that from the time… well, the first time we met, I thought: *Here's a new friend. A real* friend. Not like the friend in the poem."

"You saved my life." Ray took another gulp of whisky. "I need to know what to do. I mean, I *think* I know. But I need somebody to help me out. A sounding board."

Barry grimaced. "I'm sorry. I'm not really."

"Not really what?"

"Bored. I didn't know I was sounding like I was. Honest." He sat back and fidgeted.

"No." Ray laughed. The whisky was getting to him. Maybe the shandy was getting to Barry. "No. Not sounding bored, *sounding board.* Like a litmus test, only with sound, not acid."

It took Barry a moment to get it. "I'm stupid," he said.

"No, you're not. It's words. They let you down. They let us all down. Some of them can't make up their minds how they should sound so they sound like one another."

"Yeah," Barry sat up straight again, "I've always thought that. Some of those people at the Poets – Celia, Jim, Fred… No, not Celia, she's OK. But some of those others…"

"Yeah?"

"They don't know about words. They think words are just there to be moved around. They think words are there just to do what you tell them."

"You know different, don't you, Barry? *We* know different."

"Words are there to make you trip up, to make a fool of you. You've got to make them think they're winning sometimes, trick them into…" He hesitated, knitted his brows again, desperately sought the word.

"Positions," suggested Ray.

Barry considered it. "It's more than that. It's not just getting them together, it's fooling them that you're doing them a favour."

"Sorry?"

"You've got to make them think that you're doing it for their benefit. "They're selfish, are words. They don't do it for *your* sake, they do it for their own. So you've got to pretend, you've got to convince them that it's good for them, getting into line, meaning what you want them to mean."

Ray said: "I never thought of it like that." Then: "I want to stop these people. I know who they are. But I don't want to do anything that'll get my Dad hurt."

"Me and my Dad," said Barry, "We used to be close. We used to go to the pub together. We used to come to *this* pub." He indicated his surroundings with a sweep of his arm. "I'll never forget this place, I remember every bit of it."

"Yeah. My Dad and me, we used to be close too. Now he gives me money for Christmas like all the other Dads. I'd like to be close to him again."

Barry looked across the room over Ray's shoulder. "That bloke over there. The one in the trilby."

"Yeah?"

"Don't look."

Ray didn't look.

"That bloke over there," Barry warmed to his theme, "I think he's watching us."

"Why would he be watching us?"

"Why does anybody watch somebody else?"

"He was here when we got here."

Barry looked blank.

"So how would he know where we were going, Barry? If he was watching us?"

"He might have known this was our pub. He might have known this was where I used to come with my Dad."

Ray nodded. "What do I do, Barry? About these friends that aren't friends?"

Barry sighed. "I wrote a poem once about standing up for myself. Because sometimes I don't do that. Sometimes…" He closed his eyes and lifted his chin away from the glass. He quoted:

> *"You better watch out for me, watchers.*
> *You better watch out, got that?*
> *Remember, you watchers,*
> *Remember who I am and*
> *Watch out*
> *Because I'm coming.*
> *Hear my footstep.*
> *See my walk*
> *When I walk the walk.*
> *Watch out."*

He smiled, subsided and sat, staring into the middle distance. There was a small amount of spittle on his lip.

"I know what you mean, Barry. You mean there's a time you've got to take a chance, fight back." He quoted:

> *"Then when the dragon, put to second rout,*
> *Came furious down to be revenged on men,*
> *Woe to the inhabitants of earth!"*

Barry stared at him, wide-eyed now. "Yes. That's it. That's it exactly."

"I did Milton at school. He knew how to convince the words that it's good for them, getting into line, meaning what you want them to mean."

After that the conversation flagged. Ray thought about another drink but decided against. He was driving. He didn't want to get picked up by the law, this day especially.

Also he didn't know what more alcohol might do to Barry or even whether Barry had told him the truth about the medication. When they left, Ray dropped him off at the corner of his road and drove to the office.

He got out of the car, climbed the steps, put his key in the lock, opened the door. He passed through the front office with its grey walls, down the tiled steps to the basement office, stopped at the green four-drawer filing cabinet. He opened the top drawer, rifled through the copies of *Wisden*, Dickie Bird, Boycott, and Arthur Tetley. He rummaged behind the bottle of Bell's. Now he saw it: the thing, the Browning automatic 9mm. He picked it up gingerly and brought it out into daylight. He put it on the table. He unlocked the drawer above and took out the blue and red biscuit tin and put that on the table next to the Browning. He took a deep breath and opened the biscuit tin. The bullets stared back at him, shiny, new, beautiful. Hah! He had tricked the words into saying *beautiful*. Normally they would not have said such a thing, not dared to say it to *him* anyway. Now he had coaxed them to lose their bashfulness.

But they had told the truth. The bullets *were* beautiful, perfectly cylindrical, perfectly bright, perfectly pointed. They cried out for their beauty to be celebrated. Still, he should leave them alone for now. He had his own way of doing things.

He drove back to *The Turk's Head*. There was a bit of snow in the wind and he had to be careful. If it got too thick, if it meant his car could be tracked... But thick snow was still a long way off.

He parked in the pub car park, but near the exit this time. It was nice having a nondescript car like a Polo that everybody else had. But just to make sure of things, he picked up four handfuls of snow, moulded them into balls, threw them at the numberplates back and front, covering enough of the numbers but not in a way as might court suspicion.

He walked through the brass-handled door with its frosted glass and the legend (he could now see) *Fine ales and porter*. He went over to the bar. It was still the same two people. The nancy boy recognised him straight away.

"Hello again," said Ray.

The nancy boy smiled. Maybe he thought Ray had come back for *him*. And in a way, he had.

The man in the black suit and striped tie finished his pint. He got up, wished "Merry Christmas" to the nancy boy and winked at him. He nodded at Ray and walked out. Ray looked round the bar to make sure it was empty. Empty except for him and the nancy boy. "I'll have a whisky," he said, "and a packet of crisps."

The nancy boy moved slowly across to the optics and poured Ray a measure of Johnnie Walker. He came back again, put the glass on the bar, smiled again, said: "What flavour?"

Ray felt his heart beat faster. "Plain, please."

The nancy boy turned his back, studied the rack of crisps a couple of feet away, hesitated, searching among the cheese and onion, the barbecue beef, the prawn cocktail. Ray leaned over, wrapped the wire round the nancy boy's neck.

So fast. The nancy boy didn't even get his fingers under it. That's how good he was. Then the holding-on against the tugging, against the panic. But not for long. Easy now. The nancy boy slumped, gurgled, life ran out of him like slops out of a glass. Not like Chanelle. Not like Chanelle, who knew it was only pretend. The time for *only pretend* was over.

As he sped through country lanes back to the house, Ray was thinking of Chanelle. He felt excited and he knew she would be too. It had been a good rehearsal. A dummy run for anything he would need to do later.

33 Det Sgt Derek Rankin

RANKIN, NAKED EXCEPT for Josie's purple dressing gown with the fluffy collar, came down the stairs, ambled into the cramped kitchen with its cat bowl and overflowing bin, released with a bang the yellow Venetian blind, looked out of the window on a grey morning and a small overgrown garden dominated by a half-built patio, put on the kettle, dropped a spoonful of Nescafé and two spoons of sugar into a mug that said *Souvenir d'Antibes*, went into the lounge, switched on the light, switched on the telly, watched the news till the kettle boiled (nothing new about the Geordieland shooting then), went back into the kitchen, poured out the water, went back into the lounge with its salmon-coloured curtains and green settee, ambled across to the round, smoky-glass-topped table on tubular steel legs that was serving as a drinks cabinet, and added a slug of Bailey's Irish Cream.

"What you doin', Dez?" Josie's shrill voice from upstairs.

"Nothing."

"You havin' a drink then? Bring me a hot chocolate with a drop of brandy, eh? There's a good boy."

"I am *not* a good boy!" he shouted back. He thought about going back upstairs and giving her one. That would be the third time in 12 hours. But he didn't feel up to it. "Fuckin' Christmas," he said. He switched channels. It was *The Muppets' Christmas Carol*. Michael Caine was in it. He switched again. It was some awards programme with fresh-faced kids winning medals for being good little sods. He switched back. Evan Michael Caine was better than that.

Josie poked her head round the door. She was a short, dark-haired woman in her thirties with breasts like cantaloupes. She was wearing a very short, frilly black nightie and nothing else. She gave him one of her raucous laughs, which he quite enjoyed at the right time, then she leaned back against the door jamb so her nightie rode up a couple of inches and he could see it all. He thought for a moment: *Maybe I'll be OK.* But he knew he wouldn't.

After a bit, Josie said: "OK then. You can make breakfast. I like that Bailey's on my corn flakes. Gets the engine started."

"Make it yourself." This wasn't the first time he'd spent a night away from Mel and the kids, no, by no means. But it was the first time he'd spent *Christmas* night away. And he'd said, he'd told her: *Back by seven.* Good job she didn't believe a word he said anyway. He knew he faced a hard time, even if she did believe the stuff about following up leads in the Newcastle thing. He ought to give her a bell. But he didn't feel like a row with Mel this time in the morning. Not at Christmas anyway.

Josie went across to the drinks, thought long and hard about it, poured herself a vodka and tonic. She went into the kitchen and he heard the fridge door creaking open and the grunts of a clumsy woman trying to force an ice cube out of a plastic tray. When it finally dropped, she came back into the lounge.

"I can see you're in a good mood," she said, "Lots of Christmas spirit. Or is it that you've just not had enough of it?"

Fuckin TV. It's not like it used to be, thought Rankin. He thought: *The Sweeney.* Aaahh. Now that was the time when they had something good on telly. It had always been his favourite. That was the TV show he'd watched all through his childhood even though his Mum didn't like him staying up for it, even though you sometimes caught a glimpse of tit – *bosoms*, his Mum would say – now and then. That was the reason he'd wanted to be a copper in the first place. That Jack Regan. *"We're the Sweeney and we haven't had our breakfast."* Or something like that. The message was plain: *Don't mess with me, son.*

Rankin said: "Don't mess with me, son."

"You what?"

"He broke all the rules."

"Who?"

"Regan."

"I never liked him. All that grease on his hair. And his mind went, didn't it? Couldn't remember Princess Di's name."

Rankin looked at her. "No, no." He licked round the edge of his mug where there was still a residue of the Bailey's. "No, not *Ronald* Reagan." He put his mug down on the smoky glass top.

"Alright. If you say so."

Rankin switched off the telly. He said: "I've got to phone Mel. She'll be expecting it. Otherwise she'll phone the nick and find out…"

"As if she didn't know."

There was a muted bang from the kitchen as the cat-flap swung open and shut. Snuggins the albino Persian appeared in dislocated segments through the fluted glass of the door.

Josie pulled the door open. Snuggins looked at her with absolute animal confidence. Josie cooed. "Ooohh, my little darling! My itsy pussy love! Oose gonna have a nice bowl of left-over salmon then?" and she disappeared with Snuggins into the kitchen. Rankin heard the fridge again, then the scrape of fork on plate and the slurp-slurp sound of cat joy. Josie returned.

Rankin said: "She doesn't *know*, Josie. Get that inside your head. There's a difference between knowing and suspecting. There's a little thing called evidence." He started to think about evidence. It had never bothered Regan. Evidence could always be… *provided*. He was a lot like Regan himself, even now, even after the joy had gone out of it, when it was just a tacky job, sucking up to morons with

204

sociology degrees. In fact, that made him feel even more like Regan, now that the job had gone sour. Because Regan had to bend the rules, Regan had to face down those snotty bastards with the pips on their shoulders. You couldn't be a good copper unless you could do that. You had to live in the real world.

And what did it matter if you took a bit on the side? Whether it was the women or the cash? *The real world.* That's what the PC love-thy-neighbour bastards didn't get. All they thought about was equal opportunities, working in partnership, calling the police force the police *service*, as though you were a fuckin waiter in a fuckin caff. Fuck.

"You really gonna phone her? Wish her happy Christmas?"

"Yes." Get it over. He walked purposefully out of the room and down the hall, ran his hands through the pockets of his trenchcoat hanging on the row of pegs, found his mobile, switched it on. And then it rang. Just like that. The theme from *Goldfinger.*

"Hergie," said the voice. It was a black man and a hard *g*.

Rankin tried to recall the name. It was only a first name anyway. Then it came back to him. OK. Drugs bust, three years ago, big West Indian, thick glasses, played the harmonica in a drinking club in Chapeltown, played stuff with a touch of Larry Adler – *Rhapsody in Blue, The Theme from Genevieve.*

"Go on," said Rankin.

"Lorraine Castle," said the voice.

"Go on."

"How much?"

Hergie Ringwold. Now Rankin remembered the surname.

"Tell me."

"How much?"

205

"Cash or goods?"

A silence now, Hergie reckoning the deal, working out the best he could get. Money? What would it buy, the kind of money Rankin could give him from the Police account? When would he get it? Goods, on the other hand, would be immediate or near as damnit, because Rankin would already have them in a safe place.

"A kilo."

Rankin laughed. He let his laugh go on long after the joke was stale. He knew Hergie wouldn't hang up..

The voice said: "Look. There's four people dead."

"Let's keep it simple, let's keep it reasonable, let's keep it sane. OK?"

Silence.

"OK?"

"And that two million," said the voice. Obviously a man who knew what he was talking about.

"Might be a reward from the insurers, ten per cent split two ways."

From the other end a sigh.

From Rankin: "That's a hundred thousand for each of us."

Another sigh.

"Six ounces," said Rankin.

"Fuckin robber," said the voice. But he didn't hang up.

"Six ounces. Good stuff. No talcum powder. No Polyfilla."

Breathing. Heavy now.

"You need some pretty fast, Hergie. You got an address for me?"

"Fuckin robber."

"I knew we had a deal, Hergie. Just think about that hundred grand. Dream about it when you've got the white stuff. Now you have an address to give me." Rankin picked a ballpoint off the floor.

Hergie gave him the address. Rankin wrote it on the back of a copy of *The Sun* lying on the glass-topped table. He wrote it across the Page Three Girl but carefully avoided her nipples like the gent he was.

"The stuff. When...?"

"Next day delivery. When I've checked this out. Where are you?"

Hergie gave him another address, three streets away from the previous one. So. He'd dropped on it by accident more than likely. Suddenly got lucky. Suddenly saw somebody he recognised. Rankin didn't bother writing down the second address.

"Can't you...?"

"I'd like to. But there's a professional way of doing things. I'm sure you appreciate that, Hergie."

A silence. Then: "Yeah. OK."

"Trust me."

"I trust you."

Rankin turned off the phone. "You got no choice." He thought about his next call. When it answered, he said: "Where are you, Harry?"

"Out and about," said Harry Fountain, "A few errands."

"You got the day off after that?"

"Sort of. Me and my Kim going down the pub."

"Very domestic." He thought it through. This was still the best bet. "I need some help. Bit of strongarm maybe. Not much risk."

"Shooter?"

"Only for show. And only," he had belatedly imagined official ears tuning into his airwaves, "if you've got a licence."

"Of course I've got a licence."

"Right then."

He gave Harry a place to meet, a piece of waste ground near a derelict Edwardian house now boarded up and frequented by the usual druggies.

Harry said: "Then we go on somewhere?"

"That's right."

"But you're not giving me that."

"Not just yet."

Silence. Then: "What's in it for me?"

Rankin considered. "Maybe two hundred grand. Split two ways. Maybe."

He heard Harry whistle.

Rankin said: "Give my love to Kim. Is he still doing that weight training?"

Silence at the end of the line.

"See you," said Rankin. He hung up.

He started on up the stairs to get dressed. Then he remembered. He still hadn't phoned Mel. Well, other things got in the way, didn't they? He'd have to leave it awhile.

It was only what Regan would have done.

34 Eddie Patterson

EDDIE WAS FEELING on top of the world. A little bit drunk. Gina wasn't pleased that Eddie was a little bit drunk. But Gina could go and fuck herself with a salad server. Eddie laughed. He enjoyed the image. It was the sort of thing he always fast-forwarded to on video nights.

Eddie grinned. "I love it, mon. I love it. I go to the championships every year. I started playing in the nick. Best sentence I ever did. Lots of new words." He laughed. "Gerrit? Sentence. New words." He laughed again.

Gina said: "Ay, I bet you was a popular prisoner. I bet they all wanted to share a cell with *you*, the lifer's Billy Connolly. Never a dull bleedin moment." She snorted.

Simone looked round the room, making calculations. "Alright. We can move the chaise longue."

Eddie hesitated, grinned again. "You mean that settee?"

"Eddie," said Gina,

"OK," said Eddie. He put his Jack Daniel's down on the sideboard. "OK, we'll move the chaise longue." They moved the chaise longue, pushing it back towards the wall. They moved the table so it was a bit more central. Eddie went to the bedroom, took the suitcase down from off the wardrobe, opened it, rummaged inside, pulled out the *Scrabble* set that he'd brought all the way from Newcastle.

When Eddie returned, the others were sat round the table waiting. He laid out the board in the centre. He laid out the little wotsits that you put the letters in – he'd never had a name for them – one for each of the players. He dropped the letter tiles into the middle of the table with a grand and satisfying *whoosshh*. He looked round and smiled. He was feeling good, full of the Christmas spirit. And he didn't just mean the Dexters' Tomatin whisky which they'd enjoyed with their breakfast or the Jack Daniels that followed. He said: "Ay, I love games. And I love Christmas because that's the time for games. Wait. We gotta have a dictionary. You always need a good dictionary to settle disagreements."

"Can't we just vote?" asked Simone.

"How d'you mean?"

"Well, Eddie, I put down a word and you challenge it and we have a vote on whether it's right or not."

"Oh no, oh no, Simone. That's not on. For a start, if *I* challenged *you*, then me and Gina would vote for me, and you and Dexy would vote for you. That's family."

Gina said: "Don't count on it, Eddie."

209

"Anyway," said Eddie, warming to his theme, "it's not about democracy. It's about being right. You got to have an umpire, a referee, in any good game, and the referee here is the dictionary."

"Supposing the dictionary's wrong, Eddie?"

"How can the dictionary be wrong, Simone?"

"Different dictionaries say different things, Eddie. One dictionary might have a particular word, another one won't."

Eddie liked Simone – she was a sexy piece for her age. But she had pretensions. The first thing he'd been taught in this life was never to have pretensions, eg (that meant for instance) never use words like *democracy, faith, literature, spirituality* – all words he knew from *Scrabble* but wouldn't want soiling his lips with regular use. They were just words that meant anything you wanted them to mean, which meant they didn't mean nothing at all. Words that had meaning were words that made you actually see things when somebody said them: *cigar, shotgun, whisky, turkey* (the bird not the country because the country was too big to see the whole of just because somebody happened to say the word) and *cunt*.

"When I'm at home, Simone, I've got the best dictionary. I've got the Oxford. Hardback. In 24 volumes. Because I like to buy things, I like to own things. And when you think about it, here we are, we're using words all the time. Words are important."

Simone said: "We haven't got the Oxford."

Eddie raised his hands, fingers upwards, palms outwards. "That's not important. Not in itself. What's important is: once you agree on the dictionary, that's your referee. You never argue with the ref. It doesn't matter if there's another poxy dictionary somewhere that you dig out later on that says different. It's like video replays. They never make any difference because the ref's made his decision on the field and that's that."

"They do sometimes," said Dexy, "when it comes to fining players and such."

"Well yes," said Eddie, "that is true."

"Oh come on," said Dexy, "it's only a game."

Eddie laughed. "*Only a game!* Famous last words. I've seen people…" he paused and shook his head, "I once saw a lad get stabbed. Not so much stabbed as had his stomach cut open like surgery. A lad called Pete Simpson. Gina knows him. *Knew* him. He was a lad I used to do favours for in the personal finance trade. He puts down *prepense*. P-R-E-P-E-N-S-E. And Jackie Hamnett, who is another lad well known in credit circles, he challenges. And they get this dictionary. Paperback, it was, some American thing. Crap dictionary. Spelt *color* without the *u*, so you could tell we were gonna have trouble. And we did." He looked up at the ceiling, then back at his audience. "So the word isn't in. But Pete says it's a real word and it stays and it's worth 15 points. But Jackie says no because it isn't in the dictionary. So Pete starts to mouth off about Jackie and his family and his good lady wife and some rumours he'd heard about her and the Newcastle United reserve team. And Jackie just cuts him open then and there. So. Pete bleeds all over the table before we can get a doc. And he only lives another six months anyway because there's some complication with septicaemia, another good word for *Scrabble* by the way, which is what comes of Jackie using a dirty knife."

Gina said: "He never even *looked* clean, that Jackie, I always said so."

"Indeed you did, bonnie lass. But the funny thing was, when I got the Oxford, Volume 14, NUM to OPT, there it was. *Prepense.* It means," he hesitated, thinking hard, "*premeditated malice*. It's from Spenser's *Virgin Queen* or something."

"Let's get started," said Gina, "Biggest number goes first." She took a tile and the other three followed suit.

211

"N. That's one," said Gina.

"R. One," said Dexy.

"H. Four," said Simone.

"M. Three," said Eddie, "Simone! You go first."

They took their seven tiles and faced each other, looking to see that nobody else was looking as they placed the tiles on the wotchamacallits. There was a moment or two of silence while they worked out their best shots. Then Simone said: "OK. R-O-S-E-R-Y. Rosery."

"Simone, you don't spell rosary like that," said Dexy, "there's an A in it."

"It's a different kind of rosery. It's a place for growing roses."

"Oooh," said Eddie, "I don't know about that."

Dexy said: "You gonna challenge?"

"If you're gonna challenge," said Simone, "you be the one that fetches the dictionary. It's in the conservatory where the bookcase is."

Eddie hesitated. "Mmm. No, I believe the little lady. If she's read lots of gardening books, she'd know these things. My go." He put down his word.

"What's that then?" said Gina.

"It's *bollocks*," said Eddie, "Don't tell me you've never seen bollocks before."

Gina said: "I've *heard* some bollocks. I've heard enough being married to you. That's a rude word, Eddie mon. That won't be in the dictionary."

"Course it will, bonnie lass. If it's a good dictionary..."

"Chambers," said Simone, "Hardback. One volume."

"Suits me." Eddie turned to Gina, "If you're gonna challenge me, you gan out and get the evidence."

"In the conservatory," said Simone. She pointed.

"The conservatory," said Gina, "OK." She got up and walked very sensually (Eddie thought) in the direction indicated.

Dexy said: "You sure about this, Eddie? You sure *bollocks* is in the dictionary?"

"As I live and breathe," said Eddie.

Dexy said: "I hope she can find it alright." Then he flinched. "Oooh!"

"Dexy, you still got that heartburn?" said Simone.

"Come on, lass," shouted Eddie, "we're waiting."

Gina appeared very suddenly from the direction of the conservatory. She was not alone. A scruffy, gangly, badly dressed man was stood next to her with a gun at her head.

35 Dave Castle

"STAY! STAY WHERE you are!" shouted Dave, "Don't nobody move! I'll let her have it if you do anything stupid." He held on tight to the woman with his left hand, just underneath her breasts, fuckin breasts, a woman's breasts. He waved the gun with his right hand, then shoved it in her face.

The man he didn't know stood up, slowly, steadily. "Easy, Gina," he said. He said: "Easy, young fella." He spoke with a Geordie accent. He said: "OK. So who are you, lad? What do you want?"

Dave said: "I'm Dave Castle."

"Is that supposed to mean something to me?"

"It's supposed to mean something to Mr Dexter," said Dave, "the big man, the captain of the team. It's supposed to mean two million quid. And four people dead."

Dexy's voice wavered. "*I* didn't do the killings, lad. Not *them* killings."

"What can we do for you, Dave?" said the Geordie.

But Dave wasn't fooled. "You mean how can you make me put this gun down? To stop me doing a Charles Bronson?"

"Yeah," said the Geordie, quieter now, like a man who'd been put in his place. "That's what I mean. How can we make you put that shooter down and talk like a sensible person? Because I'm sure we can settle this thing without fireworks. All it takes is getting round a table and hammering things out."

The one who must be Mrs Dexter said: "How'd you get in here anyway? Where's that precious Harry Fountain? Where's Ray and that tart of his?"

"You shouldn't call her a tart," said Mr Dexter. He paused, embarrassed. "They went out. I dunno. Maybe she wanted to do some shopping." He paused again. "And I don't know where that bastard Harry is."

The Geordie said: "That's my fault, Dex. I sent him out on a job."

Mr Dexter said: "You did *what*? He's not yours to send out!"

Dave watched them. The bastards. The murdering bastards. He smiled. The bastards falling out. That's what he wanted to see.

The woman Dave was holding on to – the pretty dark-haired woman called Gina – said in a scared kind of voice: "Don't fight over it now, lads. Settle it later, eh?"

That made Dave grin all over. "If there *is* a later! For any of you!" He took a deep breath. "You bastards killed Dockie and Teague and them two tarts they was with that had nothing to do with any of it! You think I'm gonna sit down and play bloody *Scrabble* with people like you? You think that's all it takes to make my day?"

The Geordie fella looked sad and tired and full of the sorrows of the world. It was a look that wouldn't fool Dave, oh no. "I know how you feel, Dave. But I've got history on my side. Look at Northern Ireland. There's people sat round a table there that was shooting each other's balls off a few months ago. In the end, you gotta forget the past and make a new start. No matter what people done to you."

"I don't have to do anything, mate! Not me, not Dave Castle. You know why? Because I've got this!" He waved the gun again. "And that means *I* give the orders." Suddenly he let go of Gina who stumbled forward into the Geordie's arms. Free of her now, Dave took a good look round the room and he saw a cricket bat leaning against the wall. "What's that? What's all that then?" He pointed the gun at the bat.

Mr Dexter stepped forward. "Leave it," he said.

Dave thought: *He thinks I'm gonna shoot it. He thinks I'm gonna shoot his precious fuckin bat!* He moved towards it. "This yours, Mr Dexter? You play indoor cricket, do you? Or do you beat your wife with it?" He laughed at that one. He had always been a wit, noted for it ever since school days, ever since making trouble for the PE master, old Mr Dowdswell. Ever since calling him Penis-breath.

"Shut it!" said Mr Dexter, quiet but threatening. Threatening, that is, except that it was him, Dave Castle, who had the fuckin gun. Dave shouted: "Don't tell me to shut it, mate. Not while I'm umpiring the game." He went over to the bat. He picked it up with his free hand. He weighed it, looked along the ridge on the back, closed one eye, checked it like the sight of a rifle. "Come on, Mr Dexter, show me."

"What?" Mr Dexter couldn't make him out.

"Let's see what you use it for. Come on, Mr Bradley Dexter – this is your life!" He paused to look at the others, then back again at Mr Dexter. "I thought you liked cricket, Mr D." He threw the bat straight at Mr Dexter, took him by surprise, put the wind up his arse, except Mr Dexter caught it. "Go on. Stand at the crease, Mr Dexter." He waved the bat to indicate where he meant, at one end of the green and gold carpet.

Slowly, Mr Dexter did as he was told. He walked over to the spot. "Keep a straight bat, Mr Dexter!" shouted Dave, "Eye on the ball. We do have some balls, don't we?" Dave laughed. Oh, he was on good form today. He turned and waved the gun at Gina. "*You* come over here." Slowly, as slowly as Mr Dexter, Gina did so. "You're the bowler," said Dave, "but you're only a girl. If you got no balls, you better use something else. What about these lovely wine glasses?" He pointed the gun at the row of glasses on the cocktail bar. He said to Gina: "Pick 'em up then, love. Know how to bowl, do you? Know a googly from an off-spin, do you? Bet you get him out first time."

He turned to Mrs Dexter and the Geordie. "You two! Get this *Scrabble* shit out of the way." They moved quickly to obey him, picking up the table and all the stuff on it, carrying it off the carpet, across by the settee thing, out of the way, just as he'd told them.

Dave turned back to Gina. "OK, sweetheart, you give him a hard time." Again he indicated with the gun and Gina took up the position, glancing at the Geordie and then at Mr Dexter again. Dave said to the Geordie: "And you, mate, you can field. Right? Got that? Better not drop any catches or I might get upset." Dave turned to Mrs Dexter. "You can be the scorer, my love. If you was gonna play *Scrabble*, you must have a piece of paper and a pen." He was shouting again. "Go on, Carol Voorderman! Go get 'em!"

Mrs Dexter ran over to the table, picked up a pen and a sheet of paper. When Dave turned the gun back on Gina, she threw the wine glass underarm at Mr Dexter who hit it full on with the bat. *Splat!* The glass crashed to the floor in splinters.

"Underarm!" Dave yelled, "I don't believe it!" And he said to Mr Dexter: "Well, what you waiting for? Run! You've made *me* bloody run!"

Mr Dexter ran across the room to the other end of the carpet, turned and ran back again.

216

"Two runs!" shouted Dave, "Only two! You can do better than that!" All the memories flooded back to him now. Like Jerry, the hardman spin bowler who was as queer as they come if only he'd admit it, who was always smacking Dave with the end of a towel in the changing room after games. Come to think of it, Jerry looked a lot like Mr Dexter. Or would do when he was as old and fat and scared as Mr Dexter. Dave would make Jerry just as scared one day, make him regret all the things he'd done. Oh yes. Dave shouted: "Come on then!" once again to Mr Dexter and Mr Dexter came pounding out across the room again, then back, then just stood, shaking, breathless. "Four!" shouted Dave, "Only four? Well, I reckon that one was good for a six at least." Mr Dexter started his run again, across the room and back. He was feeling it now, no doubt of that. There was sweat sticking out like fuckin raindrops on his forehead. "Nice six, Mr Dexter. But now I think it's worth… *eight!*" Mr Dexter ran again, across and back. "A ten!" shouted Dave, and Mr Dexter ran again. "Oooh," said Dave, "You're not very fit, Mr Dexter, not very agile." He liked the word *agile*. It had a sexy sound somehow.

Mrs Dexter screamed: "Stop it!" She ran at Dave, then stopped. She still had the paper and pen in her hands.

"Did you write it down?" asked Dave, "Did you write down the score?"

Mrs Dexter stood stock steady now. "Yes. I wrote it down. Now let him stop."

This time when Dave laughed it was a real guffaw. "Let him stop! *Let him stop!* No, I don't think I will." He looked across at Gina. "Let him have another one. Overarm this time. You've got to learn to take this seriously." He said to Mr Dexter: "Better hit it, Mr Dexter. I'm the fan with the plan. It's the run or the gun." And again to Gina: "OK, my love. Let him have it."

Gina threw a second glass, overarm this time and Mr Dexter played it across to the patio window where it landed with a crash.

"I'm sorry about your glasses, Simone," said Gina, "I'm sorry about your windows."

"Don't be, Gina," said Mrs Dexter, "I expect a few breakages when we throw a party."

That made Dave laugh again. "Now," he called out, "Is he gonna run? Geoffrey Boycott considers. Is it a four? Is it a six? Can he do a century from one little ball? Come on, Mr Dexter. Go for it. Run! Run!"

"No!" shouted Mrs Dexter, "Dexy, don't!"

Dave said: "Not very fit, Mr Dexter? There. There. We all need a bit of exercise once in a while, don't we? It cleans out the system, does you a world of good."

Mr Dexter hesitated. He didn't look good at all now. The drops of sweat had turned to rivulets and the shallow puffing to wheezing. Dave thought for a moment this was the time to shoot Mr Dexter, get the game over with, run out to the car where Lorraine and Joby waited, drive away forever, make good his escape, make a new life in Australia, where the sun always shone and there were lots more men than women, big, hulking, blond men as a matter of fact, just like on *Neighbours* and *Home and Away*.

Then Gina stepped up to Dave. "What's your game, mister? Just what is it you get out of this?"

"I'm doing it because it pleases me! I'm doing it because it suits me! I can make him do anything as long as I've got *this*," he waved the gun the way he'd done before, the way he'd got used to now. Australia was far away. This was here and now. And it was fun. "I can make *anybody* do anything. You!" He pointed the gun at Gina. "I could make you take your clothes off if I wanted. I could make you strip naked! Italian housewives!" He looked hard at her face to see

the fear and horror, to enjoy that. But her face stayed the same
– sulky, bad tempered, womanish.

"Alright, then," she said, "Where do I start?

Dave was startled. "Whaddaya mean?"

"Do I start with my dress or my tights?" Gina had a silly sort of grin on her face now, like she was starting to enjoy herself as well, like maybe she didn't think Dave would shoot, like maybe she didn't *respect* Dave. "I think I'll start with my tights. It's been quite warm for the time of year and I've been feeling a bit clammy down there." She shouted across at Mrs Dexter: "You've got good central heating, Sim." Then she pulled up her dress, stuck her thumbs in the top of her tights and started pulling them down. Dave's eyes swivelled round the room. All the others were looking at Gina. Nobody was looking at *him* any more. He said: "Whattaya doing? Wait!"

Gina said: "I'm doing like you told me. I'm taking my clothes off."

"I didn't tell you to do that! I said I *could* if I wanted to." Dave listened to his own voice. It had climbed much higher than he intended. He looked back at Gina's legs, away at the wall, away at the ceiling with its little cherubs in the cornices, back at Gina's legs. He didn't want to look at Gina's legs, he suddenly felt dizzy.

That was when the Geordie jumped him.

Dave moved without thinking. He stepped to one side and smacked the Geordie hard across the side of the head with the barrel of his gun. The Georide fell like the proverbial, the old sack of potatoes. He let out a cry as he went down.

Gina screamed: "Eddie!" She ran across to him. Dave waved the gun and shouted. But he couldn't stop her. She cradled Eddie's head in her hands.

Eddie said: "I'm OK, sweetheart." He rubbed the side of his head. There was blood seeping through his hair.

"Bastard!" Gina shouted at Dave, "Bastard! Bastard!"

For a moment Dave didn't know what to say. Then it clicked. "Oh, I get it! You was trying to get my attention so your boyfriend could have a go at me! Well, it didn't work!" He was pleased. He'd had the chance to show how tough he was. He'd stayed in control.

Gina said: "He's not my boyfriend!" She was talking in a proper voice now, not shouting and screaming any more.

Suddenly Dave was angry. He didn't know why. "You bitch! I ought to... " He pointed the gun straight at Gina.

Mrs Dexter moved across in front of him. She had her fingernails pressed into her palms. "She didn't mean anything, Dave. She can't think straight. She's scared. You scared us all. That's what you wanted, wasn't it?"

Dave waved the gun at Mrs Dexter. "Don't *you* say nothing neither! You women –   you think you've got it all, don't you? You think you can do as you like. But you can't! Not any more! Oh, you're worse than they are. The men do the killing but it's the women that lead them on. Don't think I don't know! Don't think I don't know about women!" Dave let them hear his laugh again, the crazy laugh, the laugh he knew scared the shit out of them. Then he heard the noise. *Bang*! It was the back door. Somebody was coming in.

"Harry!" shouted Mrs Dexter.

And there they were. The Harry bloke, that's what Mrs Dexter called him. And with him, looking scared, looking just as scared as Godalmighty Bradley Dexter and his friends, was Lorraine.

"Lorraine!" shouted Dave. He turned the gun in the direction of Harry but Harry also held a gun. They pointed their guns at each other. They waited. They said nothing. Then Dave noticed the sports bag.

"Lorraine!" Dave shouted again. He had to stop himself shouting: *Sports bag!*

Lorraine burst into tears. "Help me, Dave!"

"Bastard!" said Dave, "What've you done to her?"

"Not as much as he's going to if you don't put that gun down," said Mrs Dexter. She moved very close to Dave. "Come on. The match of the day is over. Put it down."

Dave felt faint. He could smell his own sweat. "I'm not giving you the gun. You'll kill us both."

"OK," said Mrs Dexter, "Just point it downwards, so it can't go off by accident. That's all I'm asking. Then Harry can do the same. So it won't go off by accident. So it won't hurt your girlfriend."

"She's not my girlfriend!" Dave wasn't sure if Mrs Dexter was winding him up.

"Just rest your hand, Dave," she said, "and Harry will do the same. Let's take some of the heat out of things. Give us chance to talk."

Dave stepped back. He leaned against the cocktail cabinet, bringing the gun down just a little bit, ever so slightly, just enough to show willing, ready to make a deal maybe, but not scared, not weak, not stupid. Oh no, not ready to throw it away or anything like that. He rested his gunhand on the cabinet. He could still kill them all if he wanted. A sudden thought struck him: *Was the gun loaded?* He couldn't remember. But the other gun would be loaded. That Harry person would always have a loaded gun. He could smell his own sweat again. He could feel it trickle down his forehead. Oh God, what would Sylvester Stallone do? Or Al Pacino in *Dog Day Afternoon*?

At that point, Mrs Dexter changed things. She still had the ballpoint pen in her hand. And she pounced, stabbing him with the point of the pen, driving it home through the flesh on the back of his hand, making him scream with the pain. Making him drop the gun.

"Aaaaaggghhh!!" You never heard Al Pacino scream like that. He dropped the gun. He grabbed his hand. He fell on his knees. He burst into tears.

221

36 Bradley Dexter

BRADLEY DEXTER FELT bad. His heart was racing, his breath was coming in gulps, his head was spinning and everyone looked so far away. But he knew they'd come through! And Simone! What a woman! He saw her kick the gun across the carpet while that fuckin little queer Dave Castle stayed on his knees, holding his fuckin hand like a fuckin girl, crying his fuckin heart out.

Simone was saying: "There. There. We all need a cry once in a while, don't we? It cleans out the system, does you a world of good." She came over to Bradley. "Are you OK, Dex? You look like death." Her lovely face was shadowed with worry, not the way he liked to see her.

She hugged him and he hugged her back. "I'm OK. Out of breath, that's all." Then he thought about the cricket bat still in his hand and dropped it. Gina had picked up Dave's gun now and Eddie was getting to his feet. He went over and kicked Dave. Dave fell on his back and went on crying. Eddie turned to Bradley: "That was the job, Dex. The job I sent your Harry on." He waved a hand at Lorraine. "We got lucky with some information."

At that point, another man came in – tall, wiry, greasy-haired. He had the look of copper all over him. He also carried a gun; but when he took in the scene, he put it away. "I'm Rankin," he said. "Mr Dexter," he said.

Bradley nodded. "We'll talk about it later," he said to Eddie. Maybe Eddie wasn't so bad. Maybe he'd saved them all.

Harry stepped across to where Dave lay and also gave him a kick. This time Dave curled up in a ball. Harry said: "Yeah. Lots of things we can talk about later. But right now..." This time he stamped on Dave's head. Dave screamed. Lorraine screamed too.

Gina said sharply: "Leave it!"

Rankin turned to her. "What d'you mean – leave it? *I've* got a score to settle with this dogturd too."

Eddie said: "She said *leave it* so you leave it!" He spoke very quietly and stood quite still.

Rankin stopped in his tracks. Harry stopped waving his gun, stepped back. "Alright then. Season of goodwill, is it? Alright. I've done my bit, Mr Patterson. I've brought home the lovely lady and the lovely lolly. We had to shoot her bloody dog though."

Dave groaned. "Joby!"

Lorraine was crying too, big slurpy sobs. "It was quick, Dave. Honest! He didn't suffer!"

Dave rolled over on his side. "I loved that dog!"

Harry said: "He had stinking breath." He put his gun in his pocket.

Eddie said to Harry: "You've not opened it? Nobody's opened the bag then?"

"No way."

"Good. Ay, that's good. You've done well."

"Done well, have I?" Harry was playing the tough guy now, thought Bradley, showing he could do sarcasm. "Harry Fountain. Action Man. Mine of information. Is that it? *Bye, bye, Harry, you've done well.*"

"I'll see you're alright, Harry. I always do." Dexy was still breathless, still subdued.

Rankin said: "Harry and me, we been all over the place, asked the neighbours, checked out the stolen car, followed after Bonnie and Clyde here. It's not been easy, right?"

"Right," said Harry, "And now we've turned up two million quid..."

Eddie interrupted him. "You're good for fifty grand. You too, Rankin. I guarantee it."

Gina added her twopenn'rth. "Only not now, not this minute. There's things to be done."

Bradley could see that Harry looked unsure now. He looked at Bradley. He looked round at the others. He looked at Eddie again. "I've got your word...?"

"Yes," said Bradley. He wished his heart would stop beating so loud.

Eddie smiled. "You've got it, lad."

Eddie turned away. Harry said quickly: "OK. OK then."

Simone said: "Harry, get the dustpan and brush out of the cupboard under the stairs. No, I'll get it. And all of you stand still. I don't want anybody moving, you'll tread the glass into the carpet." She went out the door into the hall.

Gina pointed the gun at Lorraine. "That means you too, sweetheart. Just get down on your knees and stay very still." Lorraine knelt down beside Dave. He was still crying, still holding his stomach where Eddie had kicked him. Lorraine put a hand on his arm. Then she looked across at Gina. "What you gonna do with us then?"

"First," said Eddie, "we check the bag." He took a key from his pocket and picked up the sports bag.

Bradley said: "*You had a key!*" He felt gobsmacked.

"Right. You bet I did." Eddie unlocked the bag, opened it, looked inside. "OK. It's all here." Just a second. That was all he took.

Bradley said: "How d'you know it's all there? I mean, we should count it."

"Trust me. I used to be a bookie."

"So what *do* we do with this pair?" asked Gina.

"We let 'em go," said Eddie.

Bradley could hear his heart again. "We do *what?*"

"Trust me, Dexy mon. It's like Harry said. Season of goodwill. Why not? There's enough people dead over this one, enough of a fuss still to die down. And where will they gan to? Who they gonna talk to? What evidence have they got?"

Bradley thought about it. "They was here. In my home. They know me."

"*Everybody* knows you. It doesn't matter. This is your story. They came over here looking for a handout, looking for a job maybe. You turned them down. They got upset and broke a few glasses. But you can afford to be magnanimous. Also, the police will know about the car, know Rankin was asking about it. So we don't want any more bodies turning up." He turned to Harry. "Get them out of here. Off the property." He looked down at Dave as Harry started kicking him again, forcing him to his feet. "I won't say it's been a pleasure meeting you, Dave mon. But I have to say it's been useful. Now just forget it."

Dave got to his feet in spite of the kicks. Lorraine got up too and hugged him. He didn't look at her. He looked at Eddie. "Two million quid…"

"Everything," said Eddie, "Forget about everything."

"I got *nothing* out of this!" Dave's voice skipped an octave of self-pity.

"You got your life and *her* life too. I wouldn't call that nothing."

Lorraine grabbed hold of Dave, very fast, very tight. "Dave! Please! They're letting us go!" Her voice sounded like she didn't believe it. Bradley didn't believe it either.

Eddie said: "Listen to her, Dave. She's a canny lass. She's making good sense." He glanced at Lorraine. "Oh – and I'm sorry about the dog. Really." He nodded back at Harry. Eddie moved across to Dave and gave him a shove, not hard, not painful, just casual, full of contempt. Harry took out the gun again, grabbed Dave's elbow and stuck the gun in his neck.

"No! No!" screamed Lorraine.

"It's OK," said Eddie. Lorraine and Dave started moving towards the conservatory with Harry close behind.

Bradley said: "You're not really doing that?" His heart was still like a hammer.

"Yes I am."

Bradley gave it up. He sank back on the *chaise longue*. "I don't get it. They're gonna talk. Somebody is gonna believe them."

Rankin said: "I've got to get through some paperwork anyway. End of the year crime figures. Let the super know they're down again for the fourth time running." He allowed himself a smile. To show he was still on top, thought Bradley, to convince himself. "Trouble with success is – pretty soon we'll be laying people off." Rankin laughed and Eddie laughed with him. He looked around one more time then sidled off through the conservatory, taking his time.

Eddie watched them go. Dave, Lorraine, Harry, Rankin. Then he sat down next to Bradley and punched him on the shoulder, all pals together. "Sure. *Somebody's* gonna believe them. Or maybe *everybody's* gonna believe them. They're gonna believe we've got our hands on two million pounds that Dave and his mates stole from the Royal Bank of Cumbria. They'll think we're a canny pair of lads." He looked up at Gina. "Sweetheart, I think Dexy here has had a bit of a shock. He needs a drink. Go get him a whisky, sweetheart…"

"A double," said Bradley.

"A double," repeated Eddie as Gina did so, "Hey, do you wanna see two million pounds, Dex? That'll make you feel better, mon. Take a good look." He reached down, picked up the sports bag, handed it to Bradley.

Bradley looked inside. He put his hand in. He took out a small silver foil bag. "Little bags," Eddie said, "They're all labelled."

Bradley read: "£10,000 in £5 notes." He turned the sports bag upside down and lots of similar silver bags fell out. He read another one: "£50,000 in £10 notes. Is that right,

Eddie? They look like bags of tea. What is this, Eddie? I know it's the pantomime season, but..."

Eddie guffawed this time. Bradley didn't feel like joining in. He felt he was the butt of the joke, a joke he didn't understand. Finally Eddie said: "Monopoly money, Dex. Not even that. You couldn't even pass go and collect £200." He pulled out one of the small foil bags and tore it. A wad of newspaper, cut to the size of banknotes, fell out.

"I don't get it. So there's no two million? There's no money?"

"Oh, there's money alright. And a share of it for you and me, my lad. But it didn't go with Dave and his mates. It went a long time before that."

"How?"

"Flick of a switch. Press of a key. That's how it's done these days. Computers. Electronic accounting. Electronic thieving too."

Gina was back with the whisky. Bradley reached out for it, realising suddenly how thirsty he was, how his breath still kept coming in gasps.

Eddie said: "You should ask your lad Harry. He knows all about that sort of thing. He's a useful fella, I don't mind telling you. But he's wasting his time here. I think we might take him on a free transfer if it's OK with you, Dex."

A surge of anger ran through Bradley. "You can pierce his bloody nipples for all I care. But I still don't see it. Dave and his mates..."

Gina sat down opposite. Eddie said to Bradley: "Well, every so often the auditors turn up. Maybe they've got their suspicions. They're not satisfied with little numbers on a screen. They want to see the readies. Problem is: no readies. So you've got to be able to tell them where the money went. So you say: *Sorry, friend, I was robbed.*"

"So Dave and his mates..."

Eddie said: "Use some sense. Who'd ever employ a bunch of losers like that for a real job? But then it went wrong, didn't it? Because that shithead decided to do a Maxwell with the money. Only there wasn't any money. But if anybody ever found out..."

Bradley said: "I don't believe it." But he was starting to.

"Why not?" asked Eddie, "You've heard of virtual reality, mon? This is virtual crime. You've heard of fantasy football? Well, this is fantasy robbery. It's the way things are going. They even play cricket on a computer nowadays. And your good sergeant there with his paperwork...what's that?"

Gina said: "Fantasy fuckin police work."

"So," said Bradley. The whisky was steadying him, helping him make sense of it, "So the Royal Bank of Cumbria did all this. The bank I've got my bloody mortgage with?"

"Ay. More or less. Except the Royal Bank of Cumbria these days is run from a hotel room about a hundred yards from Red Square in Moscow."

Gina said: "They probably call it Blue Square now."

"And the Russians...?" asked Bradley.

"Run everything," said Gina.

Now he grasped it! And he had to show Eddie that he understood, that he was part of this exciting new world. "The Russians are coming. They're the future. I know that. Which is why you're gonna be introducing me..."

At that point Simone came back with a dustpan, small brush and broom. "I told you lot not to move. Look at you! You've even been moving the furniture."

Gina got to her feet. "Here, Sim, I'll give you a hand." She opened up the gun. "It's empty! Would you fuckin believe it! That lunatic was a... fuckin *lunatic*! He never had a chance!" She laid the gun on the cocktail cabinet and took the broom from Simone. "I don't think it's so bad, this glass. I don't think it's dangerous. It's not as if you've got small children in the house."

But Simone had turned to Eddie. "Don't let me interrupt you. It was an interesting conversation. The bit about the Russians…" Bradley wondered how long she'd been listening outside the door.

"Geography," said Eddie, "That's the important thing."

Gina chipped in. "Eddie means being well placed." She started sweeping from the edge of the carpet to the centre.

"I know what Eddie means," said Simone, "And Newcastle's well placed, is it?"

"It's closer to Norway than it is to London," said Eddie to Bradley. And to Simone: "Would you believe that?"

"Norway?" said Bradley. He wasn't keeping up with this. He took another drink.

Gina said: "The Russians like to come through Norway. They like to pretend to be Norwegian. It's one of those things."

"And," said Eddie, "they need one central person to talk to, to do the business."

"That's Eddie," said Gina.

"That's me," said Eddie.

"It doesn't have to be," said Simone.

"But it does," said Gina.

"Ay," said Eddie, "It's geography."

Bradley was sweating. He said: "This is not what I wanted to hear, Eddie…"

"We all get disappointed sometimes," said Gina.

"Some more often than others," said Simone. She was brushing the last of the glass into the dustpan. "There. It's all tidied up now. Thanks, Gina. You've been a great help."

"You can always count on me, Sim."

Bradley was getting angry now, but he tried to control it. He tried not to let it seep too much into his voice. "You come over here, you stay at my house, you poach one of my best men…"

"If it's Harry you mean, Dex, I do believe he was largely unappreciated…"

"And you tell me that I'm not good enough for these Vodka-swilling bastards?"

Eddie stood up and shrugged in the direction of Simone. He said to Bradley: "You take it so personal."

Gina said: "You shouldn't do that, Dexy."

"Don't tell my husband what he shouldn't do," said Simone, "And don't call him Dexy."

Gina touched Simone gently on the arm. "I'm sorry, I'm sure. I know it must be disappointing."

Bradley said: "I have got 23 policemen, two judges, six MPs and a bishop in my pocket. I have got drugs, robbery, gambling, corrupt unions, illegal immigrants and unlicensed drinking clubs sewn up around here. There are people in this county who live in fear of me, who tell their children to stop snivelling else they'll set me on 'em. I'm ripe for expansion, Eddie. I *need* that expansion."

Eddie shrugged again, this time in Bradley's direction. "You're a one-man band, Dexy mon. Oh, I may call you that, may I? You have no structured organisation, only a bunch of casual hangers-on. You have no surveillance network, no investment in the security industry, no proper accounting system, hardly any computers, no in-road into the banks…"

"I'm not a bloody accountant!" Bradley took another drink but it wasn't doing him any good.

"Well, you should be," said Eddie, "because we're all accountants now, mon. We all have to be canny about the figures and make them add up."

"Even the government," said Gina, "Even New Labour have got to make the books balance."

Eddie said: "I'm sorry, Dex. I'm sorry, Simone. I've got the Russians and I'm keeping them. They like the way I operate. With you, they wouldn't know where to start. You're past it, Dex."

"You had a good innings," said Gina.

"Bollocks," said Simone.

Eddie said: "That's a good word, Simone. It's in the dictionary."

Gina said: "But we can do something for Ray."

Simone was nearly at the door, taking out the broken glass. "What...?" she started.

"Ray's a good lad," said Eddie, "Smart, well dressed, good education, personable. I thought we might take him with us when we go."

Gina nodded. "He's a good boy. Not loud. Not vulgar. The Russians would like him."

"We could give him a taste of the world outside," said Eddie, "A real career."

"Also," said Gina, "it's a bit of insurance. If Ray's with *us*..."

Bradley said: "My son stays with me." He meant to say it loud, but his voice would no longer obey him.

Simone tipped the glass into a waste paper bin. She said: "Wait, Dex. Remember what we were talking about?" She sat down where Eddie had sat and took Bradley's hand. "Things changing. Finding a new lifestyle that'll give us more time together. And banking. That's where the future is. You said so. That's where Raymond's future should be."

Gina nodded. "It would avoid any trouble later on."

"And we could try Georgian next," said Simone, "like Jane Austen did. Whatever you say about Elizabethan, if people changed over, moved away from it, it's got to mean there was something better. Personally, I wouldn't *mind* Georgian."

"A planned retirement," said Eddie, "Afternoons at Headingley…"

Bradley tried to pull his thoughts together. "They're supposed to be moving to Wakefield – though I don't agree with that."

Eddie said: "We could see they *didn't* move to Wakefield. The Royal Bank of Cumbria could offer," he paused, "incentives for them to stay in Leeds."

"Try to see it our way," said Gina, "It's a great career move for Raymond. We'll look after him, won't we, Eddie?"

Eddie said to Gina: "You bet," and to Bradley: "No need to fall out. Not in front of foreigners."

Simone got up and walked across to the drinks cabinet. "We'll drink to it then. I've got another bottle of St Emilion. But we'll need some new glasses."

Gina picked up brushes and dustpan. "Show us where the broom cupboard is, Sim, and I'll bring this lot through."

Eddie sat next to Bradley again. He stuck out his hand. "Why don't we shake on it, Dex? Hey? No hard feelings." Bradley could tell he was bothered, that something was wrong. Bradley couldn't think what it was. Eddie said: "Dex? What's the matter? Dex? Dex?" His voice was suddenly loud and full of alarm and he gave Bradley a little push.

Bradley fell off the *chaise longue*.

37 Chanelle Braithwaite

IT WASN'T EASY for Chanelle to see Ray this way. But she couldn't feel sorry for herself, she couldn't let that happen. It was Ray who'd suffered the loss. Ray and Simone. She allowed herself a bit of a cry for the both of them. But not too much, not so it looked like she was hogging the attention.

She and Ray had been driving back from the visit to her Mum when they nearly collided with the ambulance. And she was thinking how the visit had gone so well, with Ray and Angela getting on like a house on fire.

Chanelle had been worried beforehand. There was a world of difference between the high rise where she and her Mum lived and the mansion the Dexters were used to. And her Mum could be funny at times, with her Tarot cards and her animal rights and her Indian head massage. But Ray had been a real gent, complimenting Angela on her ribboned hair and kaftans, listening respectfully as she related her liaison with the handsome Trinidad sax player who had been Chanelle's Dad and had then buggered back to the Caribbean. Ray had even asked her to read the poem she had written about the death of Victor, her West Highland Terrier. "I write poetry myself," Ray had said, "I've only just started though."

And then on the way back... the ambulance! And the police were there, in the Dexters' house itself – the first time they'd ever been there, said Ray. So they knew something really bad had happened.

Simone met them at the door. She looked cool and composed. She told them very simply how Mr Dexter, Ray's Dad, was dead by the time the medics got there, maybe died instantly, and how the doctor said there'd have to be a post mortem but that all the signs pointed to a heart attack. Then she collapsed into Ray's arms and he sort of collapsed too, moaning and sobbing as he clutched at his mother for comfort.

Chanelle had no idea how long they'd continued like that. But when it passed, it seemed to pass suddenly, as though they'd made up their minds to get on with things.

The police said there were lots of formalities but they could wait. The doctor asked them all – Simone, Ray, Eddie, Gina and herself – if they wanted a sedative. They all said no, though Ray asked his mother *was she sure*? She just nodded.

The police officers – one was a woman and she was the main one who talked to Simone – made cups of tea with lots of sugar. Chanelle did the washing-up afterwards with a plastic brush she found in the kitchen even though she knew Ray's Mum had a dishwasher and she normally had that man called Harry to turn the knobs.

Simone told the police it had just been her and Eddie and Gina there all afternoon playing *Scrabble*. The police considered whether the excitement generated by *Scrabble* might have been the overriding factor. They were nervous. They knew who Mr Dexter was and they must have checked on Eddie as soon as they got the chance. But there wasn't anything suspicious. These things happened, even to people like Ray's Dad.

When the police and the doctor left, Eddie and Gina said they didn't want to trespass on the family grief and they'd sort out the packing and be back to Newcastle as soon as. They went upstairs. That was when Chanelle did the washing-up. When she got back into the lounge, Ray was standing by himself, looking out of the window. "Me Mum's washing her face," he said. Then: "Those bastards tried to kill me. And when it didn't work, they decided to take me to Norway. To kidnap me, that's what it amounts to. To keep me harmless."

One of Chanelle's new year resolutions would be not to be surprised by how things turned out but to make the best of them anyway. To make the best of Ray.

Right now Ray looked... so young somehow, younger than *her* even. Chanelle said: "I'll hate it if you go away."

Ray said: "It won't be for long. You could come and see me off. You could come on the boat. For the last few minutes."

"No," she said, "I can't stand water. I get sea-sick if I take a bath instead of a shower." She put her arms round him and gave him a long, lingering kiss, using her tongue. "Oh,

I'm gonna be so worried. What's Norway like? It's cold, isn't it? It's bound to be cold."

Ray gazed down at her, tall and overwhelming now, like a chest of drawers by Salvador Dali. He said: "*Yorkshire's* cold."

"Not when I've got you." They kissed again. Right now it was more like the kiss of people who were close, really knew each other. Not as exciting as the first time they did it, but it had its compensations.

Ray pulled away. "Not now. Here's me Mum." And Simone came back into the room and hugged him. "When you go to Norway," she said, "you *will* look after yourself?"

"Course I will."

"And you *will* be on your best behaviour. It's an important job. And if it goes right..."

"I know."

"Your Dad would have been so proud of you!" Her eyes became wet again and she dabbed at them with a small white handkerchief with a strawberry motif. "I think I'll need to wash my face all over." And she went out again.

Ray gazed into Chanelle's eyes. "Don't worry. I'm a big boy now. I'm my father's son. People don't think so, but I am. It ought to be *him* sorting things out. But it isn't. Fuckin heart attack."

Chanelle nodded to show she understood. "That Eddie and Gina. I never liked them. Neither of them. Not really. She gives *me* heart attacks."

"The way they run things, nobody else can get a look in. The way I see it, the way they treated my Dad, they're well out of order. I don't think I'll be with them long."

"You gonna be mending your mountain bike?" Chanelle allowed herself the smile that showed they shared a secret.

"I was thinking about it."

"You got what you need to do it?"

"I've always got what I need. You know that."

"See you do a good job." She kissed him a third time.

Simone came back in the room. She said to Chanelle: "He won't be that long away. What'll you do while he's gone?"

"Well, I'm looking out for a bit more fashion. More up-market . Sweaters and evening gowns. And Ray says he's got friends that can get me some telly. Fairy liquid might be interested. It's cause I've got soft, smooth hands. That's something Raymond noticed about me straightaway."

Simone smiled a Mum's smile. "He's always been a sensitive lad."

Chanelle saw that Ray was looking very bashful now. She suddenly said on impulse: "I want to move away from topless. I don't think it's right for a married woman. Not dignified."

Simone said: "Ray's asked you to marry him?"

"Not in so many words." Chanelle gave Ray a bold look but he said nothing. Chanelle said: "I just decided. For the both of us. Do you mind?"

Simone said: "No, I don't mind. I think you've been good for Ray, brought him out of himself. He's needed somebody to do that. So. We'll have to start planning for the big day."

Ray looked even more awkward now. "But Dad…"

"Your Dad would have *wanted* us to plan ahead. Especially about nice things. Family things. Like weddings."

Chanelle said: "I was thinking I could have a white lace dress."

Simone nodded. "You *should* get married in white. I always distrust women that get married in any other colour."

"And it could be short at the front and I could wear white silk stockings to show off my legs. And a white suspender belt. I could have a train at the back and the bodice would be sort of see-through. But because it's lace people wouldn't really be sure. I think that sort of thing is quite dignified if it's lace."

Simone put her arm round Chanelle. "You know what *I* think? I think we should have a look at some catalogues. Before you make up your mind."

"I'd like that, Simone."

"And another thing..." Simone did another smile now, a lot warmer than the last, a lot more relaxed, "You'd better start calling me *mother*."

Epilogue: Barry Oldham

BARRY IS THE first through the front door and the first thing he does is run upstairs to put the central heating on. He presses the button that says **ADVANCE** and the little red light comes on and he starts feeling warmer already. Then he goes back downstairs and it's only then he notices the post in the porch: the New Year sales and the men from the Comforta Upholstery Cleaning Company who are bringing their special machine to this neighbourhood for the next fortnight. And the letter addressed to *him*.

He doesn't recognise the writing. And it occurs to him that nobody every writes to him anyway. Alarm fills him for a moment. Then his Mum comes through the door and says: "I'll put the kettle on. We could do with some tea."

Barry takes the letter into the living room, sits down and thinks about opening it. It's nothing official. It's not the Jobcentre or the Hospital or the Social Services. It's not an overdue notice from the Library. Thinking about the Library makes him think of Alison and her bottom. He hopes she'll be back next time he goes in with a poem.

The envelope is done in proper handwriting, not word processed. It has to be somebody he knows. It has to be... He takes a deep breath and opens it. It *is* from Ray.

His Dad comes in after putting the car in the garage. He is taking off his anorak and he says to Barry: "Get them clothes off and hang them up. You don't want to wear your outdoor clothes indoors, else you'll never feel the benefit."

His Mum comes in with the tray with the rosebud pattern and a pot of tea and three cups. She says: "Now, Ted, let's not have any arguments." His Dad looks as if he's about to start one but obviously thinks better of it and goes off to the hall to hang up his anorak.

Barry's Mum says: "But your Dad is right. You've got to look after yourself when the weather's bad. We don't

238

want…" She doesn't finish the sentence because her eyes mist up and she has to look away. Barry knows she's thinking about Andrea and the funeral they've just come back from, that's what she's doing.

Barry can see it all. She's thinking about how Andrea had fallen, in the Christmas snow, in the garden, in the night, among the sculptures that Richard had helped her set up in the hope of attracting passing art-loving motorists, among the spiky heads of *Peace in the Forest*, the broad shoulder of *The Evil of Man*, and the giraffe-like necks of *Women at the Crossroads of Destiny*. She's thinking about how Andrea had lain there all night, unable to move, unable to call out, wearing only a stained nightie. Nobody knew why she had fallen, though the empty bottle of Smirnoff might have had something to do with it. Nobody knew why the elongated man from the three-figure group *My Family* had fallen on top of her, though the hole in her nightie probably meant she had caught his sharp knee in the cotton fabric.

She's also thinking about Richard and how he's bearing up and why he didn't want to come back with them but preferred to stay in that empty house. With those sculptures still in the garden. "A monument," Richard had said and Barry understood straightaway what he meant. One day Barry's poems would be a monument to Barry. That was some consolation.

Anyway, Barry gets up and goes out to the hall and hangs up the black overcoat he bought specially. It means delaying still more reading Ray's letter and that excites him. When he gets back, the tea is poured and he takes a sip. Then he puts it down, takes a deep breath and picks up the letter again. A picture falls out. A photograph. Barry picks it up. It's weird, abstract, triangles and squares and all sorts, in all sorts of colours. Like a kaleidoscope. He reads the letter.

Dear Barry (it says)

I am writing from Norway and I enclose a snap of the fiords. Well, one fiord anyway.

Barry looks again at the picture. Now he can see it. The rocks coming out of the water. The reflection underneath. You only had to hold it the right way up to see what it was. There was a lesson in that.

I have been here a week. Already we have had a tragedy. A man called Harry who works with me disappeared and we think he has had an accident in the fiords, perhaps that same fiord in the picture. Harry and I were not very close so I am not really sad.

Barry thinks: *I should write to him about Andrea.* Death was a depressing thing but news is important in a letter.

Also I don't think you know that my father died over the Christmas. He was a great man and I miss him. Still, he led a pretty unhealthy life. I don't intend to lead that sort of life. I intend a good diet and plenty of exercise and keep up to date with technology so I can have a career of my own and sort out the competition.

That settles the matter in Barry's mind. He will certainly write about Andrea. Perhaps his Mum has a photograph somewhere of the tragic sculpture. He could send it to Ray.

Now, enough of the doom and gloom! Some good news. I am going to get married. She is called Chanelle and is a model. I will invite you to the wedding.

Barry feels something akin to an electric shock. Marriage, he knows, changes your relationships with other people. Still, the upside is that if Ray can get married, maybe Barry... He thinks of Alison's bottom again and the warm plastic smell of the photocopier. Also he has some good news of his own, or at least good news of the family: Andy and Ursula have got engaged, even set the date more or less, some time in June. "That's a shock," said his Dad, "I wonder what brought that on?" and his mother said she wouldn't be surprised if it wasn't this Andrea business.

I will be home in the spring and we will go for a drink. Though not The Turk's Head this time. I heard they had a murder there.

Death, death, death, thinks Barry. *In life we are surrounded…* He searches for a rhyme for *surrounded*. Never mind.

Most of all, the reason for this letter is that I want you to know that my whole life changed from the night I met you. I have a much more positive attitude. I think this is down to your teaching me about the power of poetry. Though I have not written any more since that night, I have been reading a lot. I particularly like Sylvia Plath. People say she is morbid but I think she has a common-sense attitude to most things. I like a lot of what she says about fathers.

Barry considers. Though this is not his own opinion of Sylvia Plath, yet it is an interesting one. Maybe he should read her again.

It is a good time for starting a new life, don't you think? It is the start of the new century after all. Some people thought the new century started in 2000 but if you think about it, you realise 2000 is just the end of the old one.

Barry can't quite see that. He thinks he'll ask Fred Whittington.

Anyway, the post here in Bergen is a bit dodgy, so I will have to end now to make the collection. You can write back at the above address which is my office. I don't want to lose touch with what is happening to my best friend.

Yours truly

Ray.

Barry's Mum says: "Are you OK, love?"

Barry's Dad says: "He's bound to be upset. We're all upset."

Barry wipes his eyes. He is thinking how good things are. He is thinking of his poem *I am the Healer* and how true it turned out to be.

There was poor Ray, his life going wrong, his knowledge of poetry minimal, and Barry came along and helped him on his way. Now Ray was a better person, more in tune with life and nature and love.

Karma. It's a two-way street, Barry thinks. Ray is a better person and so am I. Barry thinks about John and Erwin. He hasn't seen them since Boxing Day. That's a step in the right direction, then. Dr Hardy will be pleased about that, even if he doesn't show it. And Mrs Gulliver. And it was all because of Ray.

He wipes his eyes again. "I'm OK," he says to his Mum. "I'm OK," he says to his Dad. And he is. And *great* is the word that comes to mind.

Life is *great.*

OBITUARY

From the Daily Telegraph, November 5, 2003

...In the 2001 season, Yorkshire returned to form to win their first Division One Championship since 1968. Former star player Arthur Tetley, 79, told *The Daily Telegraph*: "The secret of good cricket is to hit the ball with the bat and score runs. There's no substitute for that." He described himself as "delighted" with the outcome.

In 2002, Yorkshire were relegated from Division One. As part of a carefully considered action plan, the club's General Committee was replaced by a Board of Management. Veteran player Tetley, now 80, told *The Daily Telegraph*: "That's what happens when you don't hit the ball."

Sir Arthur, knighted in the New Year Honours List, was not to survive the full 12 months. His death certificate cited pneumonia and pleurisy. But a close friend, who declined to be identified, said: "It was a broken heart that ended his innings."

Also in Nettle Books

Fiction

Heaven Scent
John Winter

A brilliantly comic novel set in the swinging sixties. Charlie wanted to be part of the sexual revolution but it sort of passed him by. But he and fellow reporters on a seaside weekly paper have something to take their minds off summers of love – when the sleepy resort is rocked by mystery explosions. Is it the Isle of Wight Republican Army?

ISBN: 978-0-9561513-6-0   **£10**

Non-fiction

Flying with a Broken Wing
Sat Mehta

The powerful story of a boy growing up in India's turbulent times. Sat Mehta was five years old when he and his family became destitute refugees, his uncle murdered during partition riots. Then Sat suffered a broken arm, complications set in and amputation seemed inevitable. Then a famous English surgeon agreed to operate…

ISBN 978-0-9561513-2-2   **£10**